Rebels of Halklyen

The thought that he was about to die kept running through his head. Deliberately, he pushed his panic aside and returned to the game he had been playing in an effort to distract himself. When he spotted someone staring boldly at him, he narrowed his eyes in an attempt to make them avert their eyes.

Turning back to meet the stranger's unwavering stare, Flint noticed that he wore a long black cloak. The man did not move when a woman in the crowd pushed past him. The motion revealed the man's chainmail and a long sword belted to his waist. A ragged white scar cut across one eye, plainly visible even across the distance. He tried to return the man's stare but it did not feel like a game anymore and it was he who dropped his gaze first.

Suddenly, a grunt of pain from the guard on his right brought him to attention. The hand cruelly clutching his arm slowly released its hold as his jailer slipped to the ground and Flint stood face to face with a strangely masked man. What was a jester doing here?

THE HAWKS

BOOK ONE:

Rebels of Halklyen

PAULA BAKER & AIDAN DAVIES

Paula Baker *Aidan Davies*

MACFAY BOOKS

Rebels of Halklyen

Text copyright © 2012 by Paula Baker and Aidan Davies

Published by MacFay Books

Printed and bound in Canada
Map art by Anna-Jo Grandbois
Set in Garamond

ISBN-13: 978-0-9917900-1-2

Chapter 1 - Changing Worlds

Flint shifted his eyes to peer up at the guard who flanked him on his right and caught sight of a man in the crowd staring steadily at him. That in itself was not so surprising; people always gathered in hordes to watch a hanging. Flint recalled how excited he had been when he joined a mob eager to watch the death of a young woman convicted of murdering her husband.

In the end though, Flint took no joy in the execution. It left him feeling hollow and somehow ashamed. His lips tightened in a grimace, as he wished that same feeling of desolation on everyone who stared so eagerly at him now.

Heedlessly, his two guards dragged him closer to the gallows. Flint's feet stumbled on the rough cobblestones, but their vice-like grip prevented him from falling. Breaking eye contact with the man in the crowd, he turned and involuntarily glanced at the thick rope dangling from the scaffold.

The thought that he was about to die kept running through his head. Deliberately, he pushed his panic aside and returned to the game he had been playing in an effort to distract himself. When he spotted someone staring boldly at him, he narrowed his eyes in an attempt to make them avert their eyes.

Turning back to meet the stranger's unwavering stare, Flint noticed that he wore a long black cloak. The man did not move when a woman in the crowd pushed past him. The motion revealed the man's chainmail and a long sword belted to his waist. A ragged white scar cut across one eye, plainly visible even across the distance. He tried to return the man's stare but it did not feel like a game anymore and it was he who dropped his gaze first.

Suddenly, a grunt of pain from the guard on his right brought him to attention. The hand cruelly clutching his arm slowly released its hold as his jailer slipped to the ground and Flint stood face to face with a strangely masked man. What was a jester doing here?

A shout from the gallows pulled his attention away. Two of the King's Guards left their positions by the gallows stairs and pushed roughly through the crowd to the fallen guard. Frantically, Flint twisted around, looking for the jester. He was gone.

The remaining guard tightened his grip mercilessly. Flint winced in pain. Standing on tiptoe, he desperately scanned the crowd. No matter how hard he searched, he saw neither the man in black nor the masked jester.

He tried to suppress a bubble of hope. Flint had heard rumours of an underground rebellion against the King. And, although he had never seen it happen, he knew stories of people being rescued from the gallows.

"Move along, boy," barked one of the new guards.

"Don't worry we'll get you safely to your hanging." An edgy laugh followed this promise. The voice beside him was gruff with tension, but there was no sign of panic.

The guard to Flint's right rapped him with the side of his blade and took a firmer hold of his upper arm. Flint tried to dig in his heels but the new guard grasped his other arm and shook him like a dog, saying, "Here boy. That's enough of that."

Something hummed past his ear and Flint flinched. The guard who had just struck him gave a sigh and collapsed at his feet.

With the fall of a second guard, panic washed over the crowd, dispersing frightened people in every direction. Glancing quickly at the King's Guard who still stood at his left, Flint was shocked when the man suddenly began to foam at the mouth. Looking more closely, Flint noticed an arrow lodged in his side. The guard crumpled to his knees and toppled over.

In an instant, Flint realized that no one was left to stop him. The fourth guard still stood a few steps away. Three men lay on the ground at his feet, either dead or dying and standing in front of him was the man with the scar across his eye. The man turned his head, looked directly at Flint, then put two fingers to his lips and let out a sharp whistle.

Desperately, Flint turned from the gallows and raced away. He dodged and ducked through the mob that now had no interest in him as people struggled to escape the press surrounding the gallows. Flint slid through the narrow gaps in the crowd and edged his way carefully around the corner to the nearest street.

Just when he felt the space open up in front of him and he could finally accelerate, a woman wearing a black hood and cloak stepped out from the shadows. He barely gave her a glance as he tried to hurry past.

His inattention cost him. Before he knew what was happening, she stepped forward and hurled a small pouch of powder into his face.

His world went black.

Flint heard the creak of an opening door and turned his face to feel the sunlight warm his eyelids. He was awake but his eyes did not want to open. Despite his curiosity, he could not overcome his weariness. Exhaustion numbed his brain.

"Don't worry, lad," said a voice near his head. "You are safe here." He forced his eyes open and after a moment, managed to bring the world into focus. An old woman wearing a white cloak leaned over him. Her green eyes peered intently into his.

As the befuddled feeling began to clear, he studied her more closely. She wore her white hair in a tidy bun on the back of her head. Focussing more clearly, he saw that the cloak looked more like a loose fitting dress held in place around her narrow waist with a leather belt. Dangling from the belt were bulging pockets in all shapes and sizes.

"You are lucky that Cadmon got to you when he did," she said. Flint was reassured by her calm voice but the message confused him. He struggled to understand what was going on and to figure out what she meant. Suddenly he recalled the man in black and the dead guards. "Where am I?" he asked. His voice sounded weak and uncertain to his own ears.

The woman smiled as she answered gently, "You are in Halklyen. Rest easy, lad. This is probably the safest place in the world for a boy like you." With that, she left the room and Flint let his heavy eyes drift closed again.

When he awoke the second time, the man he thought might be Cadmon stood in the doorway. Without moving, Flint watched him from where he lay on the cot in the corner of the small room. He noticed that this time, he was not struggling to keep his eyes open and he stared curiously at the stranger.

Flint could see that the man rested easily against the doorframe yet he looked ready to move into action at the slightest provocation. The white scar running through his eyebrow stood out in the tanned face, but the eyes that regarded him with a casual intensity showed no sign of injury.

Eventually the scarred man spoke. "You were lucky we got to you when we did. I'd only just got news of your execution that morning." He cocked his head as if in amusement and added, "And then, it was only in passing. But I thought you might be of use to us."

"What do you mean?" Flint's voice squeaked upwards as he tried to imagine the man's intentions. What possible use would they have for a thirteen-year-old boy trained in nothing but waiting tables and washing dishes? "What use am I?" he sputtered. He did not even want to think about what had happened to bring him to the point where he was taking his last steps toward the town gallows.

This appeared to amuse the man who let out a low chuckle and said, "Have you no idea of the skills you've shown? What you did was not only brave but also selfless. We're always on the lookout for combinations like that." He smiled as he said it, but he continued to study Flint with that unsettling intensity.

"What do you mean by *we*?" Flint asked cautiously. The man started to answer his question, but was interrupted by the sound of the front door opening. Flint heard people talking in the outer room and a moment later looked right into the face of the woman who had thrown the sleeping powder at him. He shrank back against the wall nervously. She gave him a sympathetic smile.

At a nod from the scarred man, she stepped inside the room and slid sideways to accommodate a third visitor. It was the man whom Flint had named "The Jester". He realized that this was not exactly the right name for the masked warrior. He certainly did not look like he would try to make Flint laugh with a good joke.

He wore the traditional jester mask with a large, painted smile, but lacked the distinctive parti-coloured tunic. In its place were a suit of leather armour and a belt studded with throwing daggers. On his left hand, he wore an odd contraption. It appeared to be a steel gauntlet with sharp, bladed claws. The few patches of skin visible through the openings in the mask were stretched and shiny.

Flint remembered when a jester accompanied the King on a visit to his master's house at Shenkar. For a spell, it had been exciting to have the King staying with them, but really all he recalled now was the endless dishes he had to wash. Everything served had to be sent out on clean platters and it seemed like the courses went on forever. That jester had carried a little sceptre and jumped around, making silly comments, attempting to keep the King laughing.

This jester did not have any jokes ready. Instead, he looked at the scarred man in silence. When he seemed to get a tiny nod of approval in return, he turned his masked face to Flint. In a voice tinged with cynicism, he said, "Welcome to *The Hawks*."

Chapter 2 - The Hawks

Flint had been training for nearly four hours. With a great effort he lifted his wooden sword for one last attempt. Cadmon thought he had potential. Flint just hoped he knew what he was talking about. So far, it just seemed like a lot of work. Cadmon was teaching him the basics of sword fighting.

At first, Flint had been thrilled when he heard that he would get to practice with a sword; even if it was just a wooden stick with a grip and a cross guard. However, when Cadmon started the practices, it was all Flint could do to keep his sword moving through the patterns that Cadmon laid out for him. The first time Cadmon handed him the practice sword and demonstrated how to stand in a balanced position, his excitement lasted for all of five minutes. Then the training became brutally tiring labour.

Cadmon showed Flint how to hold the sword and how to strike at the post planted in the ground in the middle of the training yard. He often thought that whoever decided to pad the post with a layer of blankets was brilliant, because it cut down on that jarring feeling that spun through his arm every time he made contact.

Flint quickly discovered that the best way to keep practicing for the length of time Cadmon insisted upon was to switch hands whenever his arm got tired. It did not really matter to Flint which hand held the sword.

Then there were the footwork drills. Cadmon expected him to practice on the agility track over and over again. The carefully laid out series of stones required concentration and balance to be able to cross over without missing a step. The first time Flint made it through the entire track without once losing his balance and touching the dirt, Cadmon nodded and said simply, "Good. Now you can start learning to do it quickly."

It had been over a week since Flint's sudden arrival. The rebel group seemed to accept him and when he walked past a member, he usually got a nod and a smile in his direction. Aside from that small acknowledgement, however, he did not really exist for most of them.

Except for Fleta. She was a little younger than he was and really, the only person outside of his rescuers with whom he had actually spoken. Her parents had been killed in an attack when she was only five, so she was also an orphan. Well, if he thought about it, she was not actually parentless. She lived with Egbert and his wife, Merylin who treated her like an adored granddaughter.

Flint met Fleta on his third day in Halklyen when Cadmon sent him to Egbert's forge. Apparently, Cadmon's blade was never sharpened with a whetstone; it required the attention of a smith.

Egbert created the weapon from a meteorite that Cadmon found after watching a falling star descend to a place very near to where he sat watch one night. Cadmon tracked the large rock to its resting place in the bottom a massive crater that had appeared out of nowhere. He loaded it onto a sledge and with the help of a very disgruntled mule, triumphantly delivered it to Egbert.

Initially, Egbert was unable to build a fire hot enough to soften the metal in the meteorite so he began experimenting with different techniques. He knew he would need the highest quality charcoal available, because a wood fire would never get hot enough, no matter how hard he worked the bellows.

With the help of a couple of *The Hawks* he got to work building a clamp. It was similar to the ones the villagers used to store vegetables over the winter, with one exception: the chimney in the middle of the whole arrangement.

First, they dug a rectangular hole about fifteen feet square and four feet deep. Then, Egbert placed four upright boards in the center of the hole and tied a rope around them to create the chimney. Using the logs from an immense oak tree he had cut down the previous winter from the forest surrounding Halklyen, they created a large dome of wood.

After that, they mixed the dirt from the excavation with straw and covered the entire pile of logs, ensuring that every bit was buried. Finally Egbert took a burning torch, and inserted it into the kindling-filled chimney. When that caught fire, the process of making charcoal was underway.

Then began the two-week task of closely watching the

clamp to see where it cracked. Whenever that happened, Egbert would carefully shovel more dirt to fill the hole in order to prevent the admission of any oxygen. It was this trick of preventing air from entering the clamp that caused the charcoal to form. Essentially, he was cooking the wood.

After tirelessly minding the big mound of dirt for fourteen days and nights, the pile was carefully raked out and the charcoal watched until all traces of heat had dissipated. From there, the delicate black product was stacked under cover of a lean-to that had been built against the forge for just that purpose.

Egbert used this charcoal to build a fire and with the help of a neighbour boy who busily worked the bellows, he finally built a fire hot enough to turn the meteor into molten metal and forge the blade for Cadmon's sword. He still had some of that batch of charcoal that he saved for those times when Cadmon's blade needed attention.

The day that Flint appeared in the door of Egbert's forge with the sword carefully protected in its scabbard, Fleta had been hard at work on the bellows. Her brown hair clung to her head in sweaty streaks and her face glowed red from the effort of pumping the bellows, as well as from the incredible heat that hit Flint like a wall when he stepped into the building. She glanced up and he met her brown eyes but she did not falter in her regular rhythm that maintained the bright fire where Egbert worked.

Flint studied the man while he waited. The first thing he noticed was that he really was not very tall. At thirteen, Flint was accustomed to looking up at most men. It was difficult to be certain with Egbert bent over the forge, but he did not appear to be any taller than Flint. However, he was much bigger. His arms and shoulders showed the results of his constant labour with heavy hammers. His reddish-brown hair was cut short, but he wore his brown beard long, in a style that Flint had not seen before; the sides of it were tidied into two neat braids while the middle was left to curl freely.

A pair of small blades glowed in the forge. When Egbert used a heavy pair of tongs to remove them from the fire, he glanced up and saw Flint watching him. After a brief nod, he continued with his work, alternately hammering the heated metal and thrusting it back onto the fire to bring it back to a workable state. Meanwhile, Fleta had maintained her tireless pumping.

Switching his attention to the young girl, Flint had watched her energetically work the bellows. Lean and fit, Flint guessed that she was probably about his age. Black dirt was smudged across her face and she ignored the sweat that dripped off the end of her nose. Except for that first glance when he stepped into the doorway, she ignored him too. Her whole attention focused on the blades that Egbert delicately worked with his huge hammer.

When he finally decided he had finished shaping the blades, Egbert plunged them into the tank of oily water beside the forge. Fleta stopped pumping and leaned across the bellows panting. The three of them stood listening to the steam hiss from the surface of what Flint was sure must be a pair of small daggers. Egbert watched the last of the bubbles rise to the surface and then he turned to Flint.

"I see you have *Rising Star*," he said in a satisfied tone, eyeing the sword that Flint carried. His voice carried a strange lilt that Flint had never heard before. He seemed almost to sing his words.

"Yes sir. Cadmon sent me to deliver it to you. He said you would know what to do." Flint remembered how uncertain he had felt as he delivered this message but then Egbert let out a great belly laugh.

"By the Fire of Dworgunul, of course I know what to do!" he chortled. "I made *Rising Star* didn't I? I surely do know better than that wild man, Cadmon."

At that point, Fleta had spoken up, "Is this it, then, Egbert?" She left her resting place on the bellows and crowded closer, saying, "You said you would show it to me one day. I've seen him practice with it, but it's not as if you can really see what it looks like when Cadmon is waving it around."

"And so you shall see it, my wee one," answered Egbert grandly. With that, the short man stretched out a hand for the sword and in an easy motion, drew it free of the scabbard. Both Fleta and Flint gaped in wonder at the revealed blade. Almost twice as long as Egbert's arm, *Rising Star* definitely lived up to her name. The blade shone with a rippling blue radiance and the hilt of wound silver wire looked smooth and worn. Embedded in the pommel, a gleaming sapphire completed the sword. Flint thought of his wooden practice sword and imagined what it would be like to hold such a blade.

After allowing the two children a long moment to appreciate the magnificence of the weapon, Egbert briskly slid it back into the scabbard and declared, "Well, I be not about to start on this job right now. You two run along and try not to get into too much trouble before dinner. Fleta, bring the boy home for some of Merylin's soup." With that said, he turned back to his work.

Fleta hesitated for a moment and then after a quick glance at Flint, she scooted out of the hot forge. Flint followed and soon they were strolling about the village while Fleta pointed here and there and told Flint about everything and everyone she saw. Everyone knew Fleta. They all greeted her with a smile and a quick hello.

Flint had already gained some understanding of how Halklyen was organized from listening to Cadmon. In the evenings, many different people stopped by to chat with him. It seemed that very few things were undertaken in the village without first running it by Cadmon.

Fleta took the time to fill in the details. She knew everybody's story. It was not hard to get her to tell him about Cadmon. Flint had already figured out that he was the leader of *The Hawks* but he was curious about how Halklyen came to be a village full of rebels.

"Have you met Gode, yet?" she asked. When Flint nodded, she continued with barely a breath. "Did you know that Cadmon was once Supreme Commander of the King's Guard?" Flint's face showed his surprise.

Before he could say anything, Fleta rushed on with her story. "Gode was his Lieutenant Commander and together they were responsible for the King's safety and for all of the military actions in and around Kallcunarth."

When she paused for breath, he gave a low whistle. "Supreme Commander?" he repeated. Flint was shocked to learn that the man who had taken him on as an apprentice was once the top-ranked soldier in the country. "I had no idea."

Nodding earnestly, Fleta continued her story. "I heard that he and Gode decided one day that they just could not support what was happening in the kingdom. There were too many terrible things that they were ordered to do."

Apparently, every one of the residents of Halklyen were individuals who had found that they opposed the King and all he stood for in Abbarkon. Each had his or her own particular story about how they came to believe that King Abelard was not doing his best for the people of the kingdom. Most of the stories had to do with some of the horrible things that happened so often: evil beyond mere banditry. Evil that they felt must stop.

Feeling as they did that something needed to be done to resist the King's dishonest administration, people put out feelers to learn what their friends and neighbours thought of the monarch. Word of these queries inevitably reached the ears of *The Hawks*, and the person would be spirited away to Halklyen.

A version of this story was what had happened to Flint. Except of course, he had not actually made the decision to oppose the King. Worn out by the foul treatment he received at the hands of one of the King's toadies, he had finally reacted. Nonetheless, when *The Hawks* heard his story, they arranged to save him from the hangman's noose.

Most of the people who showed up in Halklyen were trained warriors. These people were given the task of perfecting their skills and learning to work together. When necessary, they were sent on missions outside of Halklyen. Somehow, Cadmon decided that Flint would be one of these fighters. Fleta was in training too. She had begun to learn to throw daggers when she was only six years old.

Sometimes, the people who appeared in the little town were average tradespeople who could help deal with the necessities of food and equipment. There was a miller, a baker, a carpenter, a stable master, a leather worker, and of course, Egbert was the blacksmith. As well, most people kept a goat, a few pigs and chickens and planted a garden.

Cadmon's arrangement with Duke Sebastien who lived in a nearby town, provided the goods and produce that they could not grow in the land surrounding the village.

Duke Sebastien was the hope of *The Hawks*. Next in line for the throne of Abbarkon, he was a good-hearted man who ruled his duchy with intelligence and generosity. It was Cadmon's plan to help Sebastien gain his throne sooner rather than later.

Chapter 3 - Trouble

"Hey, Flint!" yelled Fleta. "Let's go find Gode." Flint was due to finish his training and Fleta knew it. She had just finished her own practice session at the throwing targets. Those first two daggers that Flint had watched Egbert craft almost three years ago were her weapon of choice although now there were six blades sheathed in her belt. He had seen her put every one of them into a target the size of a small pumpkin in less than ten seconds.

Recently, she began training with moving targets, and Flint, Asdis and Penn were often enlisted to toss leather balls into the air for her to hit. The four of them were fast friends; probably because they were the only people their age living in the forest village.

Penn was the youngest. He had just turned twelve and he worked hard to keep up with the older ones. His parents ran the bakery, but Penn had elected to practice as a warrior. Flint always knew where Penn was because he rarely stopped talking. Even if he were alone, he would keep up an unremitting chatter that let everyone around know exactly what he was thinking. It was as if his brain was linked to his mouth and that in order to think, he actually had to be speaking.

But, for all that, he was becoming a very accomplished archer. He spent hours tossing a leather ball into the air and then quickly notching, releasing and lodging an arrow into it before it touched the ground.

Asdis was the eldest at seventeen and she never let them forget it. Like her mother Gytha, who had once been a Captain in the King's Guard, she was tall, muscular, and able to wield a sword with formidable skill. Asdis always felt that she should be the leader of any expedition the quartet planned. The others learned that it was easier to let her believe she was in charge and just go ahead and do it the way they wanted without arguing with her.

Flint nodded at Fleta to acknowledge the plan to go find Gode. Then, with a quick flick of his eyes, he indicated Cadmon who stood nearby with his own sword bared. Conscientiously he ran through the sequence of moves that he had practiced all afternoon. Flint held a wooden practice sword in each hand and wielded them with confidence. Training daily for almost three years, the fighting had begun to feel like second nature. He stopped the fluid motion and turned toward Cadmon with a hopeful smile. Cadmon scowled in mock disapproval but nodded his permission.

Flint grinned. "Thanks, Cadmon," he called before sprinting across the Sparrow Hawk practice yard.

Known collectively as *The Talons,* the three elite fighting squads within *The Hawks* were *The Sparrow*

Hawks, The Vultures, and *The Eagles.* It was these warriors who were most actively involved in opposing the King's rule.

Cadmon not only served as the recognized leader of *The Hawks,* he also led *The Sparrow Hawks.* Assassins by training, they hid in the shadows and leapt at their targets with a blade. Flint dreamed of becoming one of *The Sparrow Hawks* and being sent on a mission.

Fleta thought the *Vultures* sounded more interesting. Their leader, Hulda, had been her main teacher for years. Not only an expert with daggers, she was also known for her hand-to-hand combat techniques. Hulda had arrived in Halklyen when she was barely sixteen, and already a formidable fighter. Her mother, a Captain in the King's Guard had started Hulda's training when she was barely more than an infant.

It was Hulda's mother who made the decision to search for *The Hawks,* but in the end, only Hulda made it to the remote village. Her mother had been killed by men sent to chase them down. Flint had never seen it, but Fleta told him that the reason Hulda wore her long black hair loose was so that it would cover her missing ear: a souvenir from the attack that had killed her mother.

The Vultures specialized in infiltrating high influence groups to collect information. Flint suspected that it was *The Vultures* who had arranged for his rescue from the gallows. Of course, he was unlikely to ever know for certain, because secrecy was the most important rule in Halklyen.

Gode, who, with Cadmon had founded *The Hawks,* was the leader of the *Eagles.* Highly trained warriors, they were not known for their stealth, but could wield their weapons better than any others in Abbarkon. When it came to an all-out fight, this was the squad that would be most effective.

Warriors from any of the three wings of *The Talons* could be combined together to create the most effective force for a planned mission. Over the last two years, Flint and Fleta had quietly noted the departure and return of several different groups of people.

When Gode and Cadmon first left the service of the King, they did not have a solid plan for how they would fight the evil taking over Abbarkon. They started small: whispering rumours about a rebel group that could make a difference. When it became apparent that the rumours were taking root, they went to Duke Sebastien and arranged for a home base in a forest near the duchy of Fasnul. Gradually, people started drifting into the town.

Orma had been one of the first to arrive with her daughter Cwenhild who was fifteen at the time. By chance, they were living in the woods near Fasnul for the last eight years. Before that, Orma had been a healer in Kallcunarth, but an encounter with one of the particularly frightening men from the King's Guard had sent her into hiding.

As the number of *Hawks* grew, so too did the village of Halklyen. Cottages sprouted along the edges of three separate practice squares in the forest. Each square took the name of the squad that practiced there. Sparrow

Hawk Square, being primarily used by the sword fighters, had the agility track and several practice posts that were used in sword drills, as well as space for practice matches. Watching these battles, Flint was always surprised that no one had ever been killed. *Hawks* practiced in earnest, and the warriors earned plenty of bruises. It was only the killing blow that was held back.

Flint dashed up to the front door of Cadmon's tiny cottage, which was one of the first ones built in Halklyen. Inside, he carefully leaned his practice swords in the corner of the bare room that served as kitchen, living room and bedroom. Snatching his baldric from the hook near the door, he thrust his arms through the webbing and buckled on the double sword scabbards. He finally had his own real weapons. Forged by Egbert, they were remarkable swords, although no match to *Rising Star*.

Each of *The Hawks'* weapons was created by first making it from steel and then coating it with silver. Some believed that it made them easier to sharpen, but Flint figured it was just for appearance. One of his responsibilities was to polish the silver surfaces of all the *Sparrow Hawks'* weapons. It was a most impressive thing to see the glittering shimmer of a *Hawk* blade flashing in the sun.

Flint finished buckling the baldric and shrugged his shoulders to let the load settle evenly across his back. He was still a little self-conscious about wearing the weapons, but Cadmon said that a warrior is always armed, regardless of whether he expects a fight or not.

He also said that, except in practice, drawing the weapons without intending to use them to kill was not acceptable.

Rushing back across the yard, he joined Fleta, who stood watching Cadmon exercise with the *Rising Star*. Flint stopped to appreciate the easy grace Cadmon displayed as he whipped the blue-black sword around his head in a series of careful, yet deadly moves. After a moment of admiration, both Flint and Fleta turned away by a wordless accord and began walking down the street that led to Eagle Square.

Gode was one of their favourite *Hawks*. Despite the fact that he was second-in-command only to Cadmon, he could always be counted on to start up a game of some sort. When he was not training or eating, he made a point of playing with the younger trainees. It was Gode who had made Flint begin to feel welcome with *The Hawks*. The focused and frightening fighters often left him believing that they would be as happy skewering him on one of their many swords as talking to him.

Smiling to himself, Flint reflected that Gode did not even carry a sword. Perhaps that was what made him such a favourite. Gode's weapon of choice was a large double-sided axe made of the signature silver-encased steel. Egbert had worked the blades so that they resembled the wings of a soaring hawk. Flint loved to watch Gode practice: the man was well over six feet tall and the sight of those silver wings flashing in the sun was truly impressive.

While he and Fleta searched Halklyen for Gode, they

bumped into Joris. Flint could hardly believe that Joris had been accepted into *The Hawks*. Always unpleasant and frequently cruel, he was tall and lanky with long black hair and a big scruffy beard that had not been noticeably trimmed since he joined *The Hawks* six months earlier.

As far as Flint could see, he cared for nothing but gold. Although, when he appeared in the forest outside Halklyen, he professed a great hatred for the King and so the scouts had brought him into town. Flint had heard that Joris had been a merchant in Kallcunarth and that what he really hated about the King were his tax collectors: they visited every three months and expected him to be honest about his profits.

"Hello, Joris," said Fleta warily.

"Get out of my way, girl," snarled Joris. Even though she was not actually in his path, he managed to stumble into Fleta and push her into a tree. Flint reacted without even thinking and threw a punch at Joris's face. Joris ducked and kicked out at Flint. He missed but moved in quickly for a second attempt. Suddenly, Gode was there.

"What do you think you are doing?" he boomed.

For a moment, nobody moved as Joris and Gode stared at each other. Then, Joris dropped his eyes and turned away. Sullenly, he answered, "Nothing. Just teaching the children a lesson."

"What sort of lesson might that be?" Gode spoke with a frightening intensity and Joris stiffened but did not answer him. "Never mind. Don't bother to answer that. I don't want to listen to your lies." With the tiniest of motions, he gestured with his chin. "Move along, you useless piece of filth."

Joris stiffened at the insult but then after a moment's hesitation he snorted with disgust, lifted his head and sauntered away. Knowing that he was no match for Gode, he chose to leave the fight without saying anything more.

Gode turned to Fleta and Flint. "Are you two all right?" he asked. Studying them with his warm brown eyes, he waited for their answer.

"We're fine," Fleta replied as she brushed at the dried leaves and grass that stuck to her tunic when she fell to the ground. "Thanks for getting here when you did though." She was trying to make a joke of it, but her voice shook as she spoke, "I don't think Joris likes me."

"I have a feeling that Joris is more trouble than he appears," muttered Gode.

Chapter 4 - Drill and Practice

THWAP!

One of Fleta's daggers slammed into the target.

THWAP!

Moments later a second dagger landed precisely beside the first. For the last hour, Fleta had been tossing daggers at the set of six targets. She had carefully arranged the targets so that she was surrounded; some were high and some were low but not one was closer than ten feet. She kept changing the sequence that she threw the daggers. She did not let herself plan where she would aim, but whirled and spun in opposite directions as if she fought a whole crowd of attackers.

Carefully out of range, Flint trained with his swords. After fighting for almost three years with the wooden practice swords, it had taken a while for him to get used to the weight and balance of the pair that Egbert made for him. The blades were slightly shorter than his arms and Egbert had constructed them so that they were perfectly matched. Once he got used to the new feel, Flint found they were beautifully balanced and easy to handle.

He was working on a drill that he and Cadmon had devised, where he performed a series of thrusts and parries, footwork and blocks as he imagined a whole regiment of opponents facing him. He was careful to maintain his balance as he swung the swords in opposite directions. One hand would take the role of defence and the other offence, and then in the next moment, he would switch the roles for each hand. Cadmon had realized that Flint's ability to fight ambidextrously made him a dangerous opponent and they had worked hard to capitalize on this skill in order to make Flint just that much more formidable.

Flint finished the exercise with a flourish and reached back to sheath both swords in the scabbards strapped to his back. He stood panting for a moment and then noticed that Fleta too had finished her workout and sat comfortably on a tree stump while she watched him. They had decided to take their practice outside the village to a meadow just a short walk through the woods.

Normally, Flint drilled in the Sparrow Hawk Square because Cadmon supervised his training and Fleta practiced in the Vulture Square. However, Fleta had wanted to try out her idea for the varied targets and Hulda, the leader of the Vultures and Fleta's training instructor was not prepared to authorize such a scheme.

When Fleta described her plan to the tall, pale warrior, she had watched, as the woman actually seemed to get paler at the idea that daggers would be flying wildly around the square. The meadow had been Fleta's next suggestion and Hulda, herself a skilled dagger fighter, had thought that would be a much safer option.

Flint seated himself beside Fleta on the large stump. It must have been a huge tree during its life. Most likely, it was an oak that Egbert had cut down to supply his forge with fuel. They rested in silence for a minute and then Fleta said, "I'm hungry."

"It's lunch time. Who do you think we can get to make us lunch today?" asked Flint. He and Fleta tended to roam between Orma's and Merylin's cottages when they were looking for a meal. Either one of the women would welcome them and dish up something tasty.

For a long while they sat in peaceful contemplation while they considered their options until Flint finally said, "Let's go to Orma's."

"Good idea, she makes great sandwiches!" exclaimed Fleta.

Ever since Flint awakened in Orma's house that first day after *The Hawks* rescued him from hanging, Orma had been the one around whom Flint felt most comfortable. She was the healer in the town and Cwenhild's mother. She was also one of the few people who were not actually a warrior or training to become one. She did carry a knife in her belt, and although she knew how to use it for defence, she tended to employ it for more practical matters, such as cutting sutures when she sewed up the wounds that the trainees received.

Flint slept in Cadmon's cottage. Cadmon was an expert instructor when it came to swordplay, and gifted at explaining the politics of the kingdom and *The Hawks'* plans. He was also a talented cook for quick meals and a tidy housekeeper, but Flint had always found he felt more relaxed and welcome in Orma's kitchen. Perhaps it was because she invited him to talk about his days and seemed to appreciate hearing his thoughts and questions. In Cadmon's cottage, Flint was expected to listen and learn, but he rarely had an opportunity to express his own opinion.

As they made their way to Orma's cottage, they talked about bits of conversation that they had overheard from some members of *The Talons*. People in Kallcunarth were being arrested without reason, while at the same time, there were huge increases in the number of robberies.

The King's Guard was making no efforts at all to control the banditry. Flint and Fleta speculated about whether *The Hawks* would be stepping in with some action of their own soon. It seemed that it had been a long while since there had been active duty for anyone.

When they arrived at Orma's small cottage, they could smell the mouth-watering aroma of bacon cooking. Orma knelt in the middle of her huge garden, gathering some herbs and greens. She looked up from her basket, and smiled in welcome. "Greetings of the day, Fleta. And to you, Flint."

"Greetings of the day, Orma," they chorused.

"I think I smell something wonderful," said Flint sniffing the air appreciatively.

Orma chuckled, and said, "No doubt, you two are looking for an easy meal." She held up a double handful of salad greens. "Can I interest you in one of my specialty sandwiches?"

Fleta smiled broadly. "Well, if you're sure it's no trouble," she said innocently.

Orma laughed aloud at that bit of transparent manipulation. "Come on in, you two. I thought you might drop by for a bite to eat." She led the way to the door and Fleta cocked an eyebrow at Flint and grinned as they followed her into the well-scrubbed kitchen. Orma moved toward the hearth where she had a fire going.

Taking up a large cloth to protect her hands, she reached in with tongs to remove the bacon from the three-legged frying pan that was carefully placed on top of a hot section of the fire. Then, reaching for a cloth-wrapped bundle on the table, she produced a block of delicious looking cheese and a pile of fresh buns. She began assembling three sandwiches.

"So, how was your training today?" she asked.

As she answered, Fleta did not raise her eyes from the food in front of her. "Um, exhilarating," she said.

Orma raised her eyebrows at that. "Exhilarating, hmm? Tell me about it." Fleta spent the next few minutes happily explaining her idea for practicing against a crowd of opponents. She told Orma about how, once she got the targets set up surrounding herself, and began throwing her daggers, it almost felt like she could not miss. She could sense where the targets were even when she was not looking. Making herself hit the targets in a random order each time made it so that she had to constantly turn and react without losing her balance or concentration.

Her next plan to test her focus and vision was to figure out some way to make the targets move. She did not think it would be such a good idea to enlist her friends' help with that plan. Even she could not guarantee their safety if she was constantly spinning in a circle to make the shots.

Orma listened in silence, nodding and giving Fleta her whole attention. Then, she turned to look at Flint who appeared to be ignoring Fleta's story because he was so focused on the food. Under his spellbound gaze, she put the finishing touches on each sandwich with a generous dollop of her famous mustard.

"How about you Flint?" asked Orma.

"I was practicing a routine that Cadmon helped me develop," he answered not taking his eyes from the mounded creations.

"Ah, yes. Practice is a wonderful thing," she said while handing them each a sandwich. The two famished fighters immediately pounced on their lunch. The food effectively ended any conversation during the meal. Orma watched in amusement as Flint and Fleta gave their entire attention to the sandwiches.

Chapter 5 - Invention

"Bring Fleta at noon and meet me at Hawk Hut," Cadmon said as he wiped the crumbs from the table. He and Flint were cleaning up the remains of their breakfast, which had consisted of some of Flint's favourite dried sausage and the bread that Cadmon brought home yesterday from Penn's parents' bakery. Their beds had already been neatly made and Flint was carefully sweeping the wooden floor. When he moved in with Cadmon almost three years ago, there had been just the one bed up against the far wall, but a second one had been constructed and fitted into the other corner.

"Why?" Flint did not really expect an answer, but he could not help himself. He had never been invited to the Hawk Hut before for a meeting. It was there that *The Talons* discussed what was happening in Abbarkon and made plans for missions.

Flint, Fleta, Penn and Asdis had each taken their turns at cleaning out the hut and lighting the fire before a meeting but that was as close as they had ever been. Sometimes they tried to imagine what went on behind the closed door of the large windowless hut, but it had been made perfectly clear that they were to come nowhere near the place when a meeting was in session.

Inside the spacious hut, there was enough room to accommodate all fifteen of *The Talons,* and any other people who might be important to a discussion. The large room had a hearth taking up most of one wall and comfortable benches built right up against the remaining three walls. Extra chairs ranged in front of the hearth could be pulled up to the fire for intimate chats, or turned around if the whole group was meeting.

As Flint had expected, Cadmon did not reply; he just gave him a look that spoke volumes about waiting for the right moment to get the answers he needed. However, he did allow a brief smile to pass his lips as he lifted his sword belt from the hook beside the door.

Cadmon wore *Rising Star* on his left side inside a metal scabbard that Egbert had crafted for him. The swirls and curlicues running down the side of it actually spelled out *Rising Star* but you almost had to know what it said before you could make it out.

Flint hurriedly placed the broom in its usual spot in the kitchen corner and, grabbing his own baldric, buckled it in place, before racing off to find Fleta.

He found her in Merylin's kitchen eating a leisurely breakfast of fried bread with eggs. After politely greeting Merylin, he asked Fleta to join him in the meadow when she was free. Besides the exciting news about the meeting, he wanted to show her something on which he had been working. The idea came to him after listening to Fleta tell Orma about wanting to have moving targets that she could hit with her daggers.

When Fleta got to the meadow, Flint had everything set. Climbing up into the surrounding trees, he had tied ropes that held wooden targets secured to the ends of each of them. His plan was to get all the suspended targets swinging and then head for cover while Fleta launched her daggers. She stepped clear of the woods just as Flint jumped down from the last tree. Startled, she jumped back and drew a dagger from her belt.

"Whoa, now. It's me." Flint scrambled to his feet so that she could see him, but he remained poised to dive to the side if she looked as if she was going to release the blade.

"What are you doing, jumping out of trees and trying to scare me like that?" she demanded angrily. Flint knew from experience that Fleta had a quick temper, but he was confident that it would pass when he showed her what he had set up for her.

He pointed to the target hanging from the tree he had just exited and said, "Look."

Fleta did not immediately understand what she was seeing, but when she realized what he had done, a slow smile spread across her face. "That is brilliant," she breathed.

"That's not all." Flint whirled to point at all the targets he had hung. He had found trees that formed most of a circle and the targets hung at varying heights with ropes of different lengths so that when they began moving, they would move at different speeds.

Fleta stood turning in a circle as she examined the

targets with a look of admiration. "Let's try it," she said and Flint took off running around the set of targets, batting each one with his hands as he zipped past. When they were all in motion, he dived behind a rock to watch the action. Before he was able to right himself and peak around the corner of his shelter, Fleta had already launched her six knives.

Only one of them was actually wedged in a wooden target and Fleta had a rather dazed look on her face. It had been a long time since she had missed so dramatically. She looked at Flint who was slowly emerging from his hiding spot. "This is hard," she said with amazement. And then she grinned. "What a brilliant idea! This is going to be fun. Will you start them again?"

For the next two hours, they alternated between searching in the underbrush around the trees for the missing daggers and setting the targets swinging for more practice. By the time they settled down on the stump for a break, Fleta had hit as many as four of the targets in a single round. Oftentimes, the dagger would strike the target but would fail to embed itself deeply enough to stick. However, she was beginning to learn the trick of that. She needed to hit the target dead centre.

They were reclining on the stump when Flint decided to tell her about the invitation. "Cadmon asked me to give you a message," he said nonchalantly. Then he sat back to watch for reaction.

He got it. "What? Why didn't you tell me before? Were you so concerned with your invention that you couldn't tell me the message before we started?" Fleta was always quicksilver in her moods and Flint enjoyed setting up situations where he knew he could get a rise out of her.

"We had time to kill and I thought you might enjoy the targets more if you weren't worried about the invitation." He raised his eyebrows in anticipation as he threw out this bait.

"Invitation? Flint, what are you talking about? Just tell me and stop fooling around." She turned and looked him right in the eye, demanding an answer.

"All right," he said and then took a deep breath. "Cadmon wants us to meet him at the Hawk Hut at noon for a meeting." He spoke in a rush after keeping the secret for so long. "What do you suppose he has in mind?" Flint felt good at sharing the sense of expectancy he had carried all morning.

Fleta did not say anything immediately, but turned away to contemplate the possible meanings of such an invitation. Finally, she broke her silence, "He has a mission for us." She spoke with certainty and Flint was inclined to agree with her assessment. Glancing at the sun in the sky, she continued, "Let's go. I, for one, do not want to be late."

Chapter 6 - A Task for Trainees

Fleta and Flint positioned themselves outside Hawk Hut with plenty of time to spare before noon. They watched as members of *The Talons* arrived and entered the building. It was one thing to know that they had been invited, but actually walking into the hut without Cadmon was too intimidating. They had agreed that the best idea was to wait until he got there before they tried to enter.

Just as the sun was straight overhead, Cadmon arrived from the direction of Sparrow Hawk Square. Neither Flint nor Fleta moved, but waited for some sign from him to indicate that they were supposed to join him. They were surprised when Cadmon gave them a big grin as soon as he spotted them. He headed straight for the corner where they leaned casually against a wall.

Speaking quietly, but with traces of his grin still visible on his face he said, "What are you waiting out here for? We've got a meeting to get started." Stepping over to the hut, he pulled open the door, held it wide for Fleta and Flint and then followed them in himself. Apparently, they were the last to arrive because Cadmon passed a quick look around the room and then dropped the latch down on the door. Flint and Fleta stood uncertainly by the door until he motioned for them to take a seat along the back wall. The lamps were lit in the windowless hut and they made their way slowly through the dim light. Hulda moved over to make room and they settled into place.

Cadmon did not sit down. Instead, he strode to the front of the cold hearth and turned to face the other members of *The Talons*. Without fanfare, he began speaking, "Well, we have just had word from Geir in Thalnafar. He thinks that there may be some who are becoming suspicious about him so we are going to get him out before things go wrong." Flint looked at Fleta and raised his eyebrows but neither of them said anything. Expectantly, they turned back to Cadmon as he began speaking again.

"Flint and Fleta, *The Talons* have already discussed this. We want you to take this on as your first mission for *The Hawks*." Fleta caught her breath and nudged Flint who tried to keep his face as calm as possible. "The plan is to have Geir move to a safe house just outside of Thalnafar. The woman who lives there has some strong beliefs about the King and she can be trusted to hide Geir until you get there.

"Now this is just a routine extraction: essentially, all you have to do is get to Thalnafar, find the safe house and bring Geir back here. The idea is that you will look and act completely ordinary so that you do not bring down the attention of Martokallu. You will be able to carry your weapons of course, but it will not be in any open way.

"Fleta, your daggers are easily enough concealed, but Flint, we will need to come up with a way to disguise your blades because the hilt and pommel stick up above your shoulders and cannot be easily covered with a cloak.

"If you have any questions, you need to ask them in this room. None of this is to be discussed outside of the Hawk Hut for any reason." Cadmon finished his speech and then stood waiting for the barrage he knew was coming. Flint always had plenty of questions and Cadmon rarely gave him an opportunity to satisfy his curiosity.

Excitedly, Flint blurted out the first question that jumped into his mind, "What did you mean when you said that we don't want to bring the attention of Martokallu?" Of course, both Flint and Fleta knew who Martokallu was. Or, at least they had heard stories about him; horrible stories that felt more like nightmares than anything that could possibly happen in this world.

"That is a good place to start," responded Cadmon. "Cwenhild, I think you would be best to answer this one." He turned to where Cwenhild sat with her feet comfortably tucked up under her in the corner near Fleta and Flint.

Ever since Flint awakened in that back room of Orma's cottage and recognized Cwenhild as the one who threw the sleeping powder into his face just before he blacked out, he had been extremely wary of her. He understood that it had been part of the extraction plan to ensure that he would not struggle against them as they smuggled him to safety, but he never felt completely relaxed around her.

Cwenhild nodded her head and took a moment to compose her thoughts before she began to speak. "I can imagine that you have heard stories about Martokallu and no doubt you have dismissed some of those tales as fine yarns that are best shared around an evening fire." She paused and looked straight at Fleta and then shifted her eyes sideways to stare directly at Flint. "In fact, he is our real enemy here: it is he who controls the King."

Again, Fleta felt the breath catch in the back of her throat. She had lived all her life in Halklyen and this was the first time she had ever heard the suggestion of anything like this. She always imagined that the stories of Martokallu were just that: stories to frighten small children.

Cwenhild watched their reaction before continuing, "We always talk about rebelling against the King here in Halklyen. However, within the walls of Hawk Hut, we know that our real enemy is Martokallu. Somehow, he is able to see everything that happens in Abbarkon. If he discovers you, *The Hawks* will fall. Our best weapon against him so far, has been secrecy." She paused in her story and studied her listeners again. Then, as if making up her mind, she quickly continued, "My mother works to maintain a cloak of concealment over Halklyen and the forests that surround it. This cloak prevents Martokallu from seeing Halklyen which is the only thing that keeps us safe."

Fleta and Flint shared a look of confusion as Cwenhild added, "If your identity is discovered, *The Followers* will be sent after you and they will track you here. Orma's shield relies on the fact that Martokallu does not know about us. If he knows enough to look for us, he will find us."

Flint's eyes widened at that piece of information. He always thought of Orma as a nice old lady, who was a great cook and the right person to go see if you hurt yourself or did not feel well. To imagine that she had the power to shield an entire village was overwhelming. Was she a witch? What sort of magic were they talking about?

"Basically," Cwenhild continued, "*The Followers* are Martokallu's personal army and many of them live in Abbarkon where they enforce his will." Looking at Flint, she said, "You may have seen them around when you lived in Shenkar. Your Duke was under the influence of Martokallu and *Followers* would have been near."

An image of a huge soldier jumped into Flint's mind and he remembered the horrible fear he had felt whenever the man was near. Cwenhild was still talking and he dismissed the memory so that he could concentrate on what she was saying. "No one has seen Martokallu for at least two generations, but we know that he continues to gather the reins of power in Abbarkon. He has generals in all the cities and he uses his sorcery to take over the minds of our leaders. We stand no chance in a direct fight with him and that is why we must even the odds by eliminating the most influential figureheads under his command."

40

Cwenhild stopped speaking and looked at the youngsters. Flint was shocked into silence. Every piece of information that had been revealed to him in the last half hour was staggering. He had had no idea that any of this was going on around him. To remain so ignorant of the real purpose behind all the training seemed impossible. Although, after a moment's thought, he realized that the lack of information their enemies had was *The Talons'* most powerful tool.

For a moment, he could not even think of another question to ask, but Fleta was ready. "How will we know Geir?" she asked. "If secrecy is everything, I wouldn't want to walk up to some stranger and say, 'Well, are you ready to leave for Halklyen?'"

"Another very good question," said Cadmon with a smile. "Halvor will take this one because he has the details worked out for you." He turned the floor over to Halvor who rose nimbly from his seat near the door and took the spot in front of the hearth.

Fleta knew him well from the time she had spent training with him. An amazing dagger thrower, he had begun her training when she was little more than a baby. Naturally, he did not put an actual dagger in her hand at that age, but he began teaching her to throw things accurately from the time she could walk. Before she was five, she was an accomplished juggler and because Halvor knew that agility was a major part of a dagger thrower's defence, he taught her flips and balances as well.

"I have been the one who picks up Geir's encrypted

messages," began Halvor. "I know him to see him, but we have never spoken. It was arranged that he would leave the letters for pick up in a spot on the wall where we made a little hidey-hole." He smiled to himself as he said this, and looked around at the attentive faces surrounding him.

"I would slide into town, wait until that stretch of wall was unattended and then throw a stick for Selda to fetch." At this, he wiggled his eyebrows and smiled at Fleta. Selda was the golden lab he had brought back to the village as a puppy three years ago. He had been training her to perform several unusual tricks including one he called, "Fetch". It looked like a regular game of Fetch as long as he used the words, "Get it, girl". But, whenever he called "fetch", Selda had been trained to grab the stick, lie down, wrestle with it, and refuse to return it. It worked beautifully as a diversion for any sort of mission. Using these two commands, he would have her play normally until he needed to distract people.

"Geir is a big man," said Halvor. He allowed a moment for the groans to pass through the room. Halvor was not what anyone would call a big man and he often ended up thinking everyone was tall just because he looked up to so many people. He continued with a grin, "I think you can take my word on this one. He is known as the tallest guard in Thalnafar. In fact, he is the tallest man in the whole town. Geir stands head and shoulders above a crowd and to make him even more noticeable, he has bright red hair which always seems to need a haircut." At this, Halvor preened a bit to show off his neatly barbered brown hair.

"As well, he has the skin of a red-head and his face is covered in freckles and so are the backs of his hands and arms. Because he will be in hiding, I suspect he will no longer be wearing the uniform of a King's Guard, but you should have no trouble recognizing him anyway." He executed a small bow in Fleta and Flint's direction and seated himself once again.

Fleta's next question took the words right out of Flint's mouth, "How are we supposed to get him out of town then?"

Cadmon kept a straight face as he answered with one word, "Night."

They both considered this for a moment and then nodded their heads as they realized that this really was the most sensible reply.

Flint immediately had another question, "What's our cover?"

Cadmon stood up and took the floor. "That is an easy one; you are a brother and sister traveling to visit your aunt: that would be the woman who has granted Geir refuge in her home. She had a brother who was a guard in Kallcunarth before he was killed in a skirmish." Flint thought fleetingly of the guards who died on the day when he escaped hanging. They would have had family too.

Cadmon continued, "You will need to join the road from Kallcunarth, and the easiest way to do that is to ford the river just north of here. The horses can make the crossing easily enough."

Flint felt overwhelmed with amazement. First of all, to be chosen to be part of a mission that would be just him and Fleta was incredible, but it was a rare day that he had permission to ask all the questions he wanted. After hesitating a moment, he asked, "How will I be able to hide my swords and keep them ready in case I need them?"

Cadmon glanced at Cwenhild and smiled before saying, "I think you will need to talk to Orma about that, but she'll be able to fix you up perfectly."

Flint wanted to ask more, but he knew from experience that Cadmon was not likely to explain further even given these special circumstances. He had one further question though. "When do we leave?"

"Before dawn, tomorrow morning," Cadmon replied. "And now, you have plenty to think about and much to prepare, so we will excuse you from the remainder of our meeting." Cadmon gestured toward the door. Flint and Fleta rose at once and made their way out of the hut.

Chapter 7 - Skulking

Flint reeled with excitement and he could tell from looking at Fleta that she felt the same way. They stood outside Hawk Hut uncertainly for a few moments and then, grinning happily, Flint said, "I guess we better get moving if we are going to be ready in time." He looked quickly around the square before continuing in a quiet voice, "I know where I want to go first. Did you see the look Cadmon gave Cwenhild when he said Orma had something for me?"

Joris could hear them plainly from his hiding spot behind a woodpile and he debated with himself about whether to follow them or wait for one of *The Talons* to appear. He had pretty much decided that Jaak would be the one to follow. The man just could not stop talking. Joris figured that if he were patient, one of these days he would overhear something useful. He dismissed the annoying adolescents with a shrug. They were too young to be useful, he thought and watched irritably as they walked away in the direction of Sparrow Hawk Square.

Orma was busy in her workroom when Flint and

Fleta came rushing in through her front door. "Greetings of the day, Orma," Fleta called. "We've come for a visit."

"Come on through. I've been waiting for you," answered Orma from behind the closed door. When they burst into the room, Orma was just removing a small cauldron from the fire in the huge hearth that backed onto the one in the kitchen. "Greetings of the day," she said. "Cadmon said you would be coming to call at about this time." Smiling at them over her shoulder, she set the cauldron on the table in the corner of the small room. "I imagine you are curious about how you are going to conceal those blades that you carry everywhere."

Flint stared at her in wonder, and Orma chuckled at the look on his face. "I know you just learned a few facts about how things actually work here in Halklyen, so you know about the cloak over the village but I can assure you that I am not using magic to read your mind. Cadmon let me know what was planned today, and we figured you would come here first."

Fleta asked curiously, "Do you have some sort of special hooded cloak that will hide his swords?"

"Better than that," answered Orma. "I'll show you if you don't mind leaving your blades with me for an hour or so." She was pouring the contents of the cauldron carefully into a heavy glass flask that she corked tightly. Turning, she looked expectantly at Flint who hesitated only a moment before he drew the pair of swords in a hiss of metal on metal.

"Just put them on the table," Orma said, indicating

46

her workspace. She handed Flint a pair of thick leather gloves and said, "Here, put these on." He slid them on and she handed him a small piece of folded cloth. "All right, here is what you do: tip a small amount of the potion from the bottle onto the cloth and rub every bit of your sword with it."

"It's not going to make it change colour is it?" asked Flint worriedly.

Orma laughed, and said, "Oh no, it won't change colour. Don't worry; it will not hurt those precious blades. In fact, you won't see any difference for a while, but if you come back in an hour, I can guarantee you will be impressed."

Fleta looked on with interest while Flint carefully smoothed the potion over every surface of the swords including the silver-wound hilts. "What are the gloves for?" she asked.

"Well, the potion doesn't hurt metal, but it burns skin like nobody's business. You want to be really careful with this." Orma spoke seriously, as she gave the warning.

Flint finished the job, stoppered the bottle and then removed the gloves. "Come back in an hour?" he asked. "You want me to leave them here?" He was not sure he liked that idea.

"I'll take care of them," Orma assured him. "I know you have other preparations that need seeing to. Indeed, if I may make a suggestion, the next visit you make should be to the stables. I suspect Albar will be waiting for you there."

"It seems that everyone already knows what's going on," Fleta said cheerfully. "I'm guessing that there was a big discussion before you decided that we could handle this assignment?"

Orma smiled without saying anything, and held the door wide for them to leave. "Have fun," she said quietly in parting, "but remember all of this is a secret."

Smiling and nodding their thanks, they slid past Orma and headed to the edge of town where Albar oversaw the town stables.

Most of the riding that Fleta and Flint had done was confined to the riding ring and the trails that crisscrossed the surrounding forest. They had both been along the track that they would follow in the morning. The spot where it came out beside the river was a favourite place for picnic lunches. This would be their first time crossing the river to the road.

Flint had not left Halklyen since that day almost three years ago when he woke up in Orma's house. For Fleta, a nearby village called Fasnul was the only other place she had ever been. Sebastien, the Duke of Fasnul, was a good friend of Cadmon's. The villagers of Halklyen had come to count on the supplies that could be picked up from Fasnul on a market day. Not everything they needed could be grown or made in Halklyen, so once every couple of months a delegation would be sent along to pick up necessities.

On the few occasions when Fleta went along as part of a group sent on a supply run, she had a wonderful time. They always visited on market day when the town was a place of bustling activity. Duke Sebastien had known her parents well, and he made a point of inviting Fleta up to his palace when he knew she was in town. He was a generous and easygoing man who Fleta enjoyed visiting. He could also be counted on to provide a marvellous meal.

Fleta was beginning to wonder how she felt about this mission when they walked into the stable and called out for Albar. He strolled out from a stall where he had been currying the large bay that Fleta usually rode. "Well, you be looking for a good horse," he spoke quietly and smiled gently at the pair before they had an opportunity to explain what they needed. "You be needing a few other things too I be guessing. Let's get you sorted out."

The next half hour was spent going over what they would do for their mounts while they were on the road and helping Albar to fix saddlebags with extra oats. There was room for some supplies for themselves as well, and he advised them to stop in at the bake ovens to pick up some bread to take along.

The plan was to have the two new *Hawks* each ride a horse on the way to Thalnafar, and then, taking advantage of the fact that neither of them was a heavy load, give one horse to Geir and ride double on the way back to Halklyen. For this reason, the horse that Flint was taking was not his usual gentle pony but a huge gelding named Bo. Fortunately, Bo was an easygoing horse who did not mind going for a long walk. Fleta was happy to see that she would ride Prenses, who she knew well from their happy rides on the forest trails.

Joris waited impatiently outside Hawk Hut for another three-quarters of an hour before he was rewarded with the exit of *The Talons*. They left in twos and threes and he stuck with his plan to follow Jaak who was talking and joking with Walker as they strolled away.

Sliding unobtrusively from his hiding spot, he carefully followed them. Fortunately for him, Jaak and Walker were the last to leave the hut and Joris congratulated himself on his good luck.

Watching from the shadows, Joris saw Jaak wave a farewell to Walker and enter Egbert's forge with a loud greeting. Joris was just able to tuck himself in behind the lean-to storage area when he heard Jaak burst out, "I need my weapons sharpened. It would not be good trying to assassinate Count Arjen with a blunt blade." Immediately after this announcement, the conversation at the forge dropped to an inaudible volume, but Joris had heard enough. He slipped out of the shadows and without stopping to talk to anyone, quietly made his way out of town.

Chapter 8 - Extraction

Flint felt a hand on his shoulder and he startled awake. It was dark in the room and he cast around frantically for the source of danger. "No worries, boy. It's time to get up," Cadmon said quietly. Already dressed, he moved over to the table where he had placed the makings of a big breakfast.

Flint struggled to clear his mind and suddenly it all came back to him. He and Fleta were going on a mission today! Sometimes he could not believe his luck. In some ways, it seemed a short time since he had been working as a kitchen boy and server for Duke Dedrick. At that point, it seemed like his life was an endless series of dirty dishes. He had always known that he should be grateful to have the position. His memories of the horrible hunger he had experienced in the year after his parents' death reminded him that he was lucky to have work and a place to live, but sometimes it had been hard to feel that gratitude.

The Duke was a cruel master more concerned with the food on his plate than the people who prepared it for him. He tended to let his temper go if something did not meet his standards. Flint had often been on the receiving end of those hard fists or boots and occasionally, the man would casually pick up objects to use as articles of discipline against his staff.

That is what happened the morning Flint killed the Duke. Ill from over-eating and too much drink on the previous evening, the man had been in a terrible mood. He had not even bothered to wax and curl the mustache that was his pride and joy.

When Flint's friend, Pim dropped a tray of sausages at the Duke's feet, the large man had risen from his chair and, seizing a heavy silver candlestick from the table, he had begun to beat the boy. At first, Flint had been unable to move, but as he watched, he realized that something needed to be done or Pim would die. Snatching up the matching candlestick, he brought it down across the back of the Duke's head.

Before he knew it, the Duke of Shenkar, the King's cousin, lay dead at Flint's feet. His first thoughts, however, were for Pim who lay beside the Duke, bleeding from a head wound. He was kneeling over his friend, holding a napkin to the bloody gash when a guard entered the dining room and hauled Flint to his feet.

From there, it had been a blur of dungeons and angry faces until the morning, a week later, when he found himself trudging toward the gallows. His only comfort was the news that Pim was going to be all right.

With a jolt of amazement, Flint realized that it was that one reckless moment of bravery that brought him to Cadmon's attention. Cadmon rescued him, trained him and was now sending him off to continue the rebellion against the King and it all started with one rash decision. It felt wonderful to think that he could be an important part of the whole plan.

"Well, are you going to get moving this morning?" Cadmon interrupted his reverie. "Or do I have to tell Fleta she might as well head out on her own?" Cadmon was seated at the table munching on his breakfast while he watched Flint who still lay on his cot.

"I'm up," Flint cried as he leapt from his bed. Thrusting his legs into his leather breeches, he reached for his shirt. A soft leather jerkin went over that and before he left, he would put on the new black cloak that Orma had presented to him the day before. Remembering Orma, he glanced over at his swords. The scabbards appeared to be empty but he guessed that the blades still hung where he had put them before going to sleep.

When he and Fleta returned to Orma's cottage after arranging their mounts with Albar, he had been shocked at what the potion had done. The swords were completely invisible. Moreover, she said it would last for forty-eight hours.

The cloak she made for him had two narrow slits cut into it at the shoulders to accommodate the scabbards. Unless you looked closely, there was nothing unusual to notice.

Fleta's daggers were much easier to disguise. She would be wearing a wide scarf around her waist that hid the fact that the belt she wore was studded with beautifully designed throwing knives. He and Fleta would just be two normal young people on the road to Thalnafar.

Flint wolfed down his breakfast of bread and sausage, tucked the leftovers back in the cloth bag and tied it to his belt. With wonder, he checked his blades, buckled on the baldric, settled the cloak over his shoulders and waved goodbye to Cadmon.

Cadmon gave him a quick nod and reached out a hand to grasp his shoulder. Looking Flint in the eye he said, "You'll do it boy. Just keep your eyes open."

Flint felt a rush of gratitude to hear Cadmon's confidence in him. "Thanks, Cadmon. See you tomorrow."

As soon as Flint and Fleta were out of sight, Cadmon hurried to the stables where he saddled his own horse and led it outside to wait for the rest of the team. The plan was to have *The Sparrow Hawks* and *The Vultures* take out Duke Arjen of Derflanag. The information they had received showed that Martokallu had fully taken possession of Arjen's will. They knew from previous experiences that the only way to deal with someone in Martokallu's control was to kill him.

Riding always made Flint a little sleepy. He found the rhythm of the horse lulled him into daydreaming and he constantly had to remind himself to follow Cadmon's advice about keeping his eyes open.

Fleta had been all ready to go when he passed by her

cottage just before the sun rose. Egbert and Merylin had both been outside to see her off. Fleta also wore her new black cloak. *The Talons* routinely wore black; it made it easier to disappear into the shadows when necessary.

Fleta had hugged both Egbert and Merylin and Flint had received a big hug from Merylin as well. Egbert had gripped him by the shoulder and said, "Remember, lad, if you draw those swords, be prepared to use them. You know what to do."

After that, they had hurried to the stables, saddled their horses and were riding through the forest while it was still dark.

Looking around now, Flint realized that they must be getting close to the river. Albar had insisted that as soon as they crossed the water, they should take the time to groom the horses so that they did not look wet. The idea was to join the road and pretend that they had travelled all the way from Kallcunarth.

"There it is," Fleta spoke quietly, but there was an edge of excitement in her voice. "Let's watch for a bit before we try to cross."

"Good idea," Flint answered in an equally low voice. They both dismounted well before the edge of the woods and dropped their reins to let the horses crop the foliage between the trees while they settled down to watch the river.

After several minutes, they decided that no one was around. Leading the horses out of the woods, they stopped at the stream and let them each have a drink. After another look around to reassure themselves that they were alone, they mounted up and urged the beasts into the river. Neither horse needed to swim, so Flint and Fleta were able to keep dry by lifting their feet above the water.

When they got to the far shore, they did as Albar had asked and pulled out the brushes from the saddlebags. After first using dry grass from the riverbank to wipe the horses down, they made good use of the brushes and soon the horses looked quite dry.

Fleta slipped ahead to the road where she watched until there were no travelers visible from either direction. Running back to where Flint waited with the horses, she called quietly, "It's clear. Let's go."

Once they were on the road, they kept their eyes open for other travellers, but they only saw two other groups and those were both going in the opposite direction. Flint was busy with his own thoughts and he noticed that Fleta was also preoccupied. "So far, so good," he said as they approached the gates of Thalnafar.

Fleta smiled and nodded. "I still can't believe we are doing this! I know it is not much of a mission, and we are going to be home tomorrow, but..." she ran out of words and opened both arms wide to encompass a whole feeling of exhilaration.

Flint answered, "I know what you mean. We spent all that time practicing with our weapons, and learning how to track, but I never really thought I'd get to actually do anything useful." He pictured the swords that sat invisibly in their scabbards on his back. What would happen if he needed to draw them?

"All right, we will wait here for you two to scout things out," Cadmon spoke to Jaak and Walker who were making last minute preparations for their explorations of Derflanag. The walled city had only one gate and Jaak was going to brazen his way through that way. Walker was going over the wall. Both men had amazing abilities to slide through a crowd without being noticed.

The archers, Lieve, Grove and Cwenhild, positioned themselves at the edge of the woods so that they could keep an eye on the scouts for as long as possible. Cwenhild added to her sightline by swinging up into a tree that had room to accommodate her bow. From there, they were able to see what happened when Walker reached the top of the wall and Jaak made it to the front of the line at the gate.

At almost the same moment, both men were met by *Followers*, who before speaking even a word, ran them through with swords.

Cwenhild gasped and almost fell out of her tree. Below her, Lieve spoke in an anguished voice, "We are betrayed. They must have known we were coming." He glanced back at Cadmon and Hulda, and said urgently, "We have to help them. If we all go at once, we can save them." He was prepared to sprint across the open ground, but Cadmon stopped him.

"No. I am sorry," he said quietly, "It's too late. They're gone. We must retreat and make a new plan. Somehow, they knew we were coming. For now, it is too dangerous; we would all be killed." Cadmon reached out to grip Lieve's arm. The distraught man shook him off.

Hulda spoke up, "He's right. If we attempt to force our way in now, we will all die. If we wait, we can make a difference."

Fleta and Flint had asked the woman who was sheltering Geir to wake them at midnight. They wanted to leave at a time when there would be no one else around. The hope was that if someone did happen to see them, it would be too dim to see that it was Geir who was leaving town.

Flint felt as if he had just lain down when the woman began shaking his shoulder. He struggled to wake himself up. Geir stood ready near the door and Fleta was making the last adjustments to her dagger belt. Sitting up, he hurried to fasten the webbing on his baldric after checking that the swords were still invisible.

Even with Egbert's warning, he had secretly hoped that he might get a chance to use the swords. It would be funny to watch the face of an opponent who could not see the weapon that was attacking him. Still, Cadmon would probably prefer that they did not get any action on this trip.

Outside, they found that Geir had already saddled the horses. Flint and Fleta mounted up together and Geir followed on the larger animal. Trying to make himself look smaller, the huge man hunched close to his horse's neck. Flint hoped that they did not encounter anyone because Halvor had been right. Geir was very recognizable, even in the dark.

Fortunately, within minutes, they were clear of the village and heading down the road to Kallcunarth. Now all they had to do was recognize the spot where they had to leave the road in order to cross the river.

When they joined the road the day before, Flint made a special effort to notice the landmarks, but in the dark, it was more difficult than he imagined it would be. Finally, Fleta spotted the shadowy outline of a raspberry patch that had marked the exit for her. She remembered thinking that it would offer a feast in a few days if she could return.

After checking that no one would see them exit the road, they splashed through the river and then it was an easy ride back to Halklyen. Mission accomplished.

Chapter 9 - Alarm

Cadmon and the remaining members of the assassin squad raced back home. As they rode, they talked about what had happened and realized that someone from the village must be the betrayer. Lieve guessed that Joris was behind it. He remembered seeing the ill-tempered man hanging around Hawk Hut the day before when they came out of the meeting.

"If it is Joris, we're in trouble," Dell was speaking quietly to Cadmon as they trotted along the road to Fasnul. They were almost to the point where they would enter the forest before the last stretch through the woods to Halklyen. "He knows everything about us except perhaps what Orma can do and the fact that we know about Martokallu."

"Most importantly, he knows the way to Halklyen," replied Cadmon tensely. "We don't really have a plan for an evacuation, but we need to get everyone to safety before Lorund shows up with *The Followers*. You know that will be the next step for them." One of leaders of *The Followers*, Lorund had proven himself to be completely without mercy.

"We'll have to count on Sebastien," Dell's voice was bleak. "Perhaps our people can blend in with his townspeople and no one will feel the need to reveal us." Dell knew he would not have to worry about hiding. He would be ready to fight. Hiding was not an option for him; not with his scars and the concealing mask he chose to wear.

Cadmon dropped back a pace. "Halvor," he called, "I want you and Faro to head to Fasnul. Talk to Duke Sebastien and let him know what happened. We think Joris has betrayed us and we're going to need to evacuate the townspeople to him for safety. Tell him we have about thirty people who will need shelter."

"Shall we head to Halklyen after we talk with Sebastien?" Halvor's father had been a friend of the Duke's and he spoke with the familiarity of long association.

"Plan to do that," Cadmon said as he reached out, gripped Halvor's arm and then looked across to nod at Faro. "Ride hard and keep your eyes open."

The men nodded and urged their horses ahead. Selda, Halvor's faithful dog, kept pace with them. The remaining riders watched for a moment before swinging their horses toward Halklyen.

Moments later, a man who Cadmon immediately recognized as one of *The Followers of Martokallu,* leapt out of the woods and threw himself at Hulda's horse. Pulsing blue veins showed beneath his cracked grey skin: both characteristics of a man whose mind is possessed by Martokallu.

The horse stumbled under the weight of the monster, but Hulda jumped free and rolled to her feet. Cadmon turned his head in time to see Halvor fire an arrow that went straight through *The Follower's* head. The skull exploded in a flash of blue light. Reining in, Cadmon reached down and pulled Hulda up in front of him.

"Keep going!" he shouted and everyone urged the horses forward. A second *Follower* appeared at Cadmon's side. He was running as fast as the horse. Hollow black eyes stared eagerly out of the ravaged face and Cadmon had to force his attention toward the wickedly long dagger aimed at his throat. With Hulda in front of him, he was not able to freely swing *The Rising Star*. Fortunately, Hulda had no such problems and her dagger appeared in her hands just before she buried it in the *Follower's* chest.

"Orma will know where you should stay. She always knows what to do," Fleta said to Geir as they approached Halklyen. It was quiet as they rode through the streets on the outskirts of town, toward Orma's cottage. When they dismounted in front of her neat garden, they were surprised to find that she was not at home. In fact, no one seemed to be in the streets at all.

"Where is everyone?" asked Flint. "This is strange."

"Maybe there's something going on in the square," suggested Fleta. "Let's check there."

When they got closer to the centre of the village, they realized that Fleta had the right idea. They could hear someone speaking and then the sound of a crowd answering, but they could not yet make out any words.

When they entered the square, several people turned to stare at Geir who, seated on his horse, looked like a redheaded giant. Then their attention was pulled back to Cadmon who addressed the crowd from his position on top of a barrel. Flint, Fleta and Geir had missed the beginning of the speech but they could tell from the feeling in the crowd that this was not a happy announcement.

Cadmon nodded at the newcomers then continued speaking, "Obviously, precautions need to be taken. I have already sent Halvor and Faro to talk to Duke Sebastien. We will be moving the non-warriors to Fasnul this evening. If Joris told them enough to let Duke Arjen know that we were coming, and for *The Followers* to find us on the road home, we need to act immediately to keep people safe."

Flint recoiled. *The Followers* knew where to find Halklyen? They were in trouble. Would Orma be able to shield the village if Martokallu knew they were here? From what he and Fleta had learned at the meeting, the strength of *The Hawks* came from the secrecy they had managed to maintain.

Cadmon was still speaking and Flint made himself listen. "First of all," he declared while surveying the crowd, "I need to know that Joris never made a trip to Fasnul and that he was unaware of our connection with Sebastien." He paused, giving people time to think about what might have been said in front of Joris.

Most *Hawks* were extremely aware of the need for secrecy and very little was ever said in front of newcomers. Geir was getting an earful now though. They had better hope that he was not there as a double agent.

Everyone waited in tense silence to see if that secret was breached and then Cadmon began to explain the plan. "There are twenty-one here who are not fighters. I want to get you to safety in Sebastien's village. We hope to be able to let you slip into families and homes there to make it look like you completely belong. Go home, gather what you need, and come prepared to travel tonight.

"Warriors," he continued, "come prepared to fight. We leave in thirty minutes." Nothing more needed to be said, and the crowd hurriedly dispersed.

Fleta looked in shock at Flint and said, "I'm going to see Egbert and Merylin. They aren't fighters." She considered that for a moment, and then added, "Well, Merylin isn't anyway. Egbert says that when he goes to war, he takes his hammer." She stopped and asked worriedly, "This is war isn't it?"

Flint was just as alarmed and nodded slowly. "It sounds like it," he said. Then, shaking off his fear, he announced, "I'm going to go see Cadmon and Orma. We'll meet at the stables in thirty minutes." For a moment, they both forgot about Geir as Fleta slid off the horse she shared with Flint and took off for home. At that, Flint turned to the big man and said, "You'd better come with me."

They hurried through the empty streets again. This

time though, Flint knew that everyone was inside their homes packing all that they would need to either blend into village life or head off to war.

He went to Orma's house first and was not surprised to see that Cadmon had beaten him there. Looking at the leader of *The Hawks* Flint wondered what happened so that they knew Joris had betrayed them. He noted that when Cadmon addressed the crowd, he had already been dressed for war.

Stepping forward with a grim smile, Cadmon greeted Geir. "Well, this is not the welcome we were hoping to offer. I won't go into the details, but one of our newer recruits has betrayed us to the King." Flint noticed that he did not mention Martokallu again.

"I will not complain, sir. I reckon that I can be of more use here than I was as a King's Guard in Thalnafar. I have my weapons and chainmail. I am prepared to fight."

"Thank you, Geir. I imagine we will have to take you up on that offer." Cadmon reached out and shook his hand.

Turning to Flint, he said, "Well, Flint? How did it go? It looks as if your first mission was a success." Cadmon did not quite smile, but his face almost relaxed as he looked at the young man he had been training.

"Yes, sir," answered Flint. "It went just as you said it would. We even got to sleep for five hours before we left for home." That actually got a smile from Cadmon who knew how much Flint liked to sleep.

Flint had forgotten, in the worry about *The Followers,*

just how excited he had been to tell Cadmon about the mission. Now it did not seem at all worth boasting about. He was far more interested in learning what was going on. He said, "We missed the beginning of your speech, Cadmon. Can you tell me more about what's happening?"

Cadmon looked meaningfully at Geir who cleared his throat and took a step back toward the door, saying, "I'll just go look to the horses, shall I? I guess they aren't going to get a rest yet."

When Geir closed the door behind him, Cadmon gestured for Flint to follow him into the back room where Orma was working. She paused to offer Flint a tired smile but turned back to her task immediately without speaking.

After closing this door as well, and then moving to the window where he carefully looked in both directions before pulling the shutters closed, Cadmon began his explanation, "*The Vultures* and *The Sparrow Hawks* left on a mission shortly after you did yesterday. Duke Arjen is known to be under Martokallu's control and something needed to be done."

Flint suddenly understood the reasons for Cadmon's frequent missions. It also explained the many deaths of high-placed men about whom he had heard *The Sparrow Hawks* talk. And, he realized, because of the secrecy surrounding *The Hawks*, no one ever figured out who was behind the assassinations that kept happening all around the kingdom.

Blinking at these revelations, he forced his attention

back to what Cadmon was saying. "The plan was to have Jaak and Walker slip into Derflanag to get the lay of the land and then we would take it from there." Cadmon stopped speaking for a moment and swallowed hard as he looked away from Flint.

"They were both killed when they tried to enter the town. They didn't have a chance." Flint blanched at this news and Cadmon reached out to grip his shoulder. "We believe it was Joris, who betrayed us," he continued. "He has disappeared from the village and no one has seen him since late afternoon on the day of *The Talons'* meeting. You know how he has been since he got here. We are not certain whether he came here as a double agent or if he just saw an opportunity and took it."

Once again, Cadmon stopped speaking while he watched Orma's preparations. Flint waited, sensing that there was more that Cadmon needed to say. After a long moment, he continued, "On our return route to Halklyen, there were four *Followers* who laid in ambush and attacked us. Amazingly, no one was hurt and we managed to kill all four of them."

Again, Cadmon took a long breath and exhaled slowly before looking directly at Flint, "Unfortunately, I suspect that they were still mind-linked with Martokallu until their deaths so he will know what has happened. We expect that there are going to be more of them here very shortly.

"Orma has made an addition to the cloak over the village and woods. Now it will be impossible for anyone who is not of *The Talons* even to find a trail into the woods. But there is nothing to be done about the fact that we are no longer a secret, and that means we are in open war."

Chapter 10 - Wrath

Joris was nervous. At first, it had seemed like a good idea to warn Duke Arjen that there were assassins on their way to kill him. He figured that the Duke would want to reward him for the information. He imagined becoming a favoured advisor of the Duke and having an easy life in the palace. Living with *The Hawks* had not really been his idea of a good time. They were always too concerned with training or working. No one cared at all about making money.

After hearing Jaak announce his plans, he had quietly snuck into the stables, saddled his horse and slipped out of Halklyen without anyone noticing. When he arrived in Derflanag, it had been difficult to arrange to see the Duke. Without any credentials, nobody would listen to him.

When he finally convinced the guards that he had valuable information, he had been surprised at the level of excitement his announcement had generated. Arjen immediately left the room for a few minutes and when he returned, he looked slightly crazed as he began to order the King's Guard into place.

After having spent months watching the type of

training that took place in Halklyen, Joris had warned them that the assassins would not just try to enter through the main gate. They would come over the wall or under the wall or they would find some unknown route into the town. Arjen nodded and sent men to cover the entire city wall and put a large force at the main gate as well.

The strangest thing of all was the sight of the large warriors who did not wear the blue and white uniform of the King's Guard. Most of these men wore mismatched pieces of rusty iron or bone armour with shoulder pads that might have protruding spikes or rough pieces of leather hanging off them. Gap-toothed smiles leered out of many of their helmets. Just looking at those warriors, with their cracked grey skin, made Joris realize that he was in way over his head.

Joris presumed that after he shared his information, he would be paid for his trouble, and then sent on his way, or perhaps, offered a position in the court. Instead, he found himself in a locked tower room with a view of a stretch of the wall and the main gate. He hoisted himself up onto the windowsill to watch the happenings below. It did not take long. *The Hawks* must have been only a short distance behind him.

As he gazed listlessly at the view, he suddenly saw a scuffle erupt atop the wall not far from the main gate. At almost the same moment, a ruckus sprang up at the gate itself. From where he sat, Joris saw a splash of red blood spray over the crowd at the gate while the clash on top of the wall resulted in one man falling into the city and lying still. Straining his eyes, Joris thought he recognized that braggart, Jaak, who never knew when to keep his mouth shut.

Shortly after viewing these grizzly events, Joris was startled to have the door to his tower room abruptly thrust open. Arjen himself entered the small room. "Well, it has turned out as you said. What else have you got to tell me?"

Flint and Fleta were at the back of the procession that was moving as quietly as possible through the woods. The path was really only wide enough to accommodate two people at a time and Cadmon had ordered that all of the non-warriors be paired with a warrior. The non-warriors carried the larger loads, leaving the warriors free to fight if necessary. Halvor and Faro had returned earlier with the news that Sebastien's people were willing to hide anyone who would not be joining the fight. The refugees carried whatever they would need to join in with village life.

Unable to stay quiet any longer, Fleta burst out, "I cannot believe that they think we should be the ones to take the place of Walker and Jaak. They were amazing and I'm going to miss them so much." She reached up to wipe away the tears that sprang from her eyes as she remembered her friends.

Cadmon and Hulda had taken them aside while the group was preparing to leave. It was not supposed to happen so soon, but it was no secret that the youngsters were being groomed to become members of *The Talons*. The coming war made it immediately necessary to fill the positions that the deaths of Jaak and Walker had left vacant. The leaders felt that the most qualified people were Flint and Fleta, regardless of their age.

So now, they were scouts. That was rather funny because here they were at the back of the army rather than the front but Hulda had wanted them to have a chance to talk before she put them on active duty.

"Remember that day, when we played that giant game of hide and seek with Walker and Jaak?" Flint laughed as he recalled the rules that Jaak had set up.

He had given them a twenty minute head start and said they could hide anywhere in the woods. The winner of the game would be the one who could sneak up on the other team. Flint and Fleta did have the advantage of their head start, but Jaak and Walker were expert trackers, and they had been their teachers in the woods. Using tricks that the experienced men had shown them, Fleta and Flint finally managed to creep up behind the older two scouts when they sat down to rest after four hours of wandering around the woods.

Fleta giggled in a most unwarrior-like way and said, "The looks on their faces! They were sure we had taken off and given up the game!" Then she sobered as she said, "I can't believe they're not coming back."

They were quiet for a minute, and then Flint spoke up, "I guess we better get to the front. We'll be coming out of the woods soon." Their orders had been to travel at the back until shortly before the trail entered the road to Fasnul, and then make a sweep through the woods on either side of the trail. "I'll go right, you go left. Be careful. Keep your eyes open." Without thinking, he echoed the warning that Cadmon always gave him.

If Joris had felt nervous before, now he was absolutely terrified. After his interview with Duke Arjen, he had been taken to a large room in the castle and introduced to one of those frighteningly ugly men with the sickly-looking grey skin.

Lorund was tall and muscular but he looked like no man Joris had ever seen before. There were long cracks in his skin and Joris thought he could see pulsing orange veins visible. His eyes were of the same hideous orange colour. When Arjen stepped up to introduce Joris as a useful informant, and those eyes looked at him for the first time, Joris felt his knees weaken with a fear so great that he almost fell.

Now, Joris found himself on the road to Fasnul with a company of twelve of those grey-skinned men. They called themselves *The Followers*. As far as Joris could see, they did not speak to each other. In fact, it was decidedly strange to watch as they worked together without exchanging a word.

Only Lorund and Joris were mounted. The others jogged easily along beside the horses. Without appearing to look too closely, Joris was studying Lorund. He could see that his armour was ancient. Made of rusted metal and bone, Joris could not see how it would be any use in deflecting a blade. On his left hip the terrifying man bore a large broadsword, and on his right side, he carried a coiled bullwhip. In contrast to the rest of him, both of these weapons appeared to be in good repair.

Joris's job was to lead *The Followers* to the entrance to the trail leading to Halklyen. The problem was that it was not where he thought it should be.

He was afraid to ask the Gruesome Dozen, as he had been calling them in his mind, to backtrack to see if he had missed the trail entrance. He was not sure what they would do to him if he failed to find the path for them. But, he definitely did not want to find out.

Flint moved smoothly through the woods keeping the sound of the procession of villagers on his left and watching intently for signs of any intruders. He did not want to believe that anyone could breach Orma's shield, but on his first day as a scout, he was being extra careful.

He arrived at the head of the procession and noted that they were very near the edge of the woods. After a careful look around, Flint headed back toward the trail. He wanted to ask Cadmon to halt the villagers before they came to the end of Orma's shield.

Sliding out of the woods, onto the trail right beside Cadmon, Flint spoke quietly, "Would it be all right if we stopped everyone for a minute while I scout ahead?"

Cadmon jumped in surprise and turned to Flint in astonishment. "Where did you come from?"

"I've been scouting the right side. Fleta is checking

the left. She should be here in a minute," Flint answered with a smile. He was rather proud that he had been able to approach Cadmon undetected.

As if on cue, Fleta suddenly appeared at Cadmon's other shoulder. "I saw no signs of anyone in the woods," she said. "But I think we should scout ahead before everyone continues."

A flicker of a smile crossed Cadmon's face but he merely answered, "Good idea." Turning, he quietly called a halt and the message was passed quickly down the line.

Flint and Fleta crouched in the trees at the edge of the woods, watching as a strange company of men trotted past. They recognized Joris immediately, but they could see that he was not the one in charge. The huge, man beside him with a torn black cape worn over the most battered-looking armour they had ever seen was definitely the leader. They could also see that he was angry.

Joris seemed to be looking for something. He kept talking and pointing toward the woods while the man next to him watched with growing impatience.

Suddenly, it appeared that his patience ran out. After sweeping the edge of the woods once more with eyes that Flint could see were bright orange, he turned and without warning, thrust his sword through Joris.

Chapter 11 - Revenge

Flint turned at a sound behind him. Looking back, he saw that Dell had crept up to the road as well. He was watching *The Followers'* departure. Although it was difficult to read any expression on Dell's face because of the jester's mask he always wore, Flint thought he recognized rage in his eyes.

Together, they watched until the riders were out of sight and all that remained visible on the road was Joris's lifeless body. Then, Flint, Fleta and Dell rose and turned back toward the large group of people who waited just beyond the edge of the woods.

Cadmon studied their white faces as they approached. "What is it?" he asked when he saw their expressions.

Dell answered curtly, "Joris and twelve *Followers.*" He and Cadmon shared a long look, but nothing more was said.

Fleta spoke up, "They killed Joris. It looked like he was trying to find the path, but when he couldn't, one of them just ran a sword right through him." She shuddered.

Cadmon turned to Dagur, who was the Eagle scout leading the party through the woods, and said, "Take care of the body. It looks as if Orma's shield is holding. We are going to return everyone to Halklyen.

Dell did not move as the last of the villagers disappeared into the woods. Only after the tail end of the procession trudged out of earshot did he turn his horse toward the road.

The anger he felt when he recognized the monster who destroyed his village and left him with his terrible scars still seethed through his mind. Without telling Cadmon, he made a decision. He had a mission to do. Alone.

Setting off in pursuit of *The Followers*, he knew that he would need to hurry to keep them in sight because he was not about to lose them a second time. There had been one other opportunity to track Lorund but the trail had disappeared. That would not happen again.

As he rode along, he recalled that long ago day when he first encountered Lorund. The King's Guard had been ordered to burn Dell's village because there were reports of rebellion there. False reports as far as Dell knew, but it had certainly set him on the road to rebellion.

Lorund was their leader. Dell had seen him standing, safely outside the village, watching the flames from a comfortable distance. Dell, in the meantime, was working with the other villagers to battle the fire that had been set by *The Followers*.

It seemed the whole village was burning when he and

the other cottagers had given up trying to extinguish the flames. They decided to abandon the town, and were grabbing anything they could carry before making for the outskirts.

Dell had been the one to turn back when they heard a cry for help. A woman was shrieking and calling out for her children to come out of their hut, but there was no answer. He had grabbed a wet cloth for his face and thrown himself at the door. He had managed to bring the two children out of the fire, but in the process, he was badly burned.

For a while, it looked as if he would die from his injuries, but Cadmon, Gode and Cwenhild showed up just as the flames from the village were dying down. After hearing about Dell's heroics, and speaking with Dell himself, they made the decision to take him to Orma.

From that point on, all Dell remembered was pain. It had taken several hours to move him to Orma's cottage and most of that time passed in a haze. The treatment had not been easy, either. Aside from the pain, the part that he had really hated was when she used maggots to clean out the dead skin. That had been disgusting.

Disgusting too, was the way he looked now. If he could not bear to look at himself, how could he expect others to do so? That was why he had started wearing his leather and wood mask. He had worn the same one when he worked as a street performer. At the time, he had imagined that the big painted smile would make him look happy, but he was not certain that was the result.

Most people looked startled and a little frightened the first time they saw him.

Lorund and the rest of *The Followers* were in sight now so Dell carefully pulled his horse off the road. He would need to move cautiously if he wanted to avoid being seen while he tracked the monster who had changed his life.

The next several hours became a deadly game of cat and mouse as Dell manoeuvred to keep his prey in sight while being sure he remained invisible.

It was getting dark when the Chain of Thollcrawnow came into view. The mountain range was the southernmost border of Abbarkon and cut the peninsula off from the rest of the continent.

The Followers showed no sign of slowing down as the sun set with a burst of colour in the west. It appeared that they would continue into the night. That was all right as far as Dell was concerned. It would make it easier to remain unseen.

Dawn was breaking over Dell's left shoulder when *The Followers* at last came to a stop. He quickly took cover and watched while Lorund led his men straight toward the rock face. During the night, they had finally reached the Chain of Thollcrawnow that had seemed so close when he first saw it the previous evening.

In his hiding spot, Dell's eyes opened wide with astonishment as *The Followers* began to disappear. One by one, they walked toward the mountain and simply vanished.

Long after they were gone, he continued to stare at the spot, but nothing more was visible. Worried that his long ride was for nothing, he settled down to wait and watch.

The Talons were gathered in the Hawk Hut. As usual, Cadmon was the last to enter and he glanced quickly around the room. "Where's Dell?" he asked abruptly.

Everyone looked around in surprise. Dell was known for his promptness and impatience when someone was late.

Flint answered, "The last time I saw him, we had just seen Joris killed and I think he looked angry. When you decided to bring the villagers back home, he said he would take up the rear. I haven't seen him since then."

There was a rumble of agreement, and then, looking thoughtful, Cadmon asked, "Exactly what did the man who killed Joris look like?"

Flint hesitated, "Well," he said, "he had orange eyes." He paused, expecting someone to scoff at him, but a tense silence waited for him to continue. "He had a scar across his face." He glanced involuntarily at Cadmon whose white scar was the first thing he noticed on that day Cadmon rescued him from hanging. Cadmon gave him a grim nod and he felt enough confidence to continue.

"Besides the sword he used to kill Joris, he was also wearing a long whip that was coiled at his hip." Flint thought for a minute, trying to think of a way to describe the strange armour the man had worn.

Fleta jumped in with her own description, "His

armour looked really old." She stood up as spoke and turned to look earnestly at her listeners. "It was rusty in places and parts of it were made of bone! And, his cloak? I have never seen anyone wear something so threadbare. It was more holes than cloth."

Cadmon exchanged a long look with Cwenhild. Finally, she nodded and Cadmon let out a heavy sigh before saying, "Apparently, Dell has taken on his own mission." When he saw a few mystified faces, he continued, "It is Lorund. He is one of *The Followers*. In fact, we believe that he is one of the top-ranking *Followers* and Dell has sworn to kill him."

Cwenhild picked up the story, "When rumours of rebellion in Dell's village surfaced, Lorund was sent with a company of the King's Guard to burn the village. That's where Dell got his scars. He holds Lorund responsible." Cwenhild had been around for much of Dell's healing time and she knew the rage that he felt toward Lorund.

Cadmon added, "About ten years ago, Dell managed to follow Lorund but the trail disappeared." He halted his explanation and turned away from the group. After a moment, he seemed to make up his mind and turned back to face everyone.

"I think Dell's idea to track Lorund has merit. Maybe it will lead to Martokallu himself. I propose that we send a team to trail Dell. Let's see what he has learned."

Chapter 12 - Pursuit

Cadmon had not wanted to leave the village undefended, so he chose a select group of people to shadow Dell. Flint and Fleta rode at the head of the party. They were making good use of the scouting skills that Jaak and Walker taught them.

The trail was almost twelve hours old, but they had the advantage of knowing which horseshoe track belonged to Dell's horse. Sometimes the road was so hard-packed that the trail would disappear, but soon enough, one of them would spot the telltale sign in the dust. They could see that Dell had often pulled his horse off the road into the woods and they guessed that he was staying hidden from the group he was tracking.

Gode, Cadmon's right hand man and best friend, was in charge of the mission. He had remained Flint's favourite man in *The Hawks*. Throughout the ride, he kept up a continuous barrage of jokes and stories.

Initially, Fleta thought that he was not paying enough attention, but then she noticed that he really did follow Cadmon's advice to keep your eyes open. Gode constantly surveyed everything before and behind them as they followed the scouts. He never ceased his chatter, but his eyes never rested either.

Hackett rode easily beside Gode. Almost as tall as the commander, he was a hugely muscled man with a bald head and a bushy, grey beard that more than made up for the lack of hair on top of his head. Hackett had been a volunteer for this mission. Since he lost his arm, Cadmon had not sent him out on many missions. However, Dell had been the one to rescue him from the torturers that cost him his arm.

Hackett meant to be there if Dell was in trouble. Despite the fact that he only had one arm, Hackett was a formidable opponent with the massive claymore he carried at his side.

Gytha was the fifth member of the company. She joined *The Hawks* at about the same time that Flint did and her fighting experience made her a natural member of *The Talons*. During her time as a Captain in the King's Guard, she had encountered *The Followers* on several occasions. Those meetings were part of the reason she decided that she could no longer support the King. It seemed that whenever they were around, the King's Guard was asked to do something that was mindlessly cruel or, quite simply, atrocious.

Hulda also had an excellent reason to join the group hurrying to support Dell. A Captain in the King's Guard, Hulda's mother had trained her in the art of hand-to-hand combat from the time she was a very small child. When Hulda was sixteen, her mother became so disillusioned with the King that she set off to join the rumoured rebel group.

Lorund was sent in pursuit. It enraged Hulda to recall how she had been the one who put her mother in danger when he caught up with them. She had carelessly allowed herself to be captured by one of *The Followers*. Lorund took advantage of the distraction and killed Hulda's mother.

After he killed Hulda's mother, Lorund began to torture Hulda in an attempt to find out where they were headed. Dell had showed up in time to save her before any real damage was done, but not before she lost her ear.

That was the time that Dell had been pursuing Lorund and had to let him go. No matter how much she protested that she could take care of herself, he had been determined to see her to safety.

She promised herself that this time, Dell would have his chance for vengeance and she would be there to support him.

After spending most of an hour staring at the spot where *The Followers* had disappeared into the mountain, Dell knew what he had to do.

First, he needed to care for his horse after almost twenty hours in the saddle, and he also needed to rest. He decided to take advantage of the trees and brush that grew right up to the huge rock face where Lorund and his crew had vanished.

Leading the horse deeper into the woods, he found a spring where they both could drink. He gave the horse a share of the oats he carried in his saddlebag before helping himself to some of the sausage he packed before leaving the village to go to war.

Behind his mask, he smiled grimly. To think that in the end, he was the only one to go looking for a fight.

Dell left his horse hobbled in a grassy area and settled down for a short nap. He was close to his nemesis and expected it would be impossible to sleep but he had no sooner closed his eyes then he was dead to the world.

Fleta was surprised how easily they followed Dell's trail. He had made no effort whatsoever to cover his tracks. Either he expected someone from *The Hawks* to follow him or he was so concerned with the group in front of him that he gave no thought to who might be coming from behind.

As she rode, Fleta thought back to the time when Dell rescued her during a bandit attack. He had been too late to save her parents, but he managed to get her safely back to Halklyen.

It was unusual for Fleta to travel with her parents when they were off on *Hawk* business, but since they were only going to Fasnul to see Duke Sebastien, they took their five-year-old daughter along. Perhaps they felt it was more of a family outing than a mission, and were not paying attention the way they normally did.

She remembered a happy ride through the forest with her father laughing and teasing beside her. He pointed out tracks along the way and told her the names of the birds that flew overhead. Her mother, a skilled dagger thrower, rode behind, joining in the laughter. They had just come out of the forest and entered the road to Fasnul when the attack came.

It was so sudden that her parents did not have a chance to defend themselves. Her mother's first reaction had been to dive at Fleta, pull her off her horse and throw her into the brush. Fleta managed to right herself in time to see her mother take a sword thrust in her stomach.

In the next instant, her father, who had been fighting off two swordsmen suddenly found himself facing four blades. They were too much for him and she watched as he too took a fatal wound through the chest.

Dell had been following behind. He appeared just in time to witness the death of Fleta's father. Kicking his horse to a gallop, he smashed into the four swordsmen while at the same time launching daggers at their exposed throats.

One attacker fell under the hooves of the horse. The second and third bandits were the targets of his deadly daggers. The final swordsmen felt the grip of Dell's gauntlet on his neck. Constructed of flexible metal fingers and blades that extended beyond each fingertip, it was a formidable defence and a frightening offence. The man's head ripped clear of his shoulders.

Dell dismounted then and called softly for Fleta. Shocked by what she had just witnessed, she was unable to answer at first. The thick brush hid her from him, but the moment she moved, he swooped down and swept her up in his arms.

Not even taking the time to deal with the bodies of his good friends, he whisked her back to the village and deposited her with Merylin.

From that time on, Fleta felt a huge gratitude to Dell. Although he remained a distant figure in the village, she knew that he was someone she could always count on.

They had been riding all night. After hours of peering blindly into the darkness, Fleta could see the beginnings of dawn. Gradually the landscape changed from the colourless light of the moon to the richer hues of daylight. The rising sun revealed a mountain that rose straight up out of a heavily treed area.

She had heard of the Chain of Thollcranow, and wondered if they would be heading into the mountain ranage to find Dell. For the rest of the morning, they rode straight toward the mountains but they never seemed to get any closer until at last, Fleta felt like she could reach out and touch it.

The play of light across the rock face had captured Fleta's attention and she roused herself blearily when Flint called softly to her. He silently pointed to the hoof prints that led into the trees. Apparently, Dell had left the trail. The tracks of many boots and two large horses continued toward the mountain.

Fleta turned in her saddle and without saying anything, indicated the trail with her eyes. The four *Hawks* riding behind nodded and slid off their horses.

Flint and Fleta also dismounted and guided their horses into the trees. They could see where Dell had stepped down from his horse and they carefully followed his trail.

Flint's horse gave a quiet whinny as they entered a small clearing. Dell was in the process of leaping to his feet when the other five horses came into view. After a moment of studying the faces of his friends, he lowered his left hand. This close to his enemy, he had not even removed the gauntlet that was his favoured weapon.

Sheathing the dagger he had automatically gripped with his right hand, Dell drawled, "Fancy meeting you here."

"Greetings of the day, Dell," Gode replied easily. "We thought you might need a little help." Dell passed his gaze over the faces of the people who had shown up to help him. He knew that each of them felt they owed him something. In fact, he did not believe he had done anything beyond his duty in every case. He did not like the idea that they were there to repay a debt.

"Listen," Dell declared curtly. "None of you owes me anything. This is something I can take care of on my own." As usual, Flint felt disconcerted when he looked at Dell's grinning mask. It was in contrast to the firmness of his voice.

This time, it was Hulda who answered him, "Yes, of course you can take care of it, but maybe we can help if it turns out you need a hand." In an unusual gesture, she drew back her black hair to expose her mutilated ear.

"None of you owes me anything," Dell repeated, looking away from the faces that patiently waited for him to finish. "What's done is done."

Hackett stepped forward, "I still have one good arm. I offer you its service."

For a moment, Dell felt overwhelmed by the support he was receiving. He managed to survive by keeping everyone at a distance.

Abruptly, he turned his back and moved to his horse. He made a show of adjusting the cinch belt on the saddle while he struggled to control the tightness in his throat.

Finally, he said, "I have a plan." Flint thought for a minute that he would not continue, but after checking the horse's hobbles and giving her a gentle rub on her soft nose, he turned back to the group. "Sit," he said gruffly. "I'll explain."

Chapter 13 - Hunting

Dell described to the group what he had seen when he arrived at the mountain. He did not believe that the *Followers* had actually disappeared. He expected that there was a good chance the entrance to the mountain was shielded by magic like Orma's. She had taught him that cloaking magic only worked if you did not know where to look. He hoped that because he knew where to find the entrance, he would be able to continue the chase.

His plan was to head into the mountain at nightfall. Beyond that, he had no idea what he would find on the other side of the wall. Once inside, he would figure it out. He did not mention it to his friends, but he knew that his strength lay in reacting to whatever lay in front of him rather than thoughtful planning.

"So where do we come into this plan?" asked Gode. His eyebrows were raised in doubt as he considered Dell's explanation.

"Well, as I was saying, there is no need for you to come along. I can take care of this," Dell answered. He did not intend to endanger any one of them.

"Perhaps a couple of partners would come in handy,"

pressed Gode. "Hulda and I could accompany you into the mountain, and we could leave the other four here as a rescue party in case something goes wrong." He grinned as he said this because he figured there was nothing the three of them could not handle. He also knew that Dell would like the sound of leaving the three weaker fighters to wait outside with Gytha as a guard.

Dell let his shoulders sag inside the leather armour he wore. "That might be a good plan," he admitted. "First though, everyone needs to rest. I'll take first watch." Abruptly, he turned his back on the group and moved out of the clearing to the path they had created. He proceeded to camouflage the trail the entry of seven people had created.

Left behind, the others looked at each other and Gytha said, "Well, he has a point. We've been in the saddle for over twenty hours. A quick rest would make us more useful."

Dell checked on his friends. Every one of them was sound asleep. While they slept he had prepared a tinderbox. It held enough red coals that he could use it as a dim light if he needed it inside the mountain.

Feeling rather guilty about leaving the others without a guard, he checked his dagger belt, slid the metal gauntlet onto his hand and headed out of the small clearing. He did not intend to put anyone else in danger. This was something he needed to take care of on his own.

Creeping up to the spot where he had seen *The Followers* disappear, he peered carefully at the rock. There, in the shadows, he made out the merest outline of a door. It looked as if it had been cut from the granite around it. It was hard to tell, but perhaps it was not shielded, merely well-disguised.

By pushing hard on the centre of the door, Dell succeeded in moving it inwards. It seemed to be hinged on one side. He stopped and listened carefully. When he heard no sign of any movement, he pushed the door wide enough for him to slide through.

Quickly, he closed it behind him so that the light from outside would not give him away. He expected to be left in total darkness, but as his eyes adjusted, he discovered a soft light illuminated the room. Looking around, he saw a low ceiling and the room narrowed to a hallway at the far end.

Dell crept along, staying close to the wall. He had one goal in mind: find Lorund and kill him. Before his friends arrived, he had not been particularly concerned about living through this assassination attempt. Now, though, he knew that if he did not reappear before nightfall, they would follow him into the mountain. He was not about to put them in that danger so he needed to hurry.

As he came to the end of the narrow hallway, it opened into a vast space with a ceiling so high, he could not make it out. The walls and floors had regularly placed gemstones that sparkled with reflected light. In fact, the whole area was quite bright although Dell could make out no obvious source for the illumination.

Continuing to move cautiously along the wall, Dell kept an eye open for any guards who might be nearby. He was rather surprised he had not encountered anyone yet. As he advanced through the room, he realized that the cave was a beautiful space. Along with the sparkling rocks, carvings adorned the walls. Each one was an exquisitely sculpted face and they all had an expression of longing that went right to Dell's heart.

At last, he reached the opposite side of the room and edged closer to a large wooden door that was the only exit he could make out. He had rather hoped there might be more options, but he resigned himself to the idea that he might be making a dramatic entrance. Slowly, he lifted the latch.

Expecting to be challenged the moment the door opened, he raised his gauntlet and checked that his daggers were ready. Sliding through the partly open door, he was again surprised to find no one there.

Here, the light was slightly brighter and the sparkling stones reflected myriad brilliant colours. It was as if he had entered a jewel box. This room was also huge and empty. Dell tried to imagine the purpose of such a space. He could see a carved metal door at the opposite end of the room and deciding no need for further caution was necessary, he strode boldly across the middle of the floor. At the door, he hesitated. Hearing nothing, he unlatched it and pushed it wide.

Hain sat up straight in the chair where he had been lounging. Lorund who sat across from him also immediately came to attention. No word was heard in the room, but both men listened intently to a voice in their heads. *There is an intruder. You will take care of it.*

Hain spoke aloud, "Which way?" However, he did not expect an answer. Turning to Lorund, he said, "You go to the North Entrance. I'll go South."

"Yes, sir," Lorund answered and rose to his feet with a salute. After Hain distractedly returned the gesture, he turned and hurried from the room. He was, as usual, fully armed and wearing his tattered armour.

He hurried through the corridors toward the entrance through which he had returned to the mountain fortress just hours before. Without hesitation, he burst into the first of the four anterooms Martokallu had built over the years.

The huge empty spaces served well as bait for any intruders who might make it through the first defence. Lorund tried to remember whether anyone had ever got past the rock face door. It was well shielded and impossible to find if one did not know where to look.

Drawing his broadsword, he entered the next room with a little more caution. However, he was not prepared for what occurred.

Dell leapt from where he had hidden at the sound of approaching footsteps. Even as he moved, he launched a dagger at Lorund's throat. Lorund gagged and staggered but Martokallu's power let him live.

Dell did not hesitate. He threw himself forward and

stabbed another dagger into Lorund's neck. Then, reaching with his gauntleted hand he dug his bladed fingers into Lorund's face and with a horrendous tearing sound, ripped his head from his body.

Chapter 14 - Retribution

Gode opened his eyes and stretched. He felt remarkably refreshed. He was only to have slept for four hours before Dell awakened him. Glancing around at the other sleepers, and then at the placement of the sun, he was suddenly suspicious.

Getting quietly to his feet, he checked his weapons and slid out of the clearing along the path Dell had taken. Even before he got to the end of the trail, he knew what he would find. There was no sign of Dell. He had gone on without them.

Quickly, turning back to the camp he roused the rest of the group. "Dell has gone on alone," he announced to the groggy *Hawks*. We are going with my original plan. Flint and Fleta, you stay here with Gytha and Hackett. Hulda, you come with me and we will check on Dell. If we are not back in six hours, head back to Halklyen. Do not follow us." He sent a stern look in Gytha's direction with this last command. She nodded to indicate that she understood.

Dell quickly cleaned the blades of his gauntlet on the threadbare cloak of the man he had chased for fourteen years. The blood was bright orange and the dead, staring eyes revealed that same shocking colour. Before sheathing his daggers, he gave them a hasty wipe as well, and watched as the strange colour smeared across the black cloth. It almost glowed.

Standing and surveying the room, Dell reached into his pack and withdrew a small, round grenade and the tinderbox he had carefully tended before entering the mountain.

He and Egbert had experimented with the design of the bomb and come up with a metal ball filled with a mixture of gunpowder and small pieces of sharp metal. Through a series of trials, they figured out a fuse length that allowed about fifteen seconds after it was lit.

He settled the bomb beside the door Lorund had burst through just a short time ago. Then he inserted the end of the fuse into his tinderbox. As soon as it sputtered to life, Dell turned and sprinted for the other door on the opposite wall. Just as he threw himself through the big wooden door and shoved it closed, he heard the explosion. The force of the falling rock threw him to the ground.

Not waiting to see if this ceiling would begin to fall on him, Dell lit another grenade and placed it beside the door he had just closed. Once again, he took off running and dove through the next door just in time.

This explosion shook the room he landed in and several rocks fell from the distant ceiling. He was just about to light his third grenade when he spotted two figures through the dust. He prepared to go on the attack but recognized the silhouette of Gode's war axe. There could be only one weapon where the two blades of the axe were designed to resemble a hawk in flight.

He called out, "We were just leaving." Trusting that his friends would get the message, he inserted the fuse of his third grenade into the tinderbox. As soon as the fuse began to sizzle, he thrust the bomb into a small alcove near the door and dashed across the room yelling, "Let's get out of here!"

The small red glow of the tinderbox was enough to alert Hulda and Gode. Dell's great fondness for explosions was well known and they immediately understood the reason for the rumbling that had accompanied their entry to the cave. Before Dell called out his warning, they had already turned and begun sprinting for the narrow hallway.

The three of them made it to the huge stone door at almost the same time. Frantically, they searched for the trick to opening it from the inside. Hulda found it first and thrust the lever up, causing the door to swing slowly inward.

Dell had just about decided that it was too slow when it finally reached the point where they could squeeze through. As the smallest, Hulda went first and Gode and Dell were on her heels.

There was no time to get the door closed so they dove to the either side and buried their faces in the dirt, trying to protect their heads with their arms. A huge puff of dust and rock debris followed them.

As soon as the sound of falling rock stopped, Dell

cautiously raised his head. He studied the door and debated whether to set off one final explosion. Beside him, Gode followed his gaze. Lifting one eyebrow, he gave Dell a nod.

Smiling beneath his mask, Dell took his second last grenade, touched the fuse to the tinder and wedged it carefully beside the stone door. Immediately, all three of them started running for the woods.

This time the explosion was not contained by the mountain and the sound was tremendous. It caused the rock door and the wall around it to crumble into a pile of rubble; completely cutting off any entrance or exit from the mountain.

Flint felt the earth tremble beneath him. Sitting watch just out of sight of the huge rock door where Hulda and Gode had disappeared, he got to his feet and peered around nervously.

As he gazed, he thought he saw a crack appear in the mountain and then Hulda came diving through, followed immediately by Gode and Dell. He stared in amazement as they all covered their heads just in time for another big blast. The air outside the hole filled with dust.

As soon as the worst of the dust had settled, Dell, Hulda and Gode jumped to their feet again; charging directly for Flint's hiding spot. He turned and ran with them. Moments later, a final eruption sent them stumbling into the campsite.

Fleta, Hackett, and Gytha stood near the horses. They

had decided that it would be best if they were ready to depart in an instant. After allowing the horses to drink at the stream, they had carefully saddled each one and checked that the cinches were tight.

Not wanting to hobble the horses when they might have to leave in a hurry, the three of them waited, loosely holding the reins of two or three horses each, while the horses contently grazed.

At the sound of the explosion, all seven horses lifted their heads in alarm and they might have bolted except that when they heard the noise, the three *Hawks* involuntarily tightened their grip on the reins.

The next moment, Gode, Dell, Hulda and Flint came pelting into the clearing and Dell yelled, "Let's ride!"

After a moment's confusion, everyone took control of a horse and led it from the clearing. Mounting quickly, Dell set his horse on a mile-eating canter and the others soon followed.

After a few minutes of frantic riding, they settled into the pace and Gode turned to Dell and said, "So, you want to tell us what that was all about?"

Flint thought that Dell was just going to ignore the question, but after a long moment of expectant silence, Dell took a deep breath and said, "Well, I figured it was my mission. So I took care of it."

No one asked any questions but they all waited hopefully for him to continue.

He did. Nodding at Gode and Hulda, he said, "There were three of those huge rooms that you saw. There may have been more, but just as I was about to go through another door, who should appear but Lorund?" Without hesitation, he added, "I killed him and then started setting off grenades at every doorway. I figure that if this is the only entrance to the fortress on the northern side, we may just have bought enough time to get away."

Again, no one said anything for a moment, and then Hulda asked, "If?"

Fleta thought she saw a glint of amusement in Dell's eyes and he answered with a drawled, "If."

Gode asked, "So, we are riding away in a hurry just in case any of Lorund's friends decide to follow?"

"Yep," answered Dell.

Chapter 15 - Plans

"COME TO ME," the voice boomed painfully in his head. Hain stopped his headlong charge through the fortress and wheeled about. He had been running steadily toward the Southern Entrance, methodically checking rooms that could have been accessed from there. It would have been a far quicker process if Martokalu's vision included the underground fortress. Unfortunately, he was unable to see into any sort of shelter.

Hain was very familiar with the rooms and hallways that he searched, having lived there for most of his nine hundred years. He was also accustomed to hearing the voice of Martokallu in his head. Although it was rare for it to be so loud. Something must have gone wrong.

Hain was Martokallu's second-in-command; however, he rarely left the fortress any longer. He was far too noticeable among regular humans and that worked against Martokallu's plans. Standing head and shoulders over even the tallest of men, the cracks in his grey skin regularly released flashes of yellow light. Those same swirls of power were visible when he drew his two large claymores, constructed of metal, bone and magic.

His eyes, that same disturbing yellow, showed no trace of white and seemed to observe every detail. In a manner of speaking, they did. Hain's direct link with Martokallu allowed him to see everything that *The Master* could see. At least, everything that Martokallu chose to share with him.

Finally, Hain arrived at the throne room. It was magnificent. For the last thousand years, thousands of slaves had been spent their lives labouring to excavate the giant mountain and form the rooms that made his fortress. Frequent additions and modifications gave him energy. Aside from his plans to rule Abbarkon openly, this construction was his greatest joy.

Even now, when they were so close to success, work continued. On his way through the carved hallways, Hain passed several human slaves who kept their eyes on their work without noticing him.

The throne room was immense. The ceiling disappeared into the shadows and left a feeling of space. The walls glistened with thousands of sparkling rubies and emeralds, diamonds and sapphires. There did not appear to be a source of light, yet the room was softly lit. The gems threw back a light of breathtaking beauty.

Hain ignored the splendour of the chamber. He had eyes only for the wizened monster seated in the centre of the room. The golden throne where Martokallu reclined threw shafts of brilliance that resembled sunlight.

On the table at his elbow sat a flask of wine and a half-filled glass, but he was not drinking it now. His black eyes swirled like whirlpools, draining his surroundings of all life. Humans were unable to look into them without losing themselves entirely.

When Hain entered the chamber, those eyes had been turned to the ceiling where they appeared to be intently studying something just out of sight. As Hain approached the throne, the eyes lowered to focus on him. Bowing stiffly, Hain said, "Master?"

That was the last word spoken aloud. Hain kept his eyes on the one who had been his master for almost a millennium. There was very little left of the man he had once been before he began his pursuit of power.

Underneath the robe covered with magical symbols and the armour designed to withstand any threat, Martokallu was nothing more than a black skeleton held together by his own overpowering will. Over the years, all of the flesh had been burned away and replaced by a black swirling mist.

Martokallu began to project the images of Lorund's death directly into Hain's brain. Hain watched without emotion as he saw a dagger fly directly at Lorund and then a masked man reached out with a bladed hand and the vision ended abruptly. Hain felt a flash of rage. He immediately realized that the images had come from Lorund and the reason they had stopped was that he had been killed.

He wanted to ask questions, but almost immediately, Martokallu continued to communicate what had happened next. The vision showed a woman diving through the hidden doorway of the Northern Entrance, followed immediately by a large, armoured warrior and

104

the masked man who had evidently killed Lorund. They threw themselves to the ground and dust roiled through the open door. Then the masked man bent to place a small round ball near the entrance and the three people dashed away from the rock wall.

A huge explosion brought the entrance crumbling down. Hain knew, without having to investigate that the damage would make that route impassable for months, even if they put the entire slave force to work right now.

This was bad. Rage pulsed through his mind. In order to pursue these intruders, Hain would need to take a force out through the Southern Entrance and then backtrack over the Chain of Thollcrawnow.

Powerless to stop them, he seethed as he saw the masked man and his partners join others and ride quickly away from the fortress.

He tried to console himself that it would be easy enough for Martokallu to watch where they went. A current of satisfaction ran through him. He would track them down and kill them himself. Regrettably, it would take time and that did not mesh well with *The Master's* plan.

It did not seem right to ask the horses to make another long run after the pursuit the day before. Gode called a halt when they neared Derflanag where *The Hawks* had attempted their failed execution just days ago. Hulda was the only one of the group who had been there when Jaak and Walker died.

"I never showed my face in town and they have no way of expecting us now," she said. "We didn't even know we were going to be here, so how could they?"

"Well, we were just in an underground fortress that I strongly suspect is the place where we would find Martokallu," replied Gode. "We know he can see everything. He'll know where we are."

"But we have never had any indication that they are able to communicate long distance," said Dell. He winked at Flint and added with a glint of humour, "I also suspect that we may have slowed them down a bit."

"Once again, you do not know that," argued Gode. "There could have been any number of entrances into that place."

"I just get the feeling that there would have been guards if they had more entrances. The way it was set up with those huge empty rooms makes me think that it was the only way in or out," Dell replied.

"Oh, I see. You have a feeling," Gode drawled. "Well then, that's all right."

Hulda said impatiently, "Of course it is a risk, but it is a calculated one. Chances are that they will have to dig their way out of the mountain before they can chase us. Regardless, we do have a bit of a head start. Maybe we can finish what we started here."

She lifted the saddle from her horse's back and spun to look at Gytha. "You were stationed here when you were in the King's Guard. What can you tell us?" Hulda asked.

"Umm," Gytha hesitated, not being used to giving her

opinion. "The Duke is guarded by four King's Guards at all times." She stopped and thought for a moment before adding, "Except when he is in his private garden. He gets impatient with all the security and insists that he is safe inside its walls."

She let a distinctly mocking tone creep into her voice, "Arjen likes to think he is a poet and needs time to sit and compose his verse." Looking around at her companions, she read the calculation on their faces. Realizing what they were thinking, she quickly warned them, "But you could never get him there. He has a full honour guard all around the perimeter of the garden and the top of the wall is covered with sharpened blades."

Gode shared a glance with Hulda who looked very interested. "How hard is it to get close to the wall?" he asked.

"Oh, that's not too hard. It is attached to the palace and parts of it border the market square." She looked around at her listeners and added in that same mocking tone, "Arjen also likes to be fairly close to the action." Gytha noticed the approval that Gode and Hulda were showing and she began to imagine that they might be able to accomplish something.

"Anything else?" Gode asked.

She thought for a moment and then glancing at the glint of light in the east, she said, "Well, it's market day today." Everyone looked surprised. They had been riding for most of the night, and after a moment's calculation, they realized that she was right. Morning was only a short time away.

"Can you draw me a map?" Gode asked, looking thoughtful.

"Of course," Gytha answered, bending to scratch in the dust at their feet. When she finished, they all studied it for a while and each one had questions to ask.

"All right," said Gode as the discussion drew to a close. "It sounds like we have enough information. Let me think. We are going to need a plan."

He stepped to his horse and automatically began to take care of its needs. Reaching up, he drew the bridle free from the horse's head and absently gave her a scratch beside her ears. The horse responded by nudging his pockets, searching for any treats he might have. He produced a small apple and took a brush to rub her down while she contentedly munched it. Finally, he led her to the stream and stood staring into space while she drank her fill.

Chapter 16 - Execution

Flint and Fleta carried heavy-looking packs on their backs. They had left off their leather armour and Flint felt more than a little exposed. Although he carried his swords, they were both stored atop his pack. Fleta had her daggers hidden under the scarf that she now wore everywhere ever since Orma gave it to her.

They joined the throng heading toward town for market day. Hulda, looking like a little old woman, leaned heavily on Fleta's arm. A little way behind, Gytha had also taken the "old woman" disguise, but she walked on her own beside a heavily laden Hackett. Somehow, the powerful man managed to draw attention to his missing arm and make himself appear very unthreatening. What people did not see, however, were the swords that both Gytha and Hackett wore strapped to their sides.

Gode and Dell were the least easily disguised so they chose to make themselves completely visible. Even though still some distance from the town gates, they started to throw juggling balls back and forth. In a booming voice, Gode announced their performance.

Already they had gained an audience in the peasants bringing their produce to the market. As Flint and Fleta approached the gates with Hulda, the guards were distracted by a particularly dramatic flip that Gode chose to execute at exactly that moment. Hardly bothering to look at them, the guards waved them through. The same thing happened when it was Hackett and Gytha's turn.

When Dell and Gode reached the gates, the guards actually smiled and patted them on the back as they went by. Gode returned the smile, made a joke for the men and then they too were clear.

In the market square, Gode and Dell continued their antics but Flint could see from his position at the edge of the crowd that both men were studying the situation. They positioned themselves so that they had a good view of the wall which Gytha had subtly pointed out. The eight-foot tall stone barrier, studded with wicked-looking blades, protected the Duke's walled garden.

Gytha laid out a blanket where she could keep an eye on the wall and arranged several woven bracelets that Hulda had been carrying in her pack.

Nearby, in a corner position, Fleta and Flint set up their "Grandmother Hulda" with a blanket and some polished rocks Hulda had also provided from her stores. Fleta was amazed to discover what had been packed in Hulda's saddlebags. She was learning that in order to be ready to disappear into any situation, it was best to carry a few supplies.

Fleta joined Hackett and together they strolled through the crowd, stopping to admire the many wares for sale. After a while, they settled in the one spot along the wall where no guard stood. There was one in plain sight of them on either side, but the assassins were managing to make themselves look so completely unthreatening that the guards virtually ignored them. Hackett played up his missing arm and Fleta pretended to be much younger than she was. With great enthusiasm, accompanied by bursts of excited applause, they watched while Gode and Dell performed for the crowd.

When Gode outlined the plan, the one point he had hesitated upon was making Fleta the actual assassin. "I know you don't have any experience," he had said, "but you are perfect for the job." Fleta had not hesitated, however, and accepted the role at once. Now, she was feeling some apprehension. She wanted to check her dagger belt but knew better than to draw attention to her array of weapons. Besides, she knew perfectly well that every blade was in place.

She watched Dell and Gode carefully. When they rehearsed their act before entering the town, they worked two signals into the show so that Fleta would know when the big distraction was coming.

She saw the first move. Dell was walking around in a handstand and he had just passed by Flint's position. In one fluid motion, he righted himself, grabbed Flint by the ankles and began to twirl him in a wide circle. Fleta knew what was coming next, but she did not have time to watch it.

This was her chance. Turning to Hackett, she found

that he already had his hand lowered, waiting for her to step into it.

With one easy thrust, he sent her flying into the air where she grasped the edge of the wall while at the same time, avoided the dagger-sharp spikes. She quickly flipped her feet up so that she was crouched on the wall and with a hasty glance to ensure that the guards were still looking the other way, she dropped down on the far side.

She immediately noticed how much quieter it was on this side of the high wall. After the noisy hubbub of the market, the hush of the garden was calming. Her eyes widened as she took in the beautiful view. Gytha's description had not done it justice.

She had landed behind a flowering bush of a type she had never seen before. After taking a moment to catch her breath, she crept carefully around it and spotted a paved walking path. The trail wandered off through a series of flowerbeds; each one filled with glorious blooms.

Guessing that this might be the route the poetic Duke would choose to stroll during his afternoon rest, she followed it. Gytha had said that the Duke would be unguarded during this time, yet she found her natural inclination was to move in a way that let her remain as invisible as possible. She drifted from shadow to shadow, timing her shifts to the movement of the breeze just as Walker had taught her.

When she saw the Duke, she was surprised at how harmless the man appeared. He sat in a stuffed chair with a sheet of paper and a bottle of ink balanced on a lap desk. She could hear him muttering to himself and then watched as he hastily scribbled a few words down on the paper.

By force of will, Fleta brought to mind all the stories of the horrible things that had been done at the command of this man. Steeling herself for what she had come to do, she silently drew two daggers. Lifting her face to check for wind, she rapidly threw both blades. The first one struck his throat and the second took him right in the heart. Without a sound, the Duke slumped over his desk.

Fleta froze at the thought of what she had just done. Then, remembering her friends outside the wall, she forced herself toward the dead man. She would need to retrieve her blades.

When she got close, she saw that the poem he had been writing was covered in blood. She could make out only the word, "shining". Hastily, she withdrew both blades in a rush of blood, and wiped them clean on the Duke's soft tunic.

Then, sheathing the daggers, she blended in with the shadows once again and swiftly made her way back to the place on the wall where she had entered the garden.

Without Hackett's boost, she would need some way of getting to the top of the wall. Spotting a bench, she decided it would do the job. It was manageable enough for her to lift, so she leaned it up against the wall and climbed up on it.

Now was the tricky part. Her signal was the sound of

a lark. Something she had practiced until it was difficult to tell her whistle from the real thing. She was to make her call, count to thirty and get over the wall.

Hackett would pass the signal to Gode who would then draw all the eyes of the crowd by first describing to everyone what he would do, and then, launching Flint, who would complete a double somersault in the air before being caught by Dell.

She finished her slow count and poked her head over the wall, Gode was just finishing his monologue and he reached down to grab Flint by the ankles. He began to spin in a circle letting Flint fly straight out as he turned. The crowd started to chant, "Fly, fly, fly," and as Fleta watched, Flint did just that.

She used the moment when all eyes were on Flint, to hop down beside Hackett, who easily reached out his arm to catch her. He gave her a questioning look and without meeting his eyes, she nodded back.

Chapter 17 - Success

Flint was ecstatic. The plan had played out perfectly. Immediately after Fleta hopped down from the wall, Gode had gracefully ended the show, and even passed a hat for a shower of coins. Group by group, *The Hawks* left the town and met again in the woods where they had hobbled the horses out of sight. They abandoned their disguises, repacked the saddlebags and continued toward Fasnul.

The thrill of entertaining the crowd had Dell, Flint and Gode still crowing about their success. Dell and Gode had used the disguise before, but the addition of Flint, who was an excellent tumbler, made it even better. Hackett and Gytha, as part of the audience, joined in the reliving of the performance.

Hulda dropped back to ride beside Fleta who was following quietly at the rear. "You did well," Hulda spoke softly but she watched Fleta's face carefully.

"Yes," Fleta answered tonelessly. "The plan worked. It was easy."

"Too easy?" Hulda asked. She knew what was going on inside the young girl's head. It was too easy to take a life, even when that life was making everything worse for so many people.

Fleta sighed in relief that someone understood what she had been thinking. She had spent her life training to be able to throw daggers with deadly accuracy. Now, she had put those skills to use for the first time, and it did not feel good. Not like when she hit every target that she set up.

"It's a good thing that it feels like it was too easy," offered Hulda. "We are not meant to kill. The fact that we train to be able to kill does not make it easy to accept that we have actually taken a life. We do this," she struggled to find the words, "this killing, because we have learned that it is the only way to stop the evil. However, we must remember that it is not the way we want to live our lives. We have to remember that we are killing in order to stop the killing. When we win, I never want to have to kill again."

They rode in silence for a while, and then Fleta asked, "Does this feeling go away?"

Hulda considered for a moment before she answered sadly, "No. But you get used to it."

Hain was irritated. It had been a long time since anyone had gotten the better of any of *The Followers*. To realize that Lorund had been killed so easily made him wonder if they were getting complacent. There is no way that Lorund should have walked into that room unprepared for a fight. He knew there was an intruder in the fortress. How could he have been so careless?

116

Now, Hain had to lead a squad out through the Southern Entrance. They would have to travel overland through the mountains of the Chain of Thollcrawnow. Hain knew it would be a very difficult journey with the snow still in the passes. As well, it had been over a century since Hain had even left the confines of the fortress. Missions in the outside world had been Lorund's responsibility.

He and Lorund were the only ones who had become proficient at the art of communication with *The Master*. Others might receive messages but no one else could reply. The advantages that Martokallu's vision brought to any mission were enormous. Hain could not imagine having to enter into a plan without the tremendous information that Martokallu could provide. It made *The Followers* invincible.

At least that was what he had believed until Lorund was killed so easily. Just thinking about it made Hain angry again.

They planned to head for Fasnul first and then to Kallcunarth before dropping off the road into the forest surrounding Halklyen. It felt like it had been a very long time since he had slept and Flint sent a veiled look at Gode to see if he might be considering stopping soon.

Gode caught the glance and nodded reassuringly at him. "There's a spot just up here where we can slip under Orma's veil and camp for the night," he said with a smile.

117

Flint tried not to reveal how much of a relief that news was, but Fleta sighed and said, "That is good to hear. I am so tired I keep falling asleep in my saddle even though I know I am supposed to be a scout and pay attention."

Gode chuckled and reassured her, "Well, I don't think any of us noticed. Maybe we are all falling asleep."

With that, he nudged his horse off the road and led them into the forest to a small clearing. It was evident that the spot had been used for a campsite in the past, and Flint could see a fire pit that contained the remains of a good-sized fire.

Hackett watched as Flint examined it with curiosity. "When we are under the cover of Orma's shield, there is no reason to limit ourselves to a tiny little fire that warms a meal but doesn't touch your bones. Here we can do both and if the flames get a little high, well, no matter," the one-armed man smiled as he said this and then he easily swung the saddle from his horse's back.

It was a relief to relax knowing that for the moment they were safe. As he brushed down his horse, Flint asked Gode, "Why aren't we heading directly home now? Why bother going around by Fasnul?"

Gode worked on his own horse with long sweeping strokes that removed the sweat and dust. "Well, I guess the biggest reason is so that if Martokallu is watching, we don't want him to see us disappear on this deserted stretch of road. There are a lot more people on the road to Kallcunarth and we will slip away when no one is around. Whenever we return from a mission, we avoid entering at the first opportunity. We figure that if we are careful to disappear in crowded areas, he will be less able to figure out exactly when we disappear."

"But won't he notice that we are invisible to him right now?" Flint wrinkled his brow in confusion.

Gode chuckled. "He might. What do you suppose he thinks of that? And when we reappear in the morning, will he believe that he is losing his mind?"

Flint felt himself smile in return but he was struck by the idea that Gode did not seem frightened by Martokallu. He treated all of this as if it were a big practical joke.

Everybody dealt with their horses and settled them to grazing the grass at the edge of the clearing. Fleta was the first to open her bedroll, tuck it around her and curl up in a ball. She was asleep before Flint had fully finished brushing down his horse.

The others settled down around the fire pit and Gytha quickly lit a fire from the wood Flint gathered. Instead of just eating the dried meat and biscuit that was all anybody had in their saddlebags, Hulda took a cooking pot from her pack, filled it with water and then everyone put their provisions in the pot. Hulda added a few herbs and tubers she found growing in the forest, and soon the delicious smell of stew drifted around the campsite.

After feasting on their first warm meal in days, they sat around the fire, drowsily sipping coffee. It was obvious that everyone was enjoying the feeling of safety after so many days of constant vigilance. One by one, they rolled up in their blankets and went to sleep.

Hain flinched at the roar in his head. Apparently, he was not the only one angered by the events of the previous day. As he trudged south through the endless rooms of Martokallu's fortress, he had been receiving periodic updates about the progress of the group who killed Lorund.

They had stopped at Derflanag and somehow managed to kill Duke Arjen as well. Hain was not sure that *The Master* had actually seen the assassination. It must have been very stealthily done. The Duke had been under twenty-four hour guard for several years. Martokallu's plan had depended on having the Duke in place to apply pressure from his position. It seemed that everything was suddenly going wrong.

The roar that had disturbed Hain this time was immediately followed by images of a group of riders on a road one moment and then, gone the next. Hain got the sense that this was a new experience for Martokallu. Was something going wrong with his vision?

The first thing Fleta noticed when she woke up was how hungry she was. Then, she saw that everyone else was still asleep. She felt a little guilty for her behaviour the previous evening, but she could not ever remember a time when she felt more tired. Now, however, she felt wonderful.

Quietly, she got up and reached into her saddlebag for some breakfast. It was amazing to simply sit and eat without worrying about keeping watch.

"Feeling better, are you?" Hulda asked quietly. She had silently risen from her bedroll and stood over Fleta's shoulder.

"I am," answered Fleta with a quick smile. Then in a quiet voice, she continued, "I was thinking about what you said yesterday. I think I understand. It was the right thing to do: to kill Duke Arjen. But, if I didn't feel badly about it, I would be as bad as he was. We kill to save people. He killed for power. There must be a difference."

Hulda nodded. "That doesn't make it any easier though does it?"

Fleta frowned and shook her head, "No."

"That's good, then," Hulda smiled. "When killing becomes easy, then we have lost the thing that makes us human."

Gode suddenly sat up in his bed. "Well, what do you say everyone? Shall we hit the road? I'll bet that Duke Sebastien could rustle us up a pretty good lunch if we get there in time."

Even though Fleta and Hulda were the first ones out of bed, Dell was the first one mounted and ready to go. The rest hurried to join him and soon they followed Flint out of the clearing. Fleta took up the rear and as they left the forest, she took the time to clear up any evidence of their trail into the woods.

A short ride took them to the outskirts of Fasnul.

Approaching the gates, they overtook the strangest looking procession.

Four colourfully dressed people perched atop a cart that looked nothing so much as a large wooden box painted in bright swirls of colour. However, that was not the strangest thing. Instead of horses pulling the cart, two huge beasts strolled unconcernedly in their harnesses. Each had three horns protruding from its head and bony armour across its head, chest and entire back.

There was not room on the road to pass, so Flint pulled his horse off into the ditch to get a better look. He could not stop staring. Each massive animal had one long horn projecting from the centre of its forehead and the lower jaw had tusks almost as long. They looked like they were ambling along, but Flint trotted his horse beside them just to keep up.

"What are they?" he called up to the people on top of the cart.

"They come from south of Tsaralvia. They are called Magnaosseum," answered the man wearing a yellow tunic and orange cap.

"I have never seen anything so big," cried Flint. "They are incredible!"

"You should see how much they eat. I'd trade you in a heartbeat for that horse you ride," the man laughed as Dell rode up beside Flint.

"How fast can they go?" Dell asked as he eyed the strange looking creatures.

"Well, this is their walking speed, and you can see that

it is much faster than a horse walks. I'd show you how fast they can run, but not while the cart is hooked up. The rattles would just about shake this thing to pieces. When they want to run, they can go faster than any horse. But," he added, "they can't keep it up for long. This is their best speed if you want them to go all day." The man on the cart considered Dell speculatively before asking, "What do you say, man, are you interested in a trade?"

Dell continued to study the Magnaosseum before he answered, "I might be."

Flint looked at him in surprise "Really?" he asked.

"Maybe," Dell replied evasively. "First though, I'd want to see how fast they can go." Dell was thinking of a project that he and Egbert had been discussing. These enormous, armoured animals might be just what they were looking for to complete the design.

"You just needed to ask," pronounced the man who seemed to be the leader. He continued in a booming voice that did not just answer Dell's question but addressed the crowd arriving at the town gates. "We will shortly begin an appearance in the main square and a more formal performance will take place later today, if the good leaders of this fine town approve. To add to the entertainment, should there be a large enough showground, we look forward to demonstrating the speed and power of the mighty Magnaosseum."

Chapter 18 - Wager

They rode straight to Duke Sebastien's palace where the man himself greeted them as he exited the building.

"Greetings of the day to all of you," welcomed the friendly Duke. He was well known to all of *The Hawks* except for Flint who had never made the trip to Fasnul before. Cousin to the King, and with Arjen dead, next in line to the throne, he was never one to stand on ceremony. "I just heard that a group of performers arrived in town. Was it you they were talking about?"

"No," Gode answered with a smile. "The strangest looking procession was just ahead of us on the road. I won't try to explain. I think this is one of those things that it is better to see than to hear about."

"That is just what my page told me," exclaimed Sebastien. "I must see this strange and wonderful sight. Do you know where they are right now?"

"They're planning a short show in the square," Fleta called out. She had dismounted from her horse and eagerly pushed forward in the group to speak to the Duke. "Let's go back. I don't want to miss it."

"So, young Fleta," responded Sebastien smiling down

at her. They had known each other since Fleta made her first trip to Fasnul with Gode after her parents died. His blue eyes twinkled as he teased her, "You think this will be worth our while?"

Fleta grinned, "I guarantee that you will not believe what you are about to see!"

He took up the challenge, "Oh, you guarantee it, do you? And, what if I feel that it is not up to my standards of disbelief? What do you offer as a guarantee?"

Fleta had learned from experience that the best way to deal with his taunts was to hit right back. "If you are not properly impressed, I will...," she hesitated as she desperately sought a witty reply, "I will eat your lunch for you!"

Everyone burst out laughing and Fleta blushed at her ridiculous answer. "Hopefully, it will not come to that," said the chuckling Duke. "Come, let us take your mounts to the stable and then, you may lead the way. We shall see just how impressive these visitors are."

Gode and the Duke chatted amiably as they walked toward the square. Dell walked on the other side of the Duke and occasionally threw in his own comment. Flint noticed that Hulda and Gytha did not relax their guard for a moment. Both of them walked in that vigilant and ready posture that he knew so well. Behind them, Flint found himself walking alone with Fleta for the first time since they discovered that they would be the new scouts.

"I guess it's true then," Flint said.

"What?" Fleta turned to him with a puzzled expression.

"We are *The Talons*," he answered with a smile. They had spoken of this as a dream often enough and it was amazing to find that it had actually come true.

Fleta felt the first moment of calm satisfaction she had known since she threw her daggers at Duke Arjen. "It's true." She smiled. "We are *The Talons*.

They walked in silence for a few steps and then Flint could not contain his curiosity. "What was it like?" he asked.

She knew what he meant immediately. "Killing?" she aksed grimly.

"Yes."

"Horrible," she answered so quietly that he barely heard her. "Maybe I'll tell you about it sometime." Fleta did not say anymore and soon they arrived at the square, which was so crowded that they could see nothing of the promised performance.

Hackett, who had been walking behind them, stepped up and spoke just loudly enough for both Flint and Fleta to hear, "Do not relax your guard. We do not know where our enemies are." Fleta immediately saw the wisdom of this reminder and she checked her dagger belt and sharpened her attention, checking the crowd for any who might be paying too much attention to their little group or to the Duke.

Flint too reached back with both hands to check that his swords were riding clear. He pulled both partly free and then let them drop back into their scabbards. He hoped that the decorated hilts were not too noticeable in the crowd. From that point on, Flint told himself, he would keep his attention focused for any dangers that might appear. As a *Hawk* and a member of *The Talons*, he should not need to be reminded of his duty.

It quickly became obvious that attempting to force a path through the crowd was impractical and Sebastien changed course, calling for the others to follow. He led them around the back of a tall house and knocked on the door. It took a few minutes, but finally, there was the rattle of the door opening and a face peered out.

A comical look of disbelief came over the man's face when he recognized Duke Sebastien. "My Lord," he said apologetically. "I'm sorry I took so long to answer the door. I was upstairs watching the show and didn't hear your knock."

"Simon, isn't it?" the Duke asked with a friendly smile. At the man's nervous nod, the Duke continued, "We were knocking on your door in the hope that you might invite us to come up and view the proceedings in the square."

For a moment, Simon did not reply and then, realizing what the Duke meant, he said, "Of course, of course, my lord. We would be honoured to have such a guest in our home. Please come up and see this unbelievable thing." He turned and looking back over his shoulder to see that his visitors were following, led them up a narrow flight of stairs.

Fleta looked at Duke Sebastien and mouthed the word, "Unbelievable." He grinned back at her and waggled his eyebrows.

The room on the side overlooking the square had

four children glued to the two small windows. "Children, we have guests," their host announced. "Let them have a turn at the windows."

The identical looks of disappointment on the faces of the children made the Duke smile and say, "No need to move aside, we can peek over your heads. Thank you for so graciously sharing your view." With that, he stepped up the window and looked out at the square.

When Sebastien spotted the Magnaosseums, his mouth dropped open and Fleta who had been watching for his reaction crowed, "Now try to tell us that you aren't shocked by the look of those things. I told you that you wouldn't believe what you saw!" She leaned forward to share the window with the Duke. "They say they are called Magnaosseums and they come from a place south of Tsaralvia."

"I do hate to admit defeat in a wager, but that may well be the most surprising thing I have ever seen. Not at all what I was expecting. So I guess you will not need to eat my lunch." At her stricken expression, he laughed and said, "Though, no doubt you'll be able to polish off your own lunch without difficulty."

The performers were putting on a show in the square. They had unhitched the cart and brought the two beasts into the center where they tied them to a post. Three of the troupe members performed incredible feats of agility using the Magnaosseums' backs as high platforms from which they would spring and execute perfect flips and somersaults.

The fourth member was a one-man band. Flint

recognized the fellow in the yellow tunic who had introduced himself as Gilbert. He stood on a high wooden box and had added an anklet of metal jingles to each foot, as well as a pair of small cymbals strapped to his knees. He played a lively melody on a very loud tenor shawm. His face was red from the effort of blowing into the wooden instrument that reached down almost to his knees. With his feet, he boomed out the beat on the hollow wooden box and the jingles added to the clamour. With the end of every phrase, he would add a cymbal crash with a flourish of knees.

All in all, he was almost as exciting to watch, as were the Magnaosseums who stood motionless amidst the action of the performance. Dell spoke quietly in the Duke's ear, "They have promised a display of the beasts' speed if you will allow them to use the training grounds."

"Of course I'll do that!" responded Sebastien excitedly. "Are they very fast then?"

Gode answered, "We saw them walking and in order to keep up, we had to trot the horses. The man in the yellow coat there, making all the noise, promises that they are faster than a horse but only for short distances. They can keep up the walk all day. By the way, the horses were not even a little nervous around them. Apparently, they are not a threat."

"This is fascinating," said the Duke. His face took on a thoughtful look as he continued to watch the display. "What do you suppose they would want for the pair?"

"Actually," said Gode casually, "they have already offered to trade them for a couple of horses. Apparently they eat so much that it is difficult to maintain them on the road."

Sebastien raised his eyebrows in inquiry, but did not say anything.

Understanding the implied question, Dell nodded, "We're considering it. We want to see the speed first."

Chapter 19 - Unbelievable

"Unbelievable," the Duke spoke the single word in a long, drawn-out utterance. "If I had not seen it with my own eyes, I would never have imagined that this could be true."

At the Duke's invitation, the travelling troupe moved their show to the training ground. After allowing plenty of time for all the townspeople to gather once the workday was complete, they began the demonstrations.

The Duke offered to put his fastest horse up against the Magnaosseums and they set up the racetrack around the outside of the training ground. The race was once around the track. Gode had volunteered to ride the horse while two of the performers, Wynn and Raymond, were to ride the massive Magnaosseums.

Apparently, when the travelling troupe acquired the animals, the original owners had already trained them to a saddle. Flint watched while the performers carefully fitted the odd-looking saddles onto the huge backs of their mounts. The animals stood calmly while a series of straps and clips were attached.

When Raymond finished, he looked around for

something to stand on to boost him up to the stirrup. Flint stepped forward and offered his hand.

"Have you ridden them much?" he asked the man who he had seen earlier leaping from the back of the Magnaosseum and performing a somersault before landing on the ground.

"In the towns, we like to have a race or two. On the road, we sit on the cart and rattle our brains," Raymond answered with a grin as he accepted the hand up and sprang into the saddle with hardly a twitch from the beast. "Gee up there," he said, nudging the bony sides of the animal with his heels. It began its ambling walk and quickly arrived at the starting line.

The townspeople lined the track and a big cheer went up as the three racers arrived. Flint was not sure what to expect. The Magnaosseums did not look as if they would be able to accelerate very quickly and he knew that a horse could fly off the line. The crowd quieted when Duke Sebastien stepped forward.

In a loud voice he outlined the rules of the race; as much for the benefit of the crowd as for the competitors. "I will call, 'on your mark, get set, and go'. When you hear 'go', ride as quickly as you can around the track and the first one back here is the winner. Does everyone understand?"

When the three riders nodded, he stepped back and roared, "On your mark. Get set. Go!" With the final syllable, all three animals leapt forward. It was stunning to watch how quickly the large, armoured animals accelerated, despite their bulk.

132

They were not fast enough to beat the horse to the first corner, however. Gode leaned low on the horse's neck and urged her to even more speed.

Flint could see him grinning as he rounded the corner and risked a look back at his competitors. Gode's eyes went round in surprise when he saw the Magnaosseums thundering down the track toward him. Those ferocious tusks must have looked terrifying. At that point, both horse and rider probably felt that they were running for their lives.

Before the second corner, one of the huge beasts calmly galloped into the lead. Flint could see Gode trying to get even more speed from the horse, but it was evident that she was going all out. She stayed ahead of the trailing Magnaosseum through the third corner and then, it was as if the huge animal found a new reservoir of power and shot past the horse as if she were just trotting. The two Magnaosseums crossed the finish line almost together and a good forty yards ahead of Gode and his horse.

All three riders pulled up when they crossed in front of the Duke. Flint heard the crowd cheering all around him. He realized that he too had been screaming encouragement at the racers. He was not exactly sure who he was cheering for, but it had been an incredibly exciting race. The riders trotted and then walked around one more lap of the field before pulling up in front of the Duke again.

Gode laughed as he chatted with the two Magnaosseum riders. He called out, "That was, indeed, unbelievable. Fleta, I believe that there can be no doubt you have won your bet!" Still energized from the race, he said, "I thought I had it at first, then I heard this thundering behind me and these fellows sped past us like we were standing still." He shook his head in mock dejection and patted the horse's neck. Swinging out of the saddle, he continued, "Well, I think I might want to talk to Gilbert about a trade. I just need to know how much they eat."

At that moment, Gilbert and the fourth memeber of the troupe climbed to the top of the cart they had pushed to the center of the training area after the race. "Ladies and gentlemen," he began in his booming voice. "I invite you to gather round and join us for an evening's entertainment."

Drawing a big breath, he began his one-man band performance of a jaunty tune. His music drew all the townspeople closer in anticipation of an enjoyable show. The tenor shawm he played was a remarkably loud instrument. Its buzzing tones carried easily across the open field. Beside Gilbert, the other fellow immediately joined in with an energetic clog dance.

Flint found his attention pulled between the two Magnaosseum riders hobbling the beasts in a place where they could crop the grass, and the performance that had begun. In the end, he helped Raymond and Wynn to stake each animal. The two men explained that they needed to put them far enough apart so that they would each have a large area where they could eat.

Flint watched in astonishment as the animals began to

tear the grass in huge mouthfuls. They slid their lower tusks along the ground, without once losing the rhythm of open, bite, and swallow. Flint watched in fascination for a few minutes as the beasts methodically trimmed the grass right down to the ground.

Turning back to the performance, he saw that Wynn and Raymond had made it to the cart where they each pulled out a large box like the one that Gilbert had performed on earlier in the day. They hopped up on top and suddenly there were three cloggers, dancing with an identical precision that was exciting to watch.

Gilbert increased the speed of his playing and the three dancers effortlessly went with him, maintaining a drumming beat with their feet. With a flourish, Gilbert ended his song and the crowd roared in approval.

For the next two hours, the four performers alternated between telling stories, singing songs and dancing. As the light died in the west, there was one last round of applause and then, sighing with contentment at such a fine evening, the crowd dispersed to their homes.

At least it was not winter. That was the thought that Hain kept in the front of his mind as he jogged along the barely visible path through the Chain of Thollcrawnow. They had already climbed to the top of two summits, and he knew there were three more mountains to climb before the travelling became somewhat easier.

Behind him loped a squad of twelve *Followers*. Each of the "recruits", as Martokallu called them, wore the armour that had been his in his past life. They really did not rely on the armour and none of it was well maintained, giving the squad a ragged look that might mislead an onlooker into underestimating them. In fact, many of the warriors had been ruthless killers during their time in the King's Guard and they had been chosen to join *The Followers of Martokallu* for just that reason.

They plodded uncomplaining behind Hain. There was no conversation in the ranks and none of the twelve men looked to be enjoying the journey. Hain was not either. That did not matter. The plan did.

Flint rode proudly beside Gode on their new Magnaosseums. It felt magnificent to sit atop the huge animal and feel its power under him. Different from a horse, the gait was both smoother and faster, and the view was definitely better.

After the show the previous evening, Gode and Dell negotiated a trade with Gilbert. Initially, Gilbert had been reluctant to give up the beasts, which although they ate so much, guaranteed a full crowd. In the end, though his partners encouraged him to make the trade. They had been the ones who most often were left to ensure that the Magnaosseums got enough to eat. It took a great deal of time: time they would rather spend doing almost anything else.

The trade was rather complicated. The troupe took two draft horses from Sebastien's stables and Sebastien took Gode and Flint's horses. Flint, Dell and Gode spent the evening with the troupe learning all they could about the Magnaosseums.

There was not much to know. They were herbivores and could be fed on any standing grass or hay or they liked to crop the leaves of low trees. In a day, they could eat as much as four hundred pounds of fodder. They also enjoyed the occasional meal of oats or barley. They drank about twenty-five gallons of water every day but could go most of the day without a drink at all if they had topped up in the morning.

When Flint asked what all the bony armour was for, the performers exchanged wry looks. Apparently, in the wild, during mating season, the males would challenge each other to butting contests. It would begin with the two contenders circling one another and then one would make a charge. Often it was an entire day of battering at each other with those tusks and the winner would get the girl. Fortunately, these two specimens had been neutered and were the gentlest beasts one could ever hope to find.

The two groups of travellers had departed from the gates of Fasnul together, amid much fanfare. Even Duke Sebastien came out to wave them on their way.

Fleta, Hulda, Hackett and Gytha had been Sebastien's guests the previous night, after the show. It had been a wonderful evening of chatting and storytelling. Hackett was always good for a tale or two and he had kept the Duke roaring with laughter.

For the first part of the trip, the two groups chatted amiably but the Magnaosseums quickly began to pull ahead. Since Gode was determined to be out of sight of the performers before they headed into the woods, the other riders urged their horses to a faster speed, leaving the ungainly cart trailing in their dust.

The voice in Hain's head had an exultant tone. Martokallu had located their prey once again. It was puzzling how contact had been lost and Hain could still feel the rage that had controlled *The Master* when he lost sight of the group of riders.

Obviously, he could not see everything at once and necessarily there were things that were not seen, but having something that was actually being observed disappear, was most disconcerting.

The image that Hain received now was also disconcerting. Previously, when Martokallu showed him Lorund's killers, there had been a group of seven horse riders. Now, he could see that five people were mounted on horses but two of them rode those huge beasts that came from far south of Tsaralvia. Where did they get those? He had only seen one once before and that had been in Tsaralvia ages ago.

Hain watched as the horses trotted to keep up with the Magnaosseums and then, they slowed to a stop and vanished. Not all at once, but one by one. Blinking in astonishment, at what he had seen, Hain suddenly felt a blast of rage arriving through the mind link.

Chapter 20 - Explanations

Cadmon closed the door to Hawk Hut and stepped to the front of the room. "Let's get started," he said after surveying the faces of the people sitting around on the benches. "Halvor, will you fill us in on what you have heard?"

Halvor stood up from his position in the corner. "It's not much to go on. I've only heard whispers," he began. The gathered *Talons* waited expectantly. The room was not as full as usual, because there were still seven members away on the mission that Dell had initiated by chasing *The Followers*. "I have heard it from two separate sources though, so I think there may be something to it. Both informants tell of a library that is maintained jointly by Martokallu and the King. Apparently, it was not started by this King but by his great-grandfather. It is supposed to house every book ever written."

At this pronouncement, he stopped and looked about the room. His listeners could see his excitement and he began to pace back and forth as he continued, "The decree limiting access to books dates back one hundred years, so that makes sense. My grandfather used to tell me stories about the library that his father had when he was a boy. I never really believed him when he told me of shelves filled with thousands of books." For a moment, he halted his pacing and his voice turned sombre. "He also told of a time when soldiers came to the house, pulled all those books off the shelves and burned them." Halvor looked sadly at *The Talons* as he said, "I cannot imagine why such a thing would be done."

"Do we know where the library is?" asked Dagur. He was the scout for the Eagles and had a mind that could always be counted on to focus on the important details. It made him a useful member of *The Talons* during the planning phase of any mission. He was also an expert in the mountains and his experience as a King's Guard gave him some valuable insight when they were planning missions into city strongholds.

"What I have heard is that it is almost directly south of here. The word is that it's a mountain fortress. I have general reports of where to find it, but no one seems to know exactly where it is located. I want to propose sending out a group to scout it and then," he stopped and looked around the room before continuing, "if it is feasible, I want to break in." His grin grew wide and he paused again before adding, "I need a new book."

Flint was excited to be riding into Halklyen. If you did not count the short ride into Thalnafar to pick up Geir—and he did not—then this was his first real mission. It had been a great success too. Dell had assassinated *The Follower* who he had pursued forever and Fleta had a successful assassination under her belt as well. For a moment, Flint regretted the fact that there had been no opportunity for him to even draw his own swords. Of course, when he thought about it, he knew that the success of the mission did not necessarily include personal glory.

Although, there had to be some personal glory in arriving home mounted on a Magnaosseum. He and Gode had outpaced the rest of the group once they got onto the forest trail. Flint could hear the steady footsteps of Gode's beast right behind him. He wondered if they should pull up and wait for everyone else before entering the village.

He was just about to ask when Gode spoke, "Pull up here. We'll wait for the others so we can all arrive together." Flint smiled to himself and immediately tugged on the reins of his mount, which obediently came to a stop and began to eat the branches near its head. "It's always a good idea to enter any settlement together," Gode continued, instructing the young *Talon*. "You never know what you are going to find. Not even if you think it's safe."

Flint had not even considered the possibility that something had gone wrong in Halklyen. He mentally kicked himself for not thinking like a scout. Then in the next minute, he worried that he might not find everyone safe at home. What if something had happened to Orma or Merylin? He was not worried about anything happening to Cadmon. He was too good at everything.

It did not take long before the horse riders caught up and Gode motioned them all forward again. Flint frantically scanned the shadows in every direction. He had not felt this edgy during any part of the whole mission. Here they were coming home and he felt downright frightened. He turned in his saddle to look at Fleta. The look she returned showed she was feeling some of the same anxiety.

With the horses trotting at their heels, they quickly reached the outskirts of the town. Flint spotted Penn, who carried his bow in one hand and the much targeted leather ball in the other. Faro sat nearby. They had evidently spotted them well before they emerged from the forest.

Penn jumped to his feet and dashed over to talk. "Hey, welcome back," he called. "We've been wondering when you would get here. I was just talking to Egbert today and he was thinking that you should be back by now but we weren't sure where you were going and there was no plan before you left so we didn't know exactly when to start expecting you back."

Penn would have continued but Gode interrupted him, "Have there been any new missions since we left?"

"No, but Cadmon just called a meeting in Hawk Hut and everybody went there. I know because I was practicing in Sparrow Hawk Square and Cadmon came by to tell Grove to come at about noon and it's just past noon now."

Again, Gode cut him off, "Thanks, Penn. Will you come along to the stables and help Albar take care of our animals?" he asked.

Penn stopped talking for the first time since he spotted the group and this time he truly looked at what he was seeing. Flint thought perhaps this was the only time that he had ever seen Penn speechless. Finally, he seemed to recover his breath, and asked in wonder, "What are you riding?"

Gode grinned as he swung down from his saddle, "They are called Magnaosseums. Come on, Penn. I'll tell you about them as we walk to the stables."

Penn looked pleadingly at Faro who nodded his permission. Happily, the younger boy fell in beside Gode and keeping up his continual stream of chatter, headed off to the stables.

When they finally left Penn and Albar in charge of the animals, Penn knew everything about the Magnaosseums. He had also come up with names for each of them as soon as he heard that they had not been named. Mag was the slightly larger one and Os was the other. When they left the stables to go to Hawk Hut, Penn was busily chattering away to Albar. Both worked to brush down the horses and make the Magnaosseums comfortable.

As the new arrivals made their way through the village, they called out greetings to everyone they saw. When they went past Orma's house, both Fleta and Flint ran in to say hello before hurrying back to join the group. Neither one of them wanted to miss a moment of their first meeting as real *Talons*.

Gode led the way to the entrance of Hawk Hut and

calmly pulled the door open. Flint was surprised to hear the sound of laughter cut short as people turned to see what had interrupted the meeting.

"What's so funny?" demanded Gode in mock fury.

Immediately the room erupted in a hail of greetings. The new arrivals were drawn into the room amidst welcomes and hugs that involved much clapping on the back. Flint was surprised to receive a hug from Cadmon who always remained so distant from him. He returned the hug, finding himself very glad to see the man who had been his guardian and teacher.

Soon the greetings subsided into demands for a report about their mission. Flint settled himself beside Fleta on one of the benches and listened as Dell and Gode told the story of how they tracked the *Followers* to a mountain fortress. There were murmurs of interest when Dell described the caverns filled with sparkling gems.

Gode also managed to wring a laugh from the crowd when he described how Dell avoided letting anyone accompany him into the fortress after they caught up with him. Dell seemed to smile modestly behind his mask as he acknowledged the deception.

Cadmon stepped forward and said, "Well, it appears that your mission was a success." He stopped and scowled at Dell. "But that doesn't mean that I approve of the way you went about it."

He looked as if he was going to go on chastising Dell, but Gode interrupted, "Actually, Cadmon, that was just part one of a very successful mission. Hulda, do you and Gytha want to explain the next section?"

Hulda smoothly took over the telling of the tale with a description of what had happened at Derflanag. Gytha described the defences and explained about the plan. When Hulda told about how Fleta slipped unobserved over the wall in order to assassinate Duke Arjen, Cadmon gave a start of surprise and then a look of satisfaction crossed his face. He knew he had made the right choice when he invited Fleta to become one of *The Talons.*

As Hulda wrapped up the story by telling how they slipped out of town before the death was even discovered, Cadmon again stepped forward to congratulate them on a successful mission.

Gode interrupted him, "Ah, we're not quite done the telling yet, old friend. Flint, maybe you would like to take over for the next part?"

Nervously clearing his throat as he stood, Flint picked up the story from the point just outside Fasnul. He was not as confident a speaker as everyone else seemed to be. He also found it very difficult to describe the Magnaosseums, and floundered through an attempt to give everyone an idea of just how incredible the beasts were.

Fleta saved him when she piped up from the back, "Let's just say, you have to see them to believe them." Flint grinned his thanks and continued to explain about the race they had watched and the trade they made.

This time, before Cadmon rose from his seat, he gravely looked around at the returnees with a questioning expression. Gode chuckled and said, "The end."

Cadmon stood and faced the group. "Well, I believe congratulations are in order," he said. "Three successful missions were pulled out of the air." There was a chorus of agreement. He continued sternly, "That is not to say that I condone rushing off to pursue individual missions. We work as a group here." He swept his eyes over the members of *The Talons* and stopped to regard Dell for a moment. Dell looked back unflinchingly.

It was quiet for a moment and then Gode spoke from the bench where he had made himself comfortable, "Speaking of groups, what was everyone laughing about when we arrived?"

Grove answered him, "Halvor needs a new book!"

Chapter 21 - Home

"Egbert, have you heard?" Dell spoke from the doorway of Egbert and Merylin's house. Fleta looked up in surprise from her place at the kitchen table Immedieately after the meeting she had raced home to see her guardians.

Initially, she had felt a little shy. She knew she was not allowed to say much about the missions. But Merylin and Egbert had welcomed her back so enthusiastically that she was able to forget about her trip while they filled her in about the happenings at home.

After Cadmon decided the villagers would be just as safe back in Halklyen, it had been a short trip home and a quick unpacking. Though everyone was on edge these days.

A twenty-four hour guard patrolled the village perimeter. Penn and Faro had been taking their shift when the travellers rode back into town. Egbert made large metal triangles that the watch could hammer upon if anything unusual appeared.

Twelve warriors at a time for four hours each meant that people were feeling the strain. Everyone slept with weapons ready and squads of fighters were prepared to answer a call at any time.

As well, Egbert had been working on some sort of invention. He excitedly told Fleta about its development. She was not sure that she understood exactly what he was describing or what use it could be. Merylin seemed to find the idea of this particular contraption to be rather funny. While Egbert explained, waving his hands around in an attempt to make Fleta see what he was describing, Merylin waggled her eyebrows and grinned behind his back.

Now Egbert turned to greet Dell, "Greetings of the day, Dell. Have I heard about what?" By the look of the eyes that she could see through the holes in his leather mask, Fleta guessed that Dell was smiling.

Dell looked at Fleta, "You haven't told them?"

She lifted a shoulder in a shrug and grimaced awkwardly, "We were told not to talk about it."

"I do not think that this is a secret that will remain safe," Dell answered. Now Fleta knew he was smiling. "Egbert," he said, "I believe we have a perfect enhancement to that invention we were talking about before I left."

"By the Fire of Dworgunul, what have you brought?" Egbert asked excitedly.

Fleta laughed. "I don't think we can tell you about it. We're going to need to show you. Let's just say that it is unbelievable. Come and see!"

The four of them headed off with Fleta in the lead. On the way past Orma's house, Fleta spotted Flint and

Cadmon eating dinner with Orma and Cwenhild. She called out, "Come and see!"

Flint knew exactly where they were headed. He turned and looked at the other people at the dinner table, "Have you seen them yet?"

"Seen what?" responded Orma. Cwenhild and Cadmon too, figured out what was going on. They smiled at each other as they remembered Fleta's interruption of Flint's report.

"Let's go," Cwenhild said, hastily finishing the last bites on her plate.

Orma did not look so certain. "Now? It can't wait?" she asked incredulously.

"You'll like it," Flint assured her. "Come on."

Soon there were eight of them heading toward the stables. Fleta began telling the story of the wager she made with Duke Sebastien. "Gode wouldn't tell him what he was going to see. He just told him that he needed to see it to believe it. I said it was unbelievable but he didn't think it could be."

"Well, I know you have all said that it is unbelievable, but really, from what Flint said, I imagine that it is entirely believable," said Cadmon doubtfully.

"Wait and see," asserted Fleta. She ran ahead to open the door of the stable and the others followed.

When they entered, she was standing in the dim light talking to Albar. "Wait," she said, waving her arms to prevent them from coming into the stables. "We'll bring them outside to the riding ring so you can see them properly." Cadmon made as if to step past her, but she grabbed his arm and said, "You too, Cadmon. Be patient. You'll see. It'll be worth it."

Reluctantly, Cadmon turned and said, "I just hope it can live up to the expectations you have built."

"I'm not worried," Fleta responded. "Flint, you come and help us get them ready."

"Good idea," Flint answered as he herded everyone else back outside.

When Flint and Fleta finally led the saddled Magnaosseums out to the riding ring, there were gasps of surprise from the assembled people. The crowd had grown from the original six people who accompanied Fleta and Flint. Apparently word had spread.

Fleta led Mag. who towered above her, while Flint swung into Os's saddle as soon as he was clear of the barn.

"What, in the name of all that is good, is that?" cried Orma.

Dell began to explain while Fleta used a mounting block to reach the stirrup so that she could hop aboard Mag. She and Flint began to ride the huge beasts around the ring. "They are called Magnaosseum," he said. "We traded a couple of horses for them in Fasnul. A performing troupe arrived in the city at the same time that we did. They said they got them from somewhere south of Tsaralvia. The troupe used the Magnaosseums to pull their cart, and during a performance, all they had to do was tether the animals nearby and you can imagine the crowds that would arrive."

His audience hung on every word, although their eyes

never left the sight of the armoured mounts walking calmly around the riding ring. Dell continued, "However, they were happy to make a trade because the beasts eat so much the troupers had to spend all their time trying to find enough fodder." He paused and turned to the blacksmith. "We figured that they would be the perfect addition to your new invention, Egbert."

Egbert had his eyes glued to the display in front of him, but he nodded his head enthusiastically. "By the Fire of Dworgunul, they be exactly right. Look at that armour! Nothing would stop them. Be they fast?"

"We watched them beat Sebastien's fastest horse in a quarter mile race," answered Dell. "And, when they are just walking, they go the speed of a trotting horse. It is true though that they eat a lot. But, they are happy eating any leaves they can reach, so that means they can actually graze in the forest. We should be able to keep them fed for a little while."

Cadmon spoke then, "Well, if we want to put them to use before they eat everything in sight, we had best get the next mission underway. We leave at dawn."

It seemed as if Flint had just fallen asleep when Cadmon shook him awake. "Are you sure you want to come along, boy? You just got back yesterday. Sometimes a rest is the sensible choice."

Flint wiped the sleep from his eyes and said, "I'm fine. I'll be ready in a minute." He rolled heavily to his feet and neatly tucked the corners of his blanket around his mattress.

It was barely two weeks since Cadmon promoted him and Fleta to *The Talons* and sent them off on a mission. This would be his third mission. As he strapped on his swords, he realized that he had not had an opportunity to practice with them since all this action began. He would definitely find time today to run through some drills just to get the feel again.

He grabbed up the breakfast Cadmon had left on the table and followed him out the door. Fleta would not be coming on this mission and he felt a little strange as he hurried through the dark streets past her house. She was planning to help Egbert with the new invention and Dagur was coming along as the second scout.

Albar already had the seven horses saddled and ready when Flint and Cadmon arrived at the stables. Near the door, Dell checked his saddlebags and added a few last items. Halvor's dog Selda sat patiently beside Halvor who chatted with Dagur and Cwenhild. Igon was the last to arrive.

Flint did not know the big man well, but he found him friendly enough despite the forbidding exterior he presented. Igon was an *Eagle*. A mountain of a man, he towered over everyone else in *The Hawks*. He even made Gode look up at him. His brush cut and the beard that was always on the point of becoming bushy lent him a threatening air intensified by his choice of weapons.

Two long flails hung from his wide leather belt. The handles were of polished oak and the chains, each measuring three feet long, ended in spike-covered balls.

Igon could easily swing both flails at the same time.

When one of those spike balls struck the target, it was like being smashed with a handful of daggers. To add to the terrible effectiveness of his weapons, both handles had an extra blade protruding from the bottom.

Flint had watched Igon practice in Eagle Square. Gode liked to spar with him, and he always wore full armour for the matches even though Igon never used his spike-ball flails in practice. He had another pair that, even though the balls were smoothly rounded, looked equally dangerous. If Gode missed a block with his double-headed axe, he always ended up with horrible bruises.

As soon as Cadmon checked his own saddlebags and added the bag of food he carried, he swung up in his saddle and sat surveying the rest of the group. Flint hurried to do the same and noticed that within seconds, everyone was also ready to go. Albar reached out to take hold of Selda's collar. He would take her over to Fleta later. This was not a mission where a dog would be useful.

After a nod from Cadmon, Dagur took the lead and started along the path leading into the forest. Cadmon nudged his horse in behind him and then, in single file, Cwenhild, Igon, and Halvor followed. Dell rode in front of Flint who took the responsibility for watching their rear.

Flint would have been happy to be on lead now while he actually knew where they were going. He wondered how they could possibly find a mountain fortress when their only clue was a rumour that it was somewhere in the mountains south of Shenkar. What could Cadmon have in mind? Did he have more specific instructions, which he was not yet revealing? This would not be like the last mission when they simply followed Lorund to his mountain fortress. This felt more like hunting blind.

Hain felt a roar of approval in his head. He had just left the Chain of Thollcrawnow and headed out onto the plain when Martokallu began showing him images of a group of seven riders. Hain did not recognize any of the faces. He wondered what Martokallu saw that gave him such excitement.

Then he looked more closely and realized he did in fact know two of the riders. One was the masked man who killed Lorund and the other was the boy he had last seen riding a Magnaosseum.

Once again he suffered a swell of rage at the memory of Lorund's easy defeat. His anger was divided between Lorund for being so careless and the masked man for daring to defy *The Followers*. He could sense traces of Martokallu's anger as well, but the feeling was edged with an impression of satisfaction. For the last twenty-four hours, *The Master* had been furious at having lost contact with the group of seven riders and now he had located them again. Or, at least part of the group.

What was happening with Martokallu's vision? Was it really failing? Perhaps *The Master* was losing strength. Hain considered the idea that there might be a need to replace *The Master*. He immediately suppressed the thought for fear that it might project back to Martokallu. It would not do to have *The Master* suspect that Hain wished to take over his position of power.

Hain studied the image of the seven riders, looking for clues as to their exact location. For a moment, he thought they were in the Chain of Thollcrawnow because the scene looked so similar to the landscape he had just crossed. Then he noticed they were passing by a waterfall that dropped several hundred yards into a turquoise coloured lake.

He knew that view. They were near *The Master's* library. Did they know where they were or was it just chance that brought them so close to the carefully guarded secret? Fortunately, he was only an hour away.

Chapter 22 - The Waterfall

Flint was astounded by the beauty of the small lake they had come upon in the mountains. A waterfall dropped straight down into a deep pool of water that sparkled in the afternoon sun. The noise was thunderous, and a welcome spray of water splashed across the riders and their horses. It had been a long hot day in the saddle and Flint hoped they would stop there for a rest or even as a campsite.

The first day after leaving Halklyen, they travelled through most of the daylight hours and then camped just north of Shenkar. Apparently, Flint was not the only one who had been thinking about the lack of weapons practice. As soon as they had cared for the horses, Cadmon set Halvor on watch and then called for a weapons check.

Each of the warriors chose a space and began to work through the drills that were a part of every blade master's training. It felt good to wield his swords after so long and Flint continued to practice long past the point when the others had satisfied themselves and found a place to sit and rest.

Remembering how perfect his swords felt the day

before, he hoped that Cadmon would choose to stop here. It would be wonderful to dive into that beautiful lake after training. No doubt, it would be extremely cold though. The waterfall probably came right off a glacier.

As if hearing Flint's thoughts, Cadmon turned in his saddle and called out to the riders following him. He had to raise his voice to be heard over the noise of the waterfall, "Do you want to take a break here, or shall we continue to a quieter spot?"

Dagur had been riding point for the last two days; using as his only guide a report Cadmon received from someone who claimed to have heard the story from his grandfather. Supposedly, the library door was carved right into the mountain. From there, you could see a perfect view of a pyramid-shaped mountain.

Dagur was convinced he knew of a mountain that could fit that description. The goal was to get the pyramid mountain in sight and then, try to locate the door.

Flint was impressed by the sheer immensity of the mountain range but he had begun to think that the search was rather like looking for a needle in a haystack. How could Dagur possibly find the door simply by finding the mountain? Surely, a mountain like that would be visible from a full three hundred and sixty degrees.

Cwenhild answered Cadmon's question. "I think we should stop here. It is a beautiful site and it also gives us access to a few peaks that we could climb so that we can take a look around." She looked up at the waterfall where Flint could see that there might be a possible route to the top. He decided that he would like to climb it if Cadmon would let him volunteer.

Dell agreed, "We need to get up top and the horses cannot do that. Let's stop here for the day. The horses can rest down below and some of us can climb up to take a look around. Maybe we'll have a better sense of where we are heading tomorrow."

"That sounds like a good idea," said Cadmon as he swung off his horse. "Flint, Dagur, Halvor and Cwenhild, would you like to be the ones to make the climb? The rest of us will set up a camp and watch you from below."

Igon swung heavily down from his horse. "What? You don't think I should be the one to climb that hill?" he asked with a grin. At almost seven feet tall and weighing in at over three hundred pounds, Igon was far more suited to battle than he was to clambering up a steep rock face.

Cwenhild teased him, "You can come along if you like. I think you'd be very useful on the end of a belaying rope."

"Yes, but, who would hold me when it was my turn to climb?" asked Igon with a good-natured chuckle.

"You make a good point, my friend," said Halvor. "I think I'd rather have you down here so I can wave to you when I get to the top." He reached into his saddlebag and pulled out a leather bundle that rattled when he set it on the ground. "Flint, you're with me," he called as he began untying the laces that held the bundle closed.

He deftly loosened the knots and unrolled the leather wrapper to display a collection of implements that looked like heavy iron sewing needles. Flint looked over to see that Dagur had a set of the iron tools as well. When Halvor saw the puzzled look on Flint's face, he laughed and explained, "They're belaying pins. Egbert made these beauties." He picked one up and held it out for Flint to examine. "I'm going to teach you how to climb a mountain and these little things are going to keep you from falling while you do it."

Cwenhild walked over carrying two large coils of rope that had been strapped to the back of her saddle. She hung one around Flint's neck saying, "Here you go. You might need this." With her free hand, she indicated the peak on the opposite side of the lake "You two can take the waterfall. Dagur and I will head up that face over there." As she turned away, she called over her shoulder, "Last one to the top is a rotten egg."

Flint thought that might be a signal to start hurrying, but Halvor set about climbing the rock in a very methodical manner. First, he spent some time surveying the route he had chosen. He studied it from across the lake first and then he and Flint walked around the lake to the base of the falls.

With some relief, Flint saw that Halvor did not intend to climb directly up the waterfall. Flint had imagined they might go right up the centre, through the water. He had wondered if it might be slippery. Instead, Halvor was studying a section sheltered from the cascading water.

When he seemed to have satisfied himself about the

route he would take, he turned briskly to Flint, took the rope from his hands and asked, "Have you ever gone climbing before?"

"Trees? Yes," answered Flint. "Mountains? No." He watched as Halvor's efficient fingers tied one end of the rope around Flint's waist. Halvor now wore the belaying pins in a bandolier across his chest and he had a small hammer hanging from his right hip.

"Well, the two are not so different," Halvor said. "Basically, just make sure you have at least two points that are holding your weight before you reach for a new hold." He handed the rest of the coiled rope to Flint, took the other end and tied it around his own waist. "All right. Hold the rope and let it out gradually as I go up. Make sure it doesn't snag anywhere. Now watch carefully. Step where I step and grip where I grip. Wait until I get to that first little ledge up there before you begin."

With that, Halvor began crawling up the side of the mountain. Flint watched his every move, trying to memorize exactly where he put his hands and feet. He made it look incredibly easy, but Flint suspected that it might prove more difficult than it appeared.

When Halvor reached the ledge, he selected a belaying pin from his bandolier and, using the hammer, tapped it into a small crack in the rock. Then he looped the rope around the pin and called down to Flint, "Your turn. Just take it easy and don't look down."

Flint put his hands on the holds that Halvor had used and began to make his way up the rock. He noticed that

Halvor pulled the rope up every time he made some progress. It gave him a feeling of security to know that if he lost his grip, the rope would stop him from crashing onto the rock below. He peeked over his shoulder to see how far he had made it off the ground and immediately wished that he had not. It was further than he thought and for a moment, he was paralyzed by the thought of falling.

Halvor called down to him, yelling to be heard over the noise of the waterfall, "I thought I told you not to look down. That is the number one rule of mountain climbing! Don't worry. You're doing really well and I have you on the rope. Keep going."

It was an effort of will but Flint finally convinced his muscles to start moving again. A few careful motions later, he found himself balanced on the ledge beside Halvor. His heart beat quickly and he felt a wild exhilaration as he looked down from the safety of his perch at what he had accomplished. Halvor noticed his excitement and smiled. "Incredible, isn't it?" he asked.

"Where did you learn to do this?" burst out Flint. He could not believe that he had never tried it before.

"One of the men who worked as a guard for my father was a climber. He used to take me out when I was about your age. Shall we continue?" Halvor coiled the rope again. He looped his end of the rope around the belaying pin and handed the coil to Flint. "This time, keep the friction on the rope. Let it out as I climb, just like before, but if I fall, you'll be holding me. So make sure you are ready."

With a reassuring smile, he turned back to the rock face and began to make his way steadily upwards. Again, Flint studiously watched his every move. When he stopped this time, Halvor was over two-thirds of the way to the top. He tapped another belaying pin into place and wrapped the rope around it.

As soon as everything was in place, Flint followed. His fingertips felt alive with the roughness of the rock and his feet confidently reached for toeholds.

In next to no time, he pulled himself up to join Halvor. "How are you doing? You're not getting tired are you?" Halvor asked him.

"Tired? Absolutely not," answered Flint. "This is the most amazing experience I've ever had." For a moment, he was sorry that Fleta was not here to share it with him. She would love the exhilaration of the climb. "How about you, old man? Are you getting tired?" Flint grinned as he teased Halvor, who at twenty-six was ten years older.

"I think I'll be able to make it to the top. Just be sure you have a good grip on that belaying line in case I lose my balance or something." Halvor grinned back at him and after giving the rope a good twist around the anchoring pin, he put the coil into Flint's hands again. "Up we go," he said reaching for his first handhold.

The next part looked a little more difficult. Halvor took his time in choosing hand and toeholds. As he got close to the top, he paused to consider his options: there was a lip on the stone that he needed to get over. Flint tightened his hold on the rope and watched nervously to see how he would handle it. Halvor reached up over the top with one hand and had to let one of his toeholds go.

Suddenly he was hanging from the rock lip by just his fingertips. Flint cringed as he watched Halvor swing his legs. He caught the lip with his left toe and wedged it over the top. Using his toe, he pulled himself higher, and with a huge effort, shoved his knee over the lip. In a moment, Halvor disappeared over the top as he hauled himself to safety. Flint sighed with relief.

Then, his stomach clenched when he realized that he would be expected to make the same manoeuvre. He watched the rope beside him uncoil as Halvor pulled up the slack. Flint felt the rope tug at his waist and stood up to begin the climb.

Ever since Martokallu first sent Hain the image of the seven riders near the waterfall, Hain had been pushing his squad of *Followers* to hurry. There had been no rest for anyone as they left the plains south of Derflanag and headed into the mountains. The fastest route to *The Master's* library took them through a river valley. He figured they would arrive at the waterfall very shortly.

Hain could see in the most recent vision Martokallu had sent to him, that two of the seven people were making the climb directly to the door of the library. They had definitely chosen the most difficult route by which to approach it. He wondered why they had not elected to climb up from the other side. It was a much easier path.

Chapter 23 - Triumph

Flint carefully let go of the last handhold before the lip at the top of the climb. He knew he would need to time everything carefully in order to get himself over the top the way Halvor had done. Taking a deep breath, he pushed off with his left foot and stretched his free right hand. He caught the handhold, but his left foot was dangling now.

Flint tried to imagine that he was simply hanging from a low branch in a tree, and to ignore the two hundred yard drop below him. He let go with his left hand, pushed off with his right foot and suddenly he was dangling from the top of the mountain. Remembering how Halvor had swung his leg up to grip the top, he shifted his weight to get his body swinging. Kicking upwards, he caught the edge with his toe just as Halvor had. By thrusting his right leg up, he succeeded in gripping the mountain with his knee. He tried to pull himself up with the strength of his arms, but suddenly found he could not haul his body weight those last few inches.

Flint felt himself begin to slip and hoped that Halvor had a good grip on that belaying rope. Just as the last of his strength gave out, he felt Halvor's hand grip his wrist and drag him over the top of the mountain.

They both lay on the rocky summit breathing heavily. Flint turned his head to the side and saw the rope knotted tightly around a rock. Halvor had set up a rope that would catch him in case he fell and then managed to prevent him from falling.

Crawling carefully away from the edge, Flint croaked, "Thank you. You saved my life."

"Not bad for an old man, huh?" answered Halvor. "Although, I didn't really save your life. The rope had you. I just saved you from having to make the climb again." Halvor grinned and sat up. "Well done, youngster. Check out the view from here. It's pretty dramatic."

The first thing Flint saw when he turned his eyes to admire the view, was a mountain shaped like a pyramid. He quickly looked back at Halvor, "Is it…" Could they possibly have found the entrance to the library so easily?

Halvor shrugged, "Maybe. Check out the rock wall behind us. This little plateau looked like the top from down below, but there's a long ways to go before we get anywhere near the top of this mountain."

Looking down to where they had left their companions, Flint waved and Cadmon lifted a hand in reply. From up here, he thought, they look like ants. Remembering Cwenhild's challenge, he checked to see how far she and Dagur had gotten. There was no sign of them on the mountain face that they had chosen. Evidently they beat Flint to the top.

He got up and walked toward the next rock face, which was some distance back from the waterfall. A creek flowed down to a pool that gathered the water before releasing it to tumble down to the lake below. It was quieter up here, away from the crashing waterfall, and the view was stunning. Tiny wildflowers covered the whole plateau. Everywhere he looked there was a profusion of purple with the occasional flash of red or yellow.

Halvor fell into step beside him and they silently followed the creek across the meadow. "Do you see this?" Halvor asked pointing to a trail leading off down the mountain. "It looks like an easier way to get up here. Maybe we'll take this route down."

"Why would there be a path up here?" wondered Flint. "It doesn't look like a game trail; the wear is too deep. Where does it lead?" Flint cast around looking for indications as to who would have worn the trail through to the rock. "It doesn't appear to have been used for a while. It looks ancient."

"It's hard to tell though," said Halvor. "Rock doesn't leave many clues." He followed the trail down the mountain for a few paces, then turned decisively uphill and said, "Let's see where it leads."

Relaxing against a rock, Cadmon watched as Flint disappeared over the lip of the mountain. For a moment, he thought he had seen the boy slip a little but then he swung up and over to safety. He let out a breath he had not realized he was holding and turned to survey the entrance to the pass. Somehow, he had a feeling he was missing something, but nothing was visible.

A few minutes earlier, he watched Cwenhild make it to the summit of her climb. Dagur was probably the best of the climbers that Cadmon had just watched. He seemed to crawl up the mountainside like a fly. Halvor and Cwenhild looked like very experienced climbers as well. Flint was the obvious rookie, but he had done well on the climb, if somewhat slowly and cautiously. Caution was a good thing in this case. The boy had not fallen.

Dell had taken a horse and gone off to scout around the base of the mountain. Cadmon was surprised to find his eyelids wanting to close. On the rocks beside him, Igon snored noisily. He shook himself awake and got up to check the horses.

Dell found a trail. It appeared to lead up to the mountain Halvor and Flint had climbed. The path switch-backed upwards and Dell was surprised that his horse climbed it easily. Perhaps it was a game trail worn by eons of animals making an annual trek.

He studied the ground in front of him. There seemed to be no sign of recent use, but in the alpine, a trail could be a hundred years old and still have nothing growing on it. The disturbed vegetation would have difficulty re-establishing itself in the short growing season and cool summers.

Regardless, it was easy riding and the horse patiently

laboured up the hill. By the looks of it, the trail would come out where Halvor and Flint had been headed. He wondered who would get there first.

Hain signalled to *The Followers* behind him. He knew that just around the bend, they would find the clearing with the lake and waterfall. He wanted to prepare his attack carefully.

Tentatively, he reached out with his mind, *Master, what do you see of the seven riders?*

The response was immediate. First, he saw the huge man sleeping on the ground beside six hobbled horses. *Where is the seventh horse?* he asked. In reply, Martokallu showed him the missing horse with the masked man riding it. He rode along the mountain path that led right to the door of the library.

Hain felt that rush of rage that hit him every time he saw Lorund's murderer but he took the time to search the image for the man's weapons. Nothing was immediately apparent though he seemed to have some sort of bladed gauntlet on his right hand and perhaps he had daggers concealed under his cloak.

The image shifted and he saw the young boy and a slightly older man approaching the door of the library. The boy had a pair of swords sheathed in a double scabbard on his back. The man wore a bandolier with some sort of stakes in it as well as a belt studded with daggers. The blades looked long and lethal with wicked serrated tips. No doubt, he had the skills to throw those daggers from a distance or use them equally well in hand-to-hand combat.

The next view showed a man and woman sitting at the top of a rock face. They did not appear to be doing anything other than resting and enjoying the view. The woman wore a machete strapped closely to one leg, and she carried a bow and a full quiver on her back. The man carried a large cutlass in a scabbard on his back and there might be a smaller version of the same blade strapped to his leg as well. These people were armed for war.

That takes care of six of the people, he said inside his mind. *Where is the seventh?* The image shifted to show a man standing near the waterfall, gazing up at the crashing stream. The powerful-looking warrior wore a long sword sheathed on his left side. His chainmail sparkled in the afternoon sun. While Hain watched, the man drew the blade and began to perform a series of drills that let Hain know he watched a master swordsman.

Martokallu's voice boomed in his head, *Be wary, Hain. That man was once a general in the King's Guard. You will be certain that he does not leave this place.*

Hain mentally agreed with *The Master* and returned his focus to the present surroundings.

Now that Hain was in possession of all the information about his enemy, he began to formulate a plan. His knowledge of the type of weapons that each person carried and the demonstration from the swordsman alerted him that he faced trained warriors. Knowledge that one of them had overpowered and killed Lorund, warned him that he had best not underestimate his opponents.

Even the sleeping man had to be taken into account. Hain had not missed the huge flails lying on the ground beside him. The spikes on those iron balls looked wicked enough to flay the skin off any unwary fighter.

Turning to his *Followers*, who waited patiently while he communicated with Martokallu, he began to outline his plan.

Chapter 24 - Attack

Strangely, the path they followed led directly up to a rock face and then stopped. Flint could not see any reason for an animal or a person to make a path leading nowhere. There was no sign of a cave or overhanging shelter that might explain the deeply worn path.

In bewilderment, Flint and Halvor studied the rock face intently. Behind them, they suddenly heard the sound of a horseshoe scuffing on rock.

Both turned with drawn weapons to see Dell calmly sitting on his horse watching them. "It's a door," he said.

The faces of Halvor and Flint wore identical expressions of shock and confusion. "It's a door?" echoed Halvor, turning it into a question.

Flint, however, made the connection. "Like the door you entered when you followed Lorund?" he asked, swinging around to examine the rock once again. "How does it open?"

"Apparently, you just have to know it's there," answered Dell. "Orma says the magic only really works if you don't know what you're looking for...and then,... Well, all I did was push on it."

As he spoke, Dell dismounted. "I would suggest that we prepare for a fight before we do that though." He flexed the fingers of his gauntleted left hand and examined the blades closely. Then with his right hand, he meticulously pulled each of his six daggers from its sheath, checked the blade and thrust it back again. Flint knew they were sharp because he had watched Dell endlessly hone them the night before while they sat by the fire.

Flint took the advice and reached back to draw his blades. After his climb, his arms felt the weight of the swords. Silently, he ran through a drill to regain his confidence. Halvor, too, checked his daggers. The serrated tips of each blade looked deadly.

When Halvor sheathed his weapons, he looked at Flint, and asked, "Are you ready for this?"

Flint felt a rush of excitement. This could be his first real fight. He finished his drill and returned his swords to their sheaths in a hiss of metal. He grinned as he declared, "I am ready."

"No," said Halvor. "I mean are you ready to face whatever is on the other side of that door? It might turn out to be nothing, or it could be a *Follower* intent on killing you." Halvor looked at him seriously. "You need to be ready. Ready to do everything you need to do in order to survive."

Flint sobered. "I guess so," he said uncertainly. Suddenly, he did not feel excited. He felt frightened.

Dell looked at him. "That's better," he said. "You're worried now. It is never a good thing to enter into a fight when you think it is a game. If you end up in a fight today, you are fighting for your life. Do what it takes." Dell held Flint's eyes for a minute and then liking what he saw, gave him a nod and strode toward the rock face.

Igon's eyes snapped open. He sat up and looked around for the noise that woke him. With the crashing of the waterfall, he could not immediately identify what that might have been. Then, he turned his head and saw the most terrifying sight of his life, charging directly at him.

The monster stood close to nine feet tall. His armour must have been designed to make him look even more threatening. Shoulder guards extended into serrated wings and the knee protectors included jagged projections that looked as if they could cut a person in half. In each hand, he wielded a long, deadly-looking sword. Flickering, yellow light crackled in the air surrounding the beast and his eyes were purest yellow.

Unable to convince his brain that what he saw was real, Igon sat rooted to the spot. Those yellow eyes pierced him through like an insect on a pin. Hain was almost upon him before he managed to respond.

At the last possible moment, Igon jumped to his feet with a flail in each hand, just in time to present a worthy opponent. Hain did not slow his charge. Still roaring, he attacked with both blades. Igon barely had time to get his flails whirling, but he was ready when Hain struck.

The tremendous crash alerted Cadmon to the fight and he spun away from his contemplation of the waterfall in time to see both of Hain's blades deflected by the spinning balls of Igon's flails in a flash of yellow light.

Even as he began to run toward the battle, his eyes swept the little valley for signs of other attackers. He checked the top of the cliff where he had last seen Dagur and Cwenhild resting after their climb and saw that they were already rappelling down the mountain face.

His mind clicked away. Why were there no other attackers? In his experience, *The Followers* always worked in groups. He had known immediately that the adversary Igon faced was a *Follower* of immense power and age. Seeing the two swords, he wondered if this might be the rumoured Hain. He had not been seen in the world of men for at least two generations. All the stories that Cadmon had ever heard of him were now considered legends.

While Cadmon watched, Igon lost his balance when one of his flails became entangled in the monster's right hand sword. For the moment, he suceeded in holding off the other blade, but flails were not meant for sustained, close up battle. Igon was tiring.

Cadmon saw an opening in *The Follower's* defence and hurled himself forward to join the fight. Just as he drew the monster's attention and raised his own sword to deflect a giant stroke aimed at his head, Cadmon heard the buzz of an arrow and saw it strike home in the unprotected stomach of *The Follower*.

Out of the corner of his eye, he saw Cwenhild rushing toward them, while at the same time nocking another arrow. Dagur sprinted toward the horses.

The huge monster sent a lethal stroke in Igon's direction and the big man used the flail to knock the blade sideways. Nonetheless, the flat of the sword was enough to knock him unconscious and Igon fell to the ground like a tree.

The Follower thrust the tip of one of his swords into the ground and grasped the arrow in his stomach. While Cadmon reared back for another strike, the monster pulled the arrow from his stomach. He ignored the gush of yellow blood and with a roar of rage threw it like a spear directly at the charging Cwenhild. She did not have time to dodge and the arrow nicked her thigh.

Cwenhild looked down in horror to see that her own poisoned arrow, now covered in the monster's blood, had cut her. She knew she had limited time before even the antidote would be useless. Her eyes briefly met Cadmon's and they both watched the monster drop to his knees. But, he did not relinquish his grasp on his sword.

Even on his knees, he was taller than Cadmon. For a moment, Cadmon considered his reduced opponent and then he launched himself forward again.

Cwenhild felt the first tendrils of poison reach her bloodstream. She stumbled toward the horses where Dagur hurriedly unfastened the hobbles. He caught her up just as her muscles lost their ability to hold her.

The horses tossed their heads, the nearby fight making them restless. But they were trained to battle and kept their nerves. Dagur slung Cwenhild across her horse knowing that she would be unable to hold herself upright in the saddle.

She mumbled, "In my saddlebag...the small leather sachet...with a...white flower...painted on it... Sprinkle the white powder...right in my wound." Then she closed her eyes.

Dagur dove for her saddlebag as he listened to her tortured breathing. In his haste to find the antidote, he gave no attention to the fight taking place not ten feet away. He found the bag containing her potions and quickly rifled through it, searching for the packet with a white flower painted on it.

As soon as he found it, he broke the seal on the sachet and pulled back the cloth of her leggings to reveal her wound. It was a very slight cut and the bleeding was already clotting so he used his own blade to gently scrape it open again. When the blood began to flow, he shook the white powder liberally into the cut and then took a bandage from the same bag and bound it up.

In talking with her one day, she had explained how the antidote worked. It counteracted the effects of the poison with which she coated all her weapons but it had to be used very quickly after the initial injury. It would take an hour or so before she regained consciousness. Dagur could see now that she breathed more easily already.

He turned to assess the battle. To this point, he had been so focused on Cwenhild that he had not spared a thought for Igon and Cadmon. He would have to tell them what he and Cwenhild had seen from their vantage point on the top of the cliff.

Igon lay unconscious on the ground. He had a thin line of blood seeping from a small cut on his forehead, but otherwise looked unharmed. Cadmon continued to battle with a greatly reduced *Follower*.

Despite having fallen to his knees, the monster fought with power and speed. He efficiently parried all of Cadmon's attacks and even managed to attack. It had come down to a battle of wills.

Somehow, *The Follower* forced Cadmon to stay in front of him. He had the great advantage of using two swords to Cadmon's one, but both fighters were slowing down. Watching them, Dagur was not sure that Cadmon could win.

"Cadmon, leave him," he shouted. "If he cannot stand, he cannot follow us. Help me with Igon."

Cadmon did not instantly register what Dagur said. Exhaustion had set in and he bashed away at his adversary with no thought for anything but the next move.

The distraction of thinking about Dagur's appeal almost cost him his life as *The Follower* took advantage of his loss of concentration and thrust a blade through his defence. Only his ability to step back saved him, and once out of the range of the attacker, his battle-fatigued brain understood that Dagur had the right idea.

Abandoning the fight, he ran to Igon's side and with Dagur's help, dragged him to his feet and slung him over the back of his horse. This was a far more difficult proposition than throwing Cwenhild up. Igon was more than twice the size of the small woman.

Hain teetered on his knees. With the urgent need to defend himself gone, he collapsed onto the ground. Cadmon ignored him while he struggled to settle Igon's huge body so that he could breathe comfortably.

While they hurried to get the two unconscious bodies safely loaded, Dagur quickly told Cadmon what he and Cwenhild had seen from above. "This one is not the only *Follower,*" he said. "There are twelve more and they slipped over to the trail that we saw Dell take. We have to get up there."

Chapter 25 - The Library

Dell followed the worn path right up to the wall, leaned his shoulder against the stone and pushed. A portion of the mountain swung inward with a high-pitched squeal.

They all froze and listened intently to see if the noise would bring any guards. When nothing happened, Dell slipped through the opening, followed closely by Halvor, and Flint. They entered into a huge room. Flint had expected it to be dark, but a soft glow came from the walls themselves.

Dell led the way across the room to the far side. Speaking quietly, he told them, "It's the same design as in the other mountain fortress. These big antechambers seem to be a security arrangement." Glancing sideways at Flint, he added, "They knew I was coming."

On the far side of the room, an intricately carved wooden door was set into the rock wall. They approached it carefully. When Dell reached out to test the latch, he discovered that it was not locked either. He checked to see that both Flint and Halvor were prepared before he entered the next room.

Even more brightly lit, this room had four doors

leading out of it. For a moment, Dell did not move. Flint and Halvor mimicked his stillness. Together, they stood straining to hear anything in the cavernous room. Then, satisfied, Dell silently headed for the second door on the right.

He indicated that Halvor and Flint should take cover on either side of the door. Drawing a dagger with his right hand, he nodded at the other two, his eyes asking them if they were ready. Flint and Halvor both brought their blades to a ready position and nodded back at Dell.

A solid kick to the centre of the door left Dell facing four startled men. Dressed in ancient and battered armour, they had the unmistakeable look of *Followers*. Grey skin revealed coloured light shining through long ugly cracks.

Before a word was spoken, Dell fired off a dagger, which found its target in one of the guard's throats. The man crumpled to the floor. Halvor released one of his blades and took down another. The two remaining *Followers* drew their weapons and charged.

Dell rushed forward to meet the attack, sinking his gauntlet into the exposed throat of his opponent. Flint dove forward and with a quick parry, knocked aside the powerful attack. He struggled to maintain his balance and brought his other sword around to thrust it through the ancient, armoured chestpiece. He felt a moment's resistance before his blade crunched past the man's ribs. Flint saw the look of surprise that lit up *The Follower's* eyes before he sank slowly to the floor.

Flint wrenched his blade clear and watched the seep

180

of yellow blood. Glancing over at Dell, he saw him give his gauntlet a hurried wipe. Flint too, took a moment to clean his own blade. He noticed that even as he drew the sword across the cloth trousers of the man he had killed, the glowing yellow blood began to fade.

Halvor stepped over the fallen bodies and retrieved the blades from the throats of their first targets. Neither Dell nor Halvor stopped to celebrate. After a quick look around the small room failed to reveal any other exits, they slid out the door, back into the larger chamber. Halvor eased the door shut. Perhaps it would buy them a few more minutes of secrecy.

Again, Dell froze. He listened carefully for any indications of habitation. Hearing nothing, he randomly chose to enter the next room on the right. They used the same formation to make their entrance. After hearing the thud Dell's boot made on the door, Flint worried that the noise would bring more guards. He kept his attention on the other three doors.

This time the room they entered had no evidence of any guards. It was filled with books. Overflowing shelves ran right up to the ceiling all around the outside. Amazingly, the perimeter held only a small fraction of the books stored here. At right angles to the entrance wall, dozens of bookcases ran the entire length of the huge room. Flint had never imagined there could be this many books in the entire world.

Cadmon took the reins of Igon's and Flint's horses

while Dagur grabbed the reins for Cwenhild's and Halvor's. Moving quickly, the two men sprang into their saddles. Looking back over his shoulder, Cadmon saw the huge *Follower* fall to his side. Unmoving, he lay with his feet drawn up to his stomach. He looked to be having trouble breathing.

For a moment, he considered going back and finishing off the monster, but on second consideration, he decided that is was possible *The Follower* was not dying, but only resting. Remembering the power of those arms, Cadmon was uncertain that he would be able to hold him off, never mind be the victor if the fight continued.

Making his decision, he turned his attention forward and nudged his horse after Dagur. They followed the path around the base of the rock face in the same direction that Dell had taken. Hearing a groan behind him, Cadmon looked back to see Igon stirring. He slid off his horse and walked back to where Igor's head hung down. Calmly he asked, "How are you feeling?"

His only answer at first was a long, drawn out groan and then Igon cautiously raised his hands up to head and said, "What happened?"

"That monster got through your defence is what happened," answered Cadmon. "But, don't worry; it was only a whack on the head with the side of his blade. Not much blood. Can you stand? I'll help you down. Right now we're chasing after twelve more of those *Followers* and if you're feeling up to it, I imagine we could use your help."

As he spoke, Cadmon checked in every direction for attackers. Igon pushed himself up and slid to his feet beside the horse. "I'll do," he said, testing his balance as he hit the ground. "Just a bit of a headache. I think I'll be more comfortable sitting in the saddle instead of hanging off it like a sack of potatoes." Igon swiped at the blood on his forehead, decided it was not too serious and swung up into the saddle. "Ah," he moaned, "that's better."

While Igon settled himself, Dagur checked Cwenhild's condition. At a raised eyebrow from Cadmon, he said, "She's breathing much better, but she's still unconscious. If we're riding into a fight, shouldn't we get her somewhere safe first? She told me it takes an hour for the antidote to work and I don't know if she'll be in any condition to fight when she wakes up."

"I don't want to leave her alone with that monster still alive," Cadmon said. "There's no telling how much the poison will affect him. It seemed to barely slow him down, while she quickly lost consciousness. He could take it into his mind to follow." Cadmon mounted his horse again. "I say we keep her with us, and if we run into a fight before we've found a safe place for her to recover, Igon takes her and rides."

Igon looked as if he were about to argue, but Cadmon turned a stern eye on him and said, "You just had a head injury and you may not be in top fighting condition, but you can take care of Cwenhild and save her if necessary."

Igon subsided. "Of course, sir." Cadmon did not generally use his authority in such a brusque manner and

Igon responded as he had been trained during his years as a King's Guard. "You're right. I will get her to safety. Perhaps I should take her reins?" he asked Dagur.

"Good idea," said Dagur, handing him the reins of Cwenhild's horse. "I think we should ride with our weapons drawn as well. I saw twelve *Followers* set off at a run up the mountain. Who knows whether they will set an ambush for us or if they are just trying to get through to Dell, Flint and Halvor."

Cadmon answered thoughtfully, "I agree. Everything about this attack makes me wonder. Why did only one of them stay behind to fight four of us while twelve took off up the mountain? What is up there that is so important?"

Halvor looked around at the overflowing shelves with an expression of complete bliss. "This is unbelievable," he said happily. "Forget Magnaosseums. A roomful of books like this is the definition of unbelievable. I've never even imagined such a thing." He stepped forward and randomly began pulling books off the shelves so that he could open them and peer inside. "Fairy tales. Philosophy. Weather. Geology." He carefully replaced each book he examined, but Flint could see that he was dying to take them all with him. No doubt, there would be a full load in Dell's saddlebags for the return trip.

Dell was not enticed by the books. He stood warily watching the door they had just entered. Gesturing with his head, he said, "Flint. Halvor. Check the room for other entrances. We don't want any surprises."

Halvor looked up with dazed eyes but as Dell's words sank in, he reacted. "Flint, you go left," he ordered. "Be ready. Let's sweep the perimeter of the room. Examine everything that looks as if it could be a door. I imagine they could easily conceal entrances in this place."

Guszorm led *The Followers* up the switch-backing trail at a trot. Although they had been running all day, he felt no fatigue. Hain had made him second-in-command, and ordered him to lead the other eleven *Followers* to the library. The secret must be guarded at all costs. For now, he led this group of *Followers*. His orange-red eyes glowed in anticipation of a fight.

Apparently, three men had found the entrance to the library. He hoped that the guards stationed there would need some help with this problem. More than anything, Guszorm wanted to fight. It had been so long. When he was a King's Guard as a young man, he learned the joy of killing. Since Martokallu took him on as one of his own, it had been too long since he was released to kill.

Hain had decided that he alone would take care of the four people in the small valley below. Guszorm knew it would not be difficult for Hain to kill four adversaries. A powerful swordsman, he never tired. The humans would have no chance of overwhelming him, even if they all managed to fight him at the same time. Although, that did not look especially likely since they were spread out all over the place.

Guszorm envied Hain's privilege; to have four almost-worthy opponents was fortunate. But, Guszorm and his *Followers* were getting close to the library now. Soon, it would be time to kill. Soon.

Chapter 26 - New Books

"There appears to be only one entrance into this place, Dell," said Halvor as he and Flint looped back to the spot where Dell guarded the door. "I propose that while you maintain a lookout, Flint and I have a peek at a few of these volumes and maybe choose a couple to take back with us." His tone was facetious, but he grinned in anticipation of a few minutes spent revelling in a collection that would take a lifetime to read.

"The main thing is that we know where to find the library. That was the assignment," responded Dell tersely. "I don't know if it is necessary to examine all the books right now." He stared humourlessly at Halvor. Then gesturing with his bladed fingers, he said, "We haven't even cleared the whole area. We have no idea whether it is safe."

"Just give me two minutes," begged Halvor. "We can't leave without at least getting a taste for what might be here." He looked imploringly at Dell.

"Two minutes," was Dell's curt reply and he turned back to guard the doorway.

With a quiet whoop of joy, Halvor called to Flint,

"Two minutes. Choose the five most interesting books you can find. Go." With that, Halvor dove into the shelves and began rifling through books. This time he was not as careful with his re-shelving. He opened and discarded books with reckless speed. Every time he found one he wanted, he placed it in a stack at his feet. Flint glanced over at him as he scoured the shelves and wondered whether he would be able to restrict himself to just five books.

Flint was not sure exactly what would be an appropriate choice for his five volumes. Everything looked interesting. He adopted Halvor's style and randomly seized books, opened them, scanned for subject matter and interest and then either quickly set it aside or added it to the growing pile at his own feet.

When he pulled out a folio tied with a braided ribbon, he was uncertain what it might be. Pushing the ribbon aside, he opened the cover and discovered a pile of drawings. Looking more closely, he read that they were the plans for the King's Palace in Kallcunarth.

With an exclamation of triumph, he hurriedly added it to his pile of choices, noting that he would only be able to take one more. He checked to see that Dell still kept watch and got an impatient nod from their guardian.

Flint arbitrarily chose an aisle, ran to the halfway point and snatched the first book that caught his eye. Looking hastily inside, he saw schematic drawings for odd-looking inventions. He decided that Egbert might appreciate such a book, so he took it, ran back to gather his other four selections and darted to the door where

Dell stood.

Halvor was already back, happily carrying his load of five books. "Did you get some good ones, Flint? I know these beauties are going…"

Dell interrupted his excited chatter, "They'll only be interesting if we can get out of here safely. I want you two able to carry your weapons, so figure out a way to bundle those things and let's get moving."

Halvor and Flint cast around, frantically looking for something that would serve as a sling for the books. Flint spotted it first. A pile of cloth bags, neatly folded on a shelf near the door, obviously meant for carrying books out of the library. With satisfaction they each slid a pile into a bag. At the same moment, identical looks of dismay crossed their faces when they realized they would still need a way to carry it without impeding their arms.

Halvor came up with a solution. Slipping off his belt he stuffed it through the loop handles of the bag before refastening it. Now he had the books safely out of the way. If they bumped him a bit in the back of the legs, it was all for a good cause. Flint quickly copied Halvor and soon he too stood ready with two weapons drawn and a package of books dangling from his belt.

So far, they had been lucky. Maybe there were only the four guards in the whole library. Perhaps Martokallu believed that the remote location offered the most important security. Still Dell was obviously not taking any chances.

After giving the two of them a quick examination, he grimaced, as he considered the clumsy loads they each carried. Nonetheless, he gave a brusque nod and stepped out into the large antechamber. Flint looked expectantly at the two doors in the room that they had not yet investigated, but Dell headed toward the exit. The wooden door stood ajar from their arrival. Dell silently stepped up to the side of it to listen.

Hearing nothing, he gestured for Halvor and Flint to precede him. Flint went first with his swords raised in defence. Halvor slipped through after him. Suddenly they both froze.

Flint looked at Halvor who gave him a small nod to tell him he too had heard it. The same high-pitched squeal had accompanied the opening of the mountain door when they arrived.

Dell moved quietly into the room. Flint could tell from the look of concentration in his eyes that he was listening hard, trying to determine just what they faced. Now they heard the tread of several booted feet on the rock floor.

Dell motioned them forward and advanced toward the wooden door on the other side of the room. Flint and Halvor followed on silent feet. Flint took the position just slightly behind and to the side of where the door would open, while Dell and Halvor positioned themselves so that anyone passing through the door would have to face their flying daggers.

It did not take long. A moment after they slid into position, the door burst inward. Flint found himself watching while daggers flew from Halvor and Dell's hands and found their targets in the throats of the first two *Followers* who passed through the door.

The monsters fell in a heap at their feet blocking the door for any who might follow. The first one through the door was a massive specimen with cracked grey skin. Even in death, his eyes glowed with an orange-red brilliance; the same colour as the blood flowing from his neck.

Flint heard a rumble of confusion on the other side of the door. The three men stood ready for a second wave of attack but nothing happened. Several minutes passed in tense silence until Dell quietly whispered, "They've lost their leader."

Halvor nodded, almost laughing as he said, "*Followers* without a leader are not much good." He smirked at his joke. "What do you suggest?"

"We might be able to take advantage of their disorganization," suggested Dell thoughtfully. "I don't know exactly how many of them there might be on the other side of this door, but I'm guessing from what we can hear and the few glimpses I have had, that there are no more than ten." He looked at Flint to assess how this news affected him. "It's not good odds and they know we are here. However…"

Halvor interrupted, "They have no leader and they cannot organize themselves. If we do this unexpectedly, we should be able to take them all down."

Flint struggled to control the flutter of fear threatening to overwhelm him. Ten against three? He thought back to their two previous encounters with *The Followers* and recalled that already five had died and none of *The Hawks* had even a scratch. He gave Dell a nod that he tried to imbue with confidence in their ability to triumph.

"Halvor and I go first with the throwing blades. Flint, you take anyone you can get close to. Watch your back." With that, Dell turned and moved toward the door, then abruptly stopped, turned back, and said in the same inaudible whisper, "Before we go in, I suggest that both of you leave your tails here." He looked significantly at the book bags hanging from their belts.

Halvor and Dell hustled to slip the loops of their bags free from their belts and within moments stood ready for combat. Dell gave them a nod and raising the dagger in his right hand, dived through the open door with Halvor right behind him. Before Flint made it into the room, Dell embedded two of his blades in the throats of two *Followers*.

After that, Flint did not have time to notice anything other than a huge sword and *The Follower* wielding it. Flint caught the first blow with a defensive block and pushed the blade away while at the same time, mounting his own offense with a slashing overhand that sliced across *The Follower's* cheek. The blood that spurted from the wound was a vivid yellow. Flint felt a surge of triumph and suddenly began to believe that they would win the fight.

After that, it became a mind and body numbing exchange of blows. Flint could not believe the power and strength the monster possessed. He was tiring quickly. It seemed that the lack of organization and the loss of their leader were no longer important. As soon as *The Followers* had an opponent to fight, they knew definitively what to do: kill.

Chapter 27 - Defeat

From the heavily treed trail leading up the side of the mountain, Cadmon broke above the tree line. A beautiful meadow opened up in front of him. Wildflowers and low growing green shrubs covered everything in sight. Right behind him, Dagur gave a low whistle.

"So this is what they were racing to reach? Can you see where this trail is leading? There doesn't seem to be anywhere for them to hide up here." Dagur rose in his stirrups to study the trail. "*The Followers* are right in front of us. I don't believe this trail is any more than a quarter of an hour old."

Cadmon turned back to Igon and, indicating Cwenhild with a nod of his head, he asked, "Is she conscious?"

Igon swung out of his saddle, walked around Cwenhild's horse, and gently lifted her head from where it hung limply. "Maybe, if I put a wet hanky on her face, she might wake up," he said. As he spoke, he reached for a somewhat soiled handkerchief that he pulled from a pocket in his shirt. Opening his canteen, he dribbled a little water onto the cloth and smoothed it tenderly over her forehead.

"Tell you what," said Cadmon. "I want you to stay here and see if you can get her to wake up. Dagur and I are going to follow the trail and see if we can find Dell, Halvor and Flint. Keep your flails close, but from the look of this trail, it appears that all of *The Followers* stayed on the path."

He turned his horse toward the large outcropping of rock that appeared to be the trail's destination. A thought occurred to him and he called back over his shoulder, "Keep an eye on the back trail as well. That massive *Follower* we fought was not dead. If he can get up, he might get it into his head to follow us."

Flint no longer had any conscious thoughts. Every fibre of his being focused on fighting the monster in front of him. The years of training took over and he unthinkingly countered every attack. His ability to fight with both hands thwarted all of the efforts of *The Follower*. Abruptly, something in the fight changed infinitesimally and Flint clearly saw his opening.

With a move he had practiced endlessly in Sparrow Hawk Square, his body shifted naturally into the correct positions. His left hand blocked a blow aimed at the right side of his body and he continued the spin so that his right blade made an uninterrupted sweep that went completely through *The Follower's* neck. The head bounced wetly onto the rock and a moment later the body collapsed beside it.

Immediately, Flint turned to face any additional challengers. A room full of dead bodies confronted him. He looked around in dismay until he located Dell and Halvor standing on either side of the room. Halvor looked disturbed at the devastation they had wrought, but he managed a grin for Flint. "That was quite the move that finished him off," he said. "Why didn't you do it sooner?"

All of a sudden Flint realized just how tired he was. Apparently, while he battled the single *Follower,* Halvor and Dell successfully defeated nine others between them. Flint counted four *Followers* who lay dead with daggers in their throats. Three more whose faces had been ripped off had bloody wounds in their guts as well. The final two bodies displayed the slashes of a trained dagger wielder. Halvor and Dell were both covered in various ghastly colours of blood, but, amazingly, seemed to be uninjured.

"Well done, boy," said Dell. "An impressive fight." In a flash, Flint understood that they had done their killing quickly and efficiently, and then stood by to support Flint if he needed help. They let him finish it on his own though. He felt a spasm of relief that he had survived. His sword tips dropped to the ground and he leaned against them as his legs suddenly turned to rubber.

The three *Hawks* stood in silence for a moment resting their bodies and relishing the thought that they were still alive.

Without warning, the outside door creaked open again. The bright light left Flint blinded. His fatigue disappeared in a rush of adrenaline. Without hesitation, he raised his swords and prepared for another attack. When his vision cleared, he found himself looking at the confounded faces of Cadmon and Dagur.

Hain felt a boiling rage fill his mind. The latest images from Martokallu were completely impossible. His twelve *Followers* mowed down by three puny humans? *The Followers* offered a completely ineffective defence and even the young boy held Ywaar at bay. As Hain watched, he saw the double-sword-wielding boy spin and slash at Ywaar's neck. And, just that quickly it was over.

The furious uproar in his head increased and Hain felt a desire to cradle his head against the assault. *Come home.* The two words filled his consciousness and Hain struggled to rise in order to obey.

"It looks like you didn't need our help," said Dagur admiringly, advancing into the huge room. The soft glowing light did nothing to soften the appearance of the bloody *Followers*. He nudged one body with the toe of his boot. With its freakish eyes closed, it looked far more human than *Followers* ever did while alive. "Poor brute, he said softly, "When they're just lying there like this, you can almost believe those tales that they were once humans until Martokallu possessed them."

"We've been pursuing them up the mountain path," said Cadmon. "Did they catch up to you here?"

"No," replied Dell dryly. "We were just leaving. We

thought we'd come and tell you about the library we found."

Halvor broke in with excitement, "It is incredible. There are more books in that single room than there are in all the rest of Abbarkon. Flint and I picked five each to bring back." He turned away from the carnage to retrieve the two bags from their resting place on the other side of the door. "You have to see..."

Cadmon interrupted him, "We'll have a look in a moment. First though, is the area clear?"

"We ran into four other *Followers* before we found the room with the library. They're dead," Dell said without elaboration. "There are still at least two areas we haven't explored yet. I figured that with only the three of us, we should get out before meeting any larger force." Flint thought he saw an ironic lift of Dell's half-hidden eyebrow.

Cadmon noted the sarcasm with a half grin of his own, "There are five of us now. Shall we take a look around before we clean up this mess?"

Flint realized that they could not very well leave the bodies to rot within the walls of the most remarkable library in the kingdom. They would have to drag the remains of the monsters outside and perhaps bury them.

Cadmon continued to plan a strategy. "What is the layout?" he asked Dell.

"Through the door is a huge room very similar to this one. It is in the same design as the mountain fortress in the Chain of Thollcrawnow. I think it may be a security measure. Although," he added under his breath, "it doesn't really seem to work for them." In a louder voice, he continued, "The next room is also large and it has four doors leading out from it. The first door we went through had the four *Followers*. The second door housed the library."

"We'll need to check out the other two doors if we don't want any nasty surprises," said Cadmon. "Is everyone prepared if we need to fight again?"

Flint looked as his blades. Both of them showed some wear from the beating they had taken at the hands of *The Follower*. He cleaned off the disgusting blood as best he could while Dell and Halvor retrieved their daggers from the throats of the dead bodies.

Halvor fastidiously polished his blades on the robe of one of his victims. Dell gave each dagger a quick wipe and then after examining his gauntlet for any damage, he said without any preamble, "Let's go."

Chapter 28 - The Librarian

Halvor and Dell led the way. With their throwing blades, they could take care of many dangers before anyone had to get too close. A quick look into the large antechamber told them that the room was still empty. Dell went directly toward one of the two doors they had not yet tried to enter.

Everyone moved on cat feet. Flint strained his ears for sounds that might alert them of danger. He did not think anyone else could be in the library fortress. After all the noise: first kicking in the other doors and then the battle just outside the main room. Flint imagined that an alarm would have been raised if anyone was around.

Dell paused to listen carefully before he gestured for everyone to take a place on either side of the door. Halvor had the best position for throwing his blades. As soon as everyone was in place, Dell reared back and planted his foot firmly in the middle of the door. It crashed open and Halvor moved into position with his daggers ready.

The room was small and evidently empty of any inhabitants. However, eight beds made with military neatness lined the stone walls.

"You said you killed four *Followers?*" asked Cadmon warily.

"So we did," replied Dell thoughtfully. In his next breath he gave an order. "Flint, check for other openings into the room."

Flint stepped forward cautiously and made a circuit of the cave-like space. He pushed on the wall in several places but there was no evidence of concealed entrances.

Cadmon gave a satisfied nod, and said, "Let's check the last door."

They followed exactly the same system established earlier. Again, Halvor took the best position beside the door giving him a clear shot at anyone on the other side. Stepping up to the door, Dell grimaced. In a barely audible voice, he said, "Every time I do this, I hope it's not going to be solidly latched. I just hope I get lucky again." With that fervent wish, he lunged at the door and it slammed open against the wall behind it.

Halvor spotted someone. His arm drew back to release a blade when Cadmon cried, "Hold!"

Rising from a bed against the back wall of the tiny cell was the oldest man Flint had ever seen. He wore a bedraggled brown robe, belted at the waist, and his hair and beard were completely white. Bright green eyes looked out of a face mapped with wrinkles.

When he spotted the unusual colour of the eyes, Flint immediately assumed he must be a *Follower,* however, on closer inspection he realized why Cadmon had called a halt. The man was human.

For a long moment, the old man regarded the

intruders with a perfect calm and then,in a voice rough with disuse, said, "Welcome to Oruk Library."

Cwenhild groaned as she opened her eyes. It was not the first time she had experienced the horrible effects of the poison she daubed on all of her weapons. Her mother, Orma, had insisted that she be familiar with both the effects of the poison and the antidote. Nevertheless, she could not remember ever feeling this foul.

Besides the pain in her leg where her arrow had scratched the skin, she found she had bruises on both her hips and one hand looked as if it had been stepped on by a horse. She flexed it painfully and examined the horseshoe shaped mark. The most distressing part, however, was the pounding headache. She felt as if she had been strung up by her heels and left to hang upside down.

Igon's face appeared in her field of vision. "You're awake," he said with a look of relief.

She turned her head, and realized they were no longer in the little valley by the waterfall. In fact, by the looks of things, somehow they had climbed above the tree line. "Where are we? What's happened?" she asked Igon.

He smiled to see that she was recovered enough to take note of her surroundings. "Ah, welcome back," he said. "I have been left in charge of your safety. Cadmon and Dagur went after the other three." He gave a tiny bow, waving his hand in a royal manner. "Cadmon designated me as the one most in need of a little rest myself." He rolled his eyes. "Just because of a wee head blow I took when we fought that monster."

He leaned back on his heels and took a look around the area. No one was in evidence so he turned his attention back to Cwenhild. "Are you feeling well enough to sit up?" he asked. "I was wondering when you would wake up after that ride up here on your horse."

"I assume you just tossed me over my saddle for the ride?" she asked with an ironic twist to her mouth.

He acknowledged her sarcasm with a small lift of his shoulder. "We had to get out of there in a hurry."

"That accounts for the bruises on my hips and the headache." She winced as she pushed herself to a seated position. "How do you explain this horseshoe shaped bruise on my hand?" Cwenhild held up her left hand for him to inspect.

"Ah," he said carefully. "That happened when your hand fell down and your horse stepped on it. No broken bones, I hope?" Igon grinned sheepishly. "Dagur said he tried to tuck your hands up out of the way, but he did mention that we trotted a little."

Cwenhild rolled her eyes and said, "Well, regardless of my injuries, thank you for the rescue." She looked at him seriously. "I would not have wanted to be left behind."

"Those thanks aren't really for me," Igon told her. "I was unconscious for the first bit and got to ride like a sack of potatoes for a while too." He grinned in understanding of her pains.

"Did Cadmon kill *The Follower*?"

"No," answered Igon with a frown. "Of course, I was unconscious so I didn't actually see it, but Dagur said the monster ended up fighting from his knees. Your poison didn't kill him but he seemed unable to stand. Still he fought with more power than even Cadmon was able to overwhelm. In the end, Dagur told him to run away because the monster would be incapable of following. So they grabbed us, took the extra horses and bolted up the mountain after *The Followers* chasing Dell."

"Who are you?" demanded Cadmon from his position in the doorway. He did not lower *Rising Star*, which he held ready in both hands.

"I am Galo," the old man replied simply.

Cadmon evidently did not quite know what to do with this piece of information. He hesitated for a moment before asking, "What are you doing here?"

"I live here." Again, the answer came calmly and lacked any real explanation.

"Who else lives here?" asked Cadmon trying to remain as calm as the old man.

"There are four of *The Master's Followers* who stay to guard the secret," answered Galo. "And me. That is all. May I ask, sir, who are you?"

Galo remained standing serenely in front of his bed. His calm demeanour almost caused Cadmon to relax his guard, but his casual reference to Martokallu as "The Master" brought his defensive attitude back. Instead of answering Galo's query, he posed one of his own. "You serve *The Master?*"

"No, no, no," answered the old man with a shake of his finger. "*The Followers* serve *The Master*. I serve the books."

Halvor burst forward. He gestured wildly with the blades he still held ready in his hands. "You're the librarian!" he exclaimed excitedly. "Have you read all those books?"

Galo's face crinkled into a smile and he settled himself on his bed as he said, "No, young warrior. I'm afraid that would take far more lifetimes than I have to live." He tilted his head as he considered this. "Perhaps I should become a *Follower*. Then I would have more lifetimes," he suggested musingly. Then giving his head a small shake, he continued, "No matter. I would be in no position to enjoy the books if Martokallu took my mind and will." He nodded as if that settled things and then looked up in surprise to find the men gathered in his doorway.

"Who are you?" he asked again, but this time his voice was querulous and he looked worried instead of calm. His attention had been captured by the weapons that everyone held trained on him.

Halvor sheathed his blades and nodded for everyone else to do the same. "Galo?" he said quietly. Then, moving slowly to avoid frightening the old man, he took a couple of steps into the room. "I am Halvor. I would love to have you show me your library."

Chapter 29 - Explosion

"My library? Oh, it is wonderful," said Galo happily. "You like books? We have a marvellous collection here at Oruk. In fact, I believe, there is nothing to match it in all of Abbarkon." The old man rose easily to his feet and still talking, led a fascinated Halvor off in the direction of the library.

"I guess that's Halvor's way of getting out of the dirty work," said Dell sardonically. "I suggest we get those dead bodies out of here before they get any smellier." He led the way to the room where they had killed the first four *Followers*.

Without fanfare, Dagur reached down to pick up the arms of the first body while Cadmon grabbed the feet. They braced to lift the weight of the massive monster and almost staggered when they found that the body actually weighed very little. "I think, most of the weight is in the armour," said Cadmon. "There is nothing left of him."

"There's nothing left of this armour," declared Dagur. "Careful there. It looks as if the whole thing could fall to pieces any minute. How old are these *Followers* anyway?"

Cadmon and Dagur cautiously manoeuvred out of the room. Flint tried to avoid looking at the head with its gaping throat wound and the dreadful, staring eyes. He edged out of the way, as they moved past him, then dove for the feet of the next *Follower*. He really did not want to have to carry the end with the dangling head.

Before passing through the doorway, Cadmon and Dagur set the body down and checked for any new threats. They examined the room with the two dead bodies in the doorway and the next one with ten ghastly corpses. The last thing they did before relaxing their guard was to inspect the exterior door.

By that time, Dell and Flint had caught up to them and they too set aside the body they carried in order to be able to draw their weapons.

Before releasing the door mechanism, Dell waited for everyone to move into position. With a quick thrust of the lever, the room filled with light. Flint was shocked to find that it was still daylight. Or, was it the next day already? No, the sun was setting in the west. As he thought about it, he realized that they had probably been inside the mountain for no more than two hours.

Outside, the four men stood drawing deep breaths of the fresh mountain air. "Flint, why don't you take my horse," Cadmon said, indicating the horses that they had left hobbled outside the mountain door, "and go tell Igon and Cwenhild that we will be spending the night here. You'll find them right down this path near the small pool at the top of the cliff."

"Yes, sir," Flint answered with enthusiasm. He hoped

his relief was not too evident. The idea of helping to move all those bodies was not very attractive.

By the time Flint arrived back to the library fortress with Cwenhild and Igon, the rooms had been cleared of dead bodies. Dagur, Cadmon and Dell had stacked them a fair distance from the entrance and now Dell peered up at a stone ledge directly above the ghastly pile.

"How difficult is it to get up there, Dagur," Dell asked.

"Easiest thing in the world," Dagur replied confidently.

"I suppose, the more important question is: how fast can you get down?" Cadmon asked dryly.

Dagur considered the question carefully. "Well, if I set a good belaying rope first and then light the fuse, I should have plenty of time." He stopped, studied the ledge again and added in a slightly worried tone, "If nothing goes wrong."

"What could go wrong?" Dell asked as he reached into his saddlebag and pulled out a grenade. "Here," he said handing the small bomb to Dagur, "stick this in your pocket."

Dagur delicately placed it into a canvas sack he wore over his shoulder. Then he placed a coil of rope around his other shoulder and reached for his first handhold. Before Flint even had time to dismount, Dagur had pulled himself over the top of the ledge. When he turned to look down, he caught a glimpse of Flint, Igon and

Cwenhild. "Greetings of the day," he called. "Are you feeling better, Cwenhild?"

Cwenhild nodded and said, "Almost good as new. I understand we owe you and Cadmon our thanks. It was nice waking up safe and sound." She eyed Dagur's rocky perch. "I think, though, if I want to stay that way, I should take cover." Sliding out of her saddle, she called, "Dell, how do you always find a reason to blow something up?"

"It's easy," replied Dell with a lazy shrug. "Something always *needs* blowing up."

Dagur had fastened his belaying rope in the meantime, and was ready to put the plan into action. "I think everyone should move very far away," he said. He waited while *The Hawks* all moved around the corner, out of range of any flying debris from the explosion, before he lit the fuse and gently settled the grenade into a crevice.

Grabbing the rope he quickly rappelled down to the ground and dashed for cover.

The blast sent the entire ledge crashing down onto the stacked bodies of *The Followers;* creating a rocky grave. When the dust settled, Dell strolled over to check out the results. "Well done Dagur. You've got to admit: that was much easier than trying to bury them by hand."

"Easier, maybe," replied Dagur. "But there is far less worry when you are using a shovel than when you are trying to avoid getting yourself blown up." Dagur smiled though. He looked very pleased with the outcome.

We need to decide what to do about the library," said Cadmon.

They sat in the room where they had encountered the first four *Followers*. It appeared to be a kitchen and sitting room. Although, Galo had explained that *The Followers* never ate. The food stored in the cupboards was for his use alone. Mostly it was just rice and dried vegetables. Galo also told them that *The Followers* would often bring him a rabbit or a marmot to add to the soup pot. Apparently they enjoyed hunting.

Galo busily stirred his broth over the fire in the hearth while *The Hawks* sat comfortably at the large table. The old man had boasted that he would make them the best soup they had ever tasted.

"What do you mean, decide what to do about the library?" Halvor burst out, jumping to his feet. He was astonished at Cadmon's words. "We must preserve it. This place holds the wealth of the kingdom. It is a collection of all written knowledge. I cannot…"

"Whoa, there," Cadmon interrupted him. "I was not suggesting that we need to get rid of the library. I only meant that we need to make a decision about who will stay to help Galo and guard the collection."

"Oh," said a subdued Halvor before dropping back into his chair. "I'll stay," he added quickly.

"That sounds like a good idea," Cadmon replied with a quiet smile. He clearly had expected this response. "Is there anyone else who would choose to remain here?"

Igon nodded his big head. "I'll stay. Halvor will need

someone who isn't lost in a book to take care of things."

"I'll stay too," said Dagur. "I know that Asdis is ready to take an active role as a scout and she is well trained." He smiled in satisfaction as he said this. Along with Fleta and Flint, she had been a star pupil.

Cadmon's smile widened and he said, "Well, that was easily settled. The rest of us will leave at daylight."

Flint squirmed in his chair and said, "Can we still take a couple of books with us? I found some really interesting things. One book is a story about an adventure and I think Fleta would like to read it. I also found a book with a whole lot of schematic drawings of some inventions that I thought Egbert would like to see. I even found something that isn't really a book but it looks like it might be the actual plans for the King's Palace."

Dell sat up straighter when he heard that. "Plans for the palace?" he asked. "May I take a look at those?"

Chapter 30 - Homecoming

I t had been a much faster trip coming home than it had been getting there, but Flint felt ready to burst with impatience by the time they arrived back in Halklyen. Mostly he missed Fleta. She was the closest friend he ever had. After spending every day together since he arrived in Halklyen, it had been strange to go on this mission without her. The whole time he was away, he had been thinking about things to tell her. He also knew that she would love the book he brought back for her.

Dell and Cadmon had been enormously interested in the palace plans that he chose by chance on that hurried dash through the library. From the whispered discussion they had while eagerly turning pages, Flint figured that they were plotting something. When they finished studying the drawings in that folio, Dell asked Galo if he knew of any more materials like it in the collection.

The old librarian was delighted to have patrons interested in delving into his library. "Of course, of course, my friends," he answered. A quick glance at the volume they were studying gave him all the information he needed to continue. "This particular folio was put together after the construction of the original palace, but as you know, there have been several renovations through the centuries and all of those plans are stored here as well." He led them effortlessly to the exact shelf he needed and selected two other volumes that encased building plans.

Cadmon was flabbergasted at the ease with which Galo could find the information. Research for *The Hawks* had always been a time-consuming process requiring much travel and the careful building of safe contacts with people. To have such material immediately accessible was pure luxury. Suddenly, he understood just why Martokallu had ordered the confiscation and destruction of all the books. Such information was power.

In the end, they decided to carry fourteen books away from the library to share with the people of Halklyen. The book that Flint chose with Egbert in mind was a favourite of Dell's. He spent hours poring over it on the trip back; even reading it as he sat in the saddle. Flint guessed that Dell's first visit would be to Egbert's forge.

They entered the village from the same route they used when they returned from the trip to the Chain of Thollcrawnow. Flint looked around for the expected watch keeper. Sure enough, Penn pelted toward them carrying his bow and leather ball. As he skidded to a stop he called, "I just told Fleta, you're back! She's coming right away!"

Even as Penn spoke, Flint could see Fleta flying around the corner of the last street. "I told Penn to let me know the minute you came in sight," she said breathlessly. "I've been waiting for you to get here. You are not going to believe what Egbert built. I've been helping him in the forge and we have been working day and night to get it finished." She still wore the heavy leather apron that protected her clothes when she helped at the forge. Flint guessed that the brief run to meet him was not the only reason her face was so red and sweaty.

Suddenly she realized that three people were missing from the returning group. She interrupted her cheerful chatter to ask with a frown, "Wait, has something happened?"

Flint had been grinning happily, as he sat in his saddle listening to Fleta's enthusiastic welcome. For a moment, he did not realize what she meant with her anxious question.

Cwenhild answered her, "Everyone is fine, Fleta. Actually, we had a tremendously successful mission." She paused before announcing, "We found the library." When Fleta looked momentarily confused, she explained, "Halvor, Dagur and Igon stayed behind to guard it."

Dell added sardonically, "Igon and Dagur stayed to guard. Halvor stayed to read."

Fleta's smile returned. "Oh, what a relief," she said. "For a minute…" Her face became grave as she followed her own line of thoughts.

Penn had no such reservations. "What did you bring back this time?" he asked. "Last time it was the Magnaosseums and they have been eating like crazy. Already everything around the village is pruned back as high as they can reach."

In the excitement of the trip, Flint had hardly spared a thought for the Magnaosseums. He saw Dell and Cadmon exchange a look and he knew they too wondered how much longer the large animals could be supported here in the small forest.

"We brought books," Cadmon answered and then before Penn had time to interrupt with more questions, he said, "Fleta. Flint. Go round up *The Talons*. We will meet in Hawk Hut in half an hour. Penn. Well done with the watch duty. Keep it up."

Flint swung down from his saddle and sent Cadmon a questioning look. The older man reached out his hand to take the reins. "You've done well, boy," he said. "I'll take your horse up to the stable. Now go find *The Talons,* and bring Asdis too."

In Cadmon's terms, this was an enormous compliment and Flint felt a rush of pride. As he fell into step beside Fleta, she began to pelt him with questions, which he took great pleasure in answering. He had saved up two weeks' worth of stories and she made an excellent audience.

If not quite routine, Flint felt these meetings of *The Talons* had begun to be almost comfortable. Cadmon let him report on the first entry into Oruk Library. It had been easier than the first time when he described the Magnaosseums.

Guessing that he might have to speak in the meeting,

he had paid attention to how he told Fleta about all that he had seen. When he stepped to the front of the room, he tried to imagine that he was telling the story only to Fleta who sat smiling throughout his entire presentation.

"Now," said Cadmon, after everyone had heard the tale, "we need to decide the next step. First of all, I think we need to send a larger fighting force to defend the library. That massive *Follower* we fought wasn't dead when we left him, and when we returned to the valley, he was gone. I have no doubt that he will return with more *Followers*. I would not leave Igon and Dagur to fight them on their own. Even if Halvor could get his nose out of a book long enough to be useful, I think they could use some reinforcements." He paused at the ripple of laughter that passed through the room: Halvor had said that the reason for the mission was to get him a new book. "Any volunteers?"

Asdis was one of the first to stand and her mother Gytha joined her. Soon Hackett, Faro and Grove had also agreed to go. Pleased, Cadmon nodded and said, "Dell drew a fairly decent map that should allow you to easily find your destination. Take enough supplies to last everyone for three months. Leave at dawn." The five volunteers trooped out to prepare for their mission. Asdis grinned madly as she passed Flint and Fleta. They both gave her a quiet word of congratulations and wished her luck.

Cadmon resumed the meeting as soon as they left. "The next order of business, I'll leave to Gode to explain."

Flint felt as if it had been ages since he saw Gode. It looked strange to see him without his customary grin. He wondered what could be so serious as to stop Gode from smiling. The man stepped up, cleared his throat and began, "Some of us have been working toward this day for sixteen years. The time has come." He paused before announcing quietly, "We are going to assassinate the King."

His listeners reacted with a hiss of indrawn breaths. This had always been the ultimate plan. Get rid of the King and replace him with someone who had not been corrupted by Martokallu's power. Everyone leaned forward on the benches, eager to hear the plan.

Chapter 31 - The Hawk

This would be Flint's fourth mission and the first time he had any opportunity for real preparation. They did not plan to leave for a week so there was much to be done. Right after the meeting, Flint and Fleta went to visit Egbert along with Dell and Cadmon. Fleta was practically bursting in her excitement to tell them about the invention she had helped Egbert build.

Flint listened, mystified, as Fleta explained the progress of the construction. Apparently, Dell and Cadmon were both in on the plan because they seemed to understand exactly what she described. However, even with the preliminary explanations, Flint could not quite comprehend the contraption that met his eye in the open square outside the foundry.

It was immense. And it looked like a bird. The fat, round body, built with sheet metal hammered out to give the effect of feathers, hung between two long steel springs attached to heavy steel wheels.

Two enormous wings, sturdily attached with a set of hinged pins, protruded from either side of the rounded body. With its wings extended, the machine easily measured twenty feet across. At the front, a long pointed shaft projected directly out of the body. It was so obviously the head and beak of the bird that Flint smiled at the effect Egbert had created. The beak was at least fifteen feet long and ended with a tip that looked like a drill.

There was no doubt that Egbert was a master armourer, never satisfied with building a serviceable suit of armour when he could create a great work of art. All of his skills had been put to work in the construction of the war machine he called, *The Hawk*.

Looking more closely, Flint saw slit holes cut at varying levels around the body, so perfectly arranged that they appeared as highlights in the feathers. Shafts wide enough to accommodate the Magnaosseums projected from the extended wings. Studying the vehicle, Flint tried to imagine what exactly Dell and Egbert had in mind.

He did not need to wait long to find out. Egbert was only too happy to explain. Starting with the exterior, he took his visitors for a tour. "The wings fold up," he said. "We be needing to travel on the roads and across the bridge."

Ducking under the wings he stepped over to the front of the body where he indicated another set of hitches. "Look here," he continued. "The shafts can be removed from the wings and reattached to the front of the chassis." He looked around at his audience and grinned. "You be wondering how could we go anywhere looking like this? Imagine driving a bird through the countryside!"

His smile widened as he explained, "I built these wooden sides which we be keeping in place until it be time to get to work." He indicated some brightly painted wood panels leaning against the side of the forge. "It be looking just like that performing troupe's cart you told me about."

Swinging away from the panels, he opened his arms in a sweeping gesture, and said, "Now, it'll be a wee bit crowded, but you have to see the inside." Eagerly, Egbert led the way around to the back. Concealed within the tail feathers were steps that led to the top of the bird's body. He climbed up and knelt beside a hatch. Easing the latch aside he lifted a small round door.

Grimacing, he turned to look down on the group below and said, "By the Fire of Dworgunul, this hole fits me like a pair of old pantaloons." He let his legs drop down and gingerly started to squeeze his belly through. Wincing as he came to a stop, he sucked his belly in, and said breathlessly, "I measured it so that I could get inside. I needed to be careful. If I made it too big, it could weaken the design." He chuckled merrily. "The rest of you should find it an easy entrance but I wouldn't want to be trying to get through here after one of Merylin's wonderful roast dinners."

After a little squirming, his head disappeared into the body of the bird. His booming laugh echoed out of the hole and the bird bounced on its springs as he moved aside to allow others to follow him. Dell went first and Flint heard him give a long, low whistle. Cadmon dropped through the hole next and Flint waited impatiently for him to move over so that he could slide in himself.

He had barely touched the floor when he felt Fleta slip in beside him. It took a moment for his eyes to adjust to the semi-darkness but soon he found himself making the same admiring whistle that Dell had just done.

It really was a tiny space; especially with five people crammed into it. Egbert had fashioned metal seats and positioned them around the outside of the cavity. Flint saw that everyone else had already chosen a place to sit, so he hurriedly slid into the empty spot.

Instead of facing inward, like the inside of a coach, the seats all faced outward. Each one had a window slit right in front of it as well as one above. Flint found that if he put his eye up close to the hole, he had a wide view of the square outside. Looking upward, he realized that the opening offered an excellent exit for an archer's arrow.

Egbert proudly pointed out the conveniences of his design. Flint had been right: the slits were not just for observation. The seats were specifically designed so that a person could use a short bow and fire directly through the opening. "Anyone riding inside this old bird will never be worrying about getting hit by a regular arrow," Egbert said. "The slits be too small to accommodate anything but these beauties." He reached into a centrally mounted bucket and pulled out an arrow with a tip barely wider than the shaft. Even the feather fletching on the end was a smaller cut than normal.

"How do they fly?" asked Cadmon picking one up to examine it more closely.

"They have an accurate range of about seventy-five feet." Egbert answered. He grinned and winked at Flint. "Of course, it do depend on who be shooting the arrow."

"Can the driver see well enough to direct the Magnaosseums?" Dell asked.

Egbert, who had been sitting in the driver's seat, shifted aside. "See for yourself," he said as he struggled to his feet. Dell traded positions with him after an awkward dance where each man vied for the space he needed to move.

Dell finally settled into the forward seat and gazed through all of the slits available to him. "There are good sight lines to the left and right and a very good view of what is directly in front of *The Hawk*. I can even see what is going on above me," he reported as he peered through a slit in the ceiling. Looking down, he spotted two circular holes on either side of his seat. "Are these for the reins?" he asked.

Pleased to have such an appreciative audience, Egbert agreed, "Exactly. When the Magnaosseums be hooked in the traces attached to the wings, the reins come back through those holes and you can loop them around these saddle horns," he said, indicating two small hook-like devices directly in front of the driver's chair.

"How does the tunnel drill work?" asked Cadmon.

Egbert's eyes lit up. "Show them, Fleta," he said happily.

Fleta had chosen her seat carefully. Now, she settled her feet on two strange devices and started to pump them up and down. Flint could see that her feet actually moved in a circle to rotate a gear, which in turn moved a chain that disappeared into the "beak" of the bird. Her feet spun so quickly that they appeared as a blur. Flint could hear something else moving inside the shaft.

"You be recalling the drill on the end of the beak that I showed you before we came inside?" called Egbert in the manner of a magician. "Fleta's efforts be causing it to spin rapidly. The drill itself be coated in diamond dust. We already determined that with the additional strength of the Magnaosseums, we be able to drill through rock in about ten minutes. I expect that it be an even shorter time if we end up having to drill through a brick wall."

He leaned back in satisfaction as Fleta let the spinning come to a gentle stop. "Flint, maybe you would like to crawl out through the beak?" he suggested. "You be finding a set of latches at the end that disconnect the drill and allow you to exit *The Hawk*."

Flint rose from his seat at the rear and squeezed himself through the central space. Careful not to brush against the arrows sticking out of the bucket, he slid past Dell who still sat in the driver's seat.

The opening at the front, between the holes for the reins, was certainly not large enough to allow Egbert to fit. Probably, not even Dell, who was not a very big man, could squeeze through. But Flint easily managed the short trip through the metal passageway.

He could see nothing, but the feel of the chain led

him to the end of the drill where he discovered a set of four latches. Struggling in the pitch darkness to figure out how to unfasten it, the drill head suddenly dropped free and dangled from the chain. Squinting his eyes against the bright light, he hopped out into the fresh air.

He poked his head back in the shaft and called out, "It works just like you said. What's it for?" Almost immediately, he pulled his head back as a roar of laughter echoed down the metal tube. Flint felt a little disgruntled to find everyone laughing so uproariously at him.

A moment later, Fleta stood beside him. "That's what I have been trying to tell you," she said excitedly. "For years, *The Hawks* have been trying to get close enough to the King for an assassination, but it never works. Dell realized that there's no way to do it by stealth so he began trying to imagine another way. When he saw the Magnaosseums, the idea he had been thinking about started to make sense. Their bony armour gave him the idea for a direct attack on the walls."

When Flint still looked puzzled, she continued, "Don't you remember? Cadmon, Dell and Egbert sat and talked about this for a long time before you left on the last mission to the library." Her grin was infectious and Flint found himself smiling as well, although he did not recall listening to discussions about an armoured bird.

He nodded and waited for her to continue, but she just smiled and nodded her head as if encouraging him to understand. Finally he burst out, "Yes, but what is it for?"

Fleta's smile disappeared when she realized that she had not made herself clear. She frowned as she tried to figure out a way to let Flint visualize what was planned. "All right," she said. "Picture this. We drive directly at the city wall surrounding the palace and then fight off any challengers while we drill like mad." She was practically dancing in excitement. Her brown eyes sparkled. "When the drill breaks through the wall, you and I are going on a mission."

Chapter 32 - New Weapons

Suddenly, Flint recalled the books they brought back from the library. No doubt, Cadmon and Dell had hoped to find some useful information all along when they set out on that mission. After all, what other reason could there be for blindly hunting down a library that may have been nothing more than a rumour?

He understood now what a fortunate find the palace plans had been. They would be able to pinpoint the exact location on the wall that would lead to a room where he and Fleta could begin their mission. Without that key piece of information, there could be no hope of successfully breaking through the wall in a safe spot.

He wondered if *The Hawk* beak was even long enough to get through the outer wall. Thinking about it, Flint decided that they probably had enough information gathered from other sources to have a good idea about how thick the wall was.

The schematic drawing book had proven to be full of strange new weapons. Flint imagined some of those inventions might make *The Hawk* even more effective. One in particular had fascinated Dell: a drawing of a bow that could fire several arrows in a rapid succession.

Flint imagined *The Hawk* driving toward a solid wall while at the same time, arrows fired repeatedly at any moving targets. It might be one of the most terrifying, not to mention confusing, sights a King's Guard could ever see.

All at once, Flint understood what Fleta had meant when she said that they would be going on a mission. He and Fleta would be the ones to kill the King.

After the tour of *The Hawk*, Dell and Egbert sat huddled over the book of schematic drawings again. When it became apparent that they would be busy for a while, Fleta pulled Flint aside. "Are you hungry?" she asked.

As soon as she mentioned it, Flint realized that he had not eaten since before arriving in the village. And that had only been the last of some very hard bread and cheese. "I'm starving," he said.

"Come on. I was invited to have dinner with Orma tonight and I'm sure she'll be happy to see you too." Fleta eagerly set off toward Orma's cottage and Flint hurried to keep up.

"What are we having? Dry meat and potatoes?" he asked. This was an old joke. Orma was a good cook but one of the first times that she invited Flint to join her for dinner, something had gone wrong. Distracted by a potion that she was working on, the pot roast had been forgotten. When it was time to eat, they sat down to a meal that included meat cooked so long, it was just short of shoe leather. Now whenever they dined with Orma, they liked to tease her with the reminder of that meal.

Fleta laughed and Flint felt a rush of happiness. It was wonderful to be back in Halklyen just walking around the streets with Fleta. The last four weeks had been an incredible whirlwind of missions. It seemed to Flint that he had been in a state of tension ever since that first mission to rescue Geir. That seemed like forever ago.

When they arrived at the cottage, they found Cwenhild already seated at the kitchen table. Orma greeted Flint like a long lost son, crossing the room in three quick strides and wrapping him in a bear hug. Flint found he was very glad to see her and returned the hug.

"I have been hearing about your adventures, young man," she said. Holding him at arm's length, she stopped and gazed seriously into his eyes. "Are you all right?"

At first, he did not understand her concern. "Am I all right?" he asked in surprise. "It was Cwenhild who got hurt!" Orma continued to calmly study him and he realized that Cwenhild must have told her the whole story. "You heard about my battles?" he asked more soberly.

Orma nodded solemnly, and said, "Cwenhild told me you fought admirably. Are you sleeping well since then? No nightmares?"

Flint glanced over at Fleta and saw her studying him with alarm. "No nightmares," he answered uncomfortably then added, "I won both fights."

Orma studied his face for a moment longer, and then

smiled. "Good," she said as she dropped her arms and stepped toward the hearth. Over her shoulder she added, "You come and see me if you want to talk about it though." She looked over at Fleta. "I guess you two are hungry?"

Flint laughed, feeling the relief of leaving the subject of the gruesome deaths. "We were hoping for some dry meat and potatoes!" he teased.

Flint woke in his own bed. Stretching comfortably, he glanced over and saw that Cadmon was already gone. Judging by the sun breaking through the window, he knew it must be well past dawn; the latest he had slept since coming to Halklyen. Suddenly, he recalled that he was supposed to meet Fleta and Cwenhild. After a delicious dinner the night before, they had agreed to meet after breakfast.

By the time Flint hauled himself out of bed and grabbed some food, he knew he was going to be late. Sure enough, when he finally arrived in Vulture Square, Fleta and Cwenhild were already hard at work.

"It's about time, sleepy head," called Fleta. "I was beginning to think you weren't going to show up. I know how you feel about projectiles."

Every *Hawk* practiced on all available weapons and Cwenhild had trained both Fleta and Flint on the use of a bow and arrow. Fleta was a good shot: all her practice with daggers had refined her aim and made her very effective. Flint however, had not put in the time with it.

He found he struggled to make the unbelievably complex mental calculations that are part of aiming. He could hit a target if it was big enough though, so he figured that he could still be useful.

Fleta handed him a short bow, a twin to the one she held. He flexed it experimentally and found that it was very stiff. She saw his surprise at how hard it was to pull, and said, "It needs to be a little firmer than a long bow because it is so short." With that, she drew an arrow from the bucket by her side, smoothly nocked it and drew the bow string back to her cheek. Seconds later, the arrow was embedded in the red circle drawn on the straw target. "Watch and learn, my friend," she said with a satisfied chuckle. "Watch and learn."

With a sigh, Flint picked up his own bow, nocked and fired an arrow. It flew harmlessly past the target and he groaned in frustration. Fleta chose to say nothing and they spent the next hour firing then retrieving arrows.

When Flint's arrows finally started finding their way to the target, Fleta felt it was safe to speak again. "Can you believe that we have only been part of *The Talons* since the beginning of the summer?" she asked. "It seems like ages since all we had to do was train every day.

Flint smiled and agreed, "That's funny. I was just thinking the same thing. I can't even remember what it felt like to believe that I'd had a hard day just because I trained for a few hours."

Fleta grimaced, and said, "I've been so busy in the forge since you left that I haven't trained at all. Egbert has had us working from dawn to dusk so that *The Hawk* would be ready. Actually, we had no idea when you would get back and we just finished it the day before yesterday." As she spoke, she casually reached back and removed an arrow from the quiver she wore. Barely taking time to aim, she shot it dead centre in the target.

"Did you know we found the building plans of the wall of Kallcunarth and the King's Palace?" Flint asked as he reached down to the bucket for his own arrow. "There is a place on the wall, which Dell has been studying ever since he got his hands on the plans." The arrow struck the edge of the painted circle and he felt a moment of elation.

Fleta turned an intense gaze on him. "They have a plan for a way in?"

"I think so," he answered. Flint tried to remember what it was that had so fascinated Dell. "There is a small guards' barracks right at the spot that he showed Cadmon. It was only large enough for four people. That must be what they are planning. If we can drill through there, the wall is not likely as thick because the barracks are built right inside the wall."

"That was the part I was most worried about," admitted Fleta. "Just picture it, we smash through the wall and then you and I are supposed to crawl out, and then what?" She lifted her hands helplessly. "I was imagining that we would come out and there would be a hundred guards watching us."

"This is too important," Flint said with certainty. "When we hit that wall, we will know everything about it. I think Dell and Cadmon have been planning something like this for a long time. But they were always missing the key piece of information. Things are moving forward now because we have the building plans. This is what they have been preparing for since *The Hawks* began."

Flint groaned. Cwenhild had pronounced that it was not enough that he could hit a large target. He needed to be able to hit a small target with confidence. For three hours, he had been shooting sets of eight arrows, running seventy-five feet to pick up the arrows, running back and firing again. He hated to admit it but it might have helped.

Initially, none of his arrows even made it near the target. Then he started to hit the straw most times. When forty arrows in a row all landed inside the red circle and a couple even hit the black dot in the middle, he began to feel some confidence. "Did I actually say that I thought a day of training sounded easy?" he asked wearily. He rubbed his arm where the muscles protested after pulling the forty-pound bow all day.

Cwenhild insisted that Flint practice standing up until he could hit the target easily. She kept saying that he needed to develop instinctive aiming so that he could hit the target every time. Since Fleta could already hit the target every time, she practiced while sitting in a chair.

It was Cwenhild's promise that tomorrow he would be able to practice while sitting in a chair that had brought on the groan. At that point, he was not even sure if he would be able to draw a bow the next day.

Fleta laughed at the look on his face. "Don't worry, Flint. You won't have to try shooting through the slits in the practice *Hawk* until at least the day after tomorrow," she assured him with a smile.

In preparation for the attack on the King's wall, Fleta and Egbert rigged a wooden shield with slits cut in it just like the real *Hawk*. Hulda and Cwenhild practiced with it for a while between offering suggestions to Flint. For the last hour or so, Fleta had been firing through the slits and it had not looked easy.

"I think we have it figured out," Hulda said. She examined the slotted shield thoughtfully. "It is very odd to shoot when you cannot see everything around your target. I've found that if you get both eyes lined up with the slit, your shot is far more accurate."

"Well, Flint," Cadmon drawled from a point just behind Flint's shoulder, "have you become an expert archer?"

Flint turned, startled to find that Cadmon had managed to sneak up on him. "Yes, sir," he answered quickly. Then smiling, he added, "Cwenhild has not had an easy task trying to teach me to shoot accurately, but her 'practice makes perfect' adage seems to be working."

"Let's see," said Cadmon, nodding at the bow Flint had just unstrung.

Fleta giggled at the expression on Flint's face. "What's the matter, Flint? Are you tired?" she teased.

Flexing the bow against his leg, he stretched the linen

bowstring into place. "Me, tired?" he said dryly. "No way. You want to see some shooting? Check this out." In one smooth motion, he notched an arrow, raised the bow to shoulder height, sighted at the target, pulled the string back to his jawbone, released and watched as the arrow struck the red target. He turned nonchalantly and raised an eyebrow at Cadmon.

"That was impressive," Cadmon complimented. "Excellent. I guess it's all right then if I pull you away from archery for a while so you can come and train with the swords now?"

The look on of dismay on Flint's face was so comical that Fleta, Cwenhild and Hulda burst out laughing and even Cadmon had to smile. "Come on boy," he said. "You'll love the feel of the swords after all this shooting. There's nothing like a good solid hit with a blade."

Fleta stood watching as Cadmon led Flint away like a prisoner being taken to his execution. She was still smiling when she heard the hissing sound of Hulda's blades being drawn. "The man has the right idea," said Hulda as she settled into a balanced stance ready for attack. "A little blade practice would be perfect right now."

Fleta's smile disappeared in an instant and she reached for her own daggers.

Chapter 33 - Repeating Bow

Egbert carefully set the box on the ground and flipped open the latches. With a flourish, he raised the lid, and his audience crowded in to see the treasure he revealed. Nestled in the sheep's wool padding, was the most complex bow Flint had ever seen. It had none of sleekness and grace of the long bow Grove used or the shorter variant with which Flint and the other *Talons* had been practicing.

This bow looked thick and heavy. A small wooden box sat on a center shaft with the arms of the bow mounted perpendicularly to it. Everyone watched with interest as Egbert gently removed the bow from its bed and tucked the center shaft under his arm.

Then, aiming at a straw target at the far end of the square, he grasped the lever above the box and pulled it back. Every time he pulled the lever, a small arrow was released. Within ten seconds, a scattered cluster of fifteen shafts had hit the straw target.

The accuracy of Egbert's shooting was not exactly noteworthy, but the speed of the shots brought a gasp from the assembled audience. Hulda recovered her speech first. "May I try it?" she asked eagerly, reaching to almost tug the contraption out of Egbert's hands.

"I could scarce credit it myself when I finished it last night and tried it out," he said as he put the machine gently into Hulda's hands. "I followed the schematics exactly, when I built it, but I had no idea what it would actually do. On the plans, the little arrows be called bolts. They be exactly half the size of a regular arrow. I know, because I used the arrow shafts we bought earlier this year and just cut them in half.

"The hardest part be reloading the cartridge," he continued, "So I built an extra one. If you had two people working together with one person loading cartridges and one just shooting, you could do an awful lot of damage in a short period of time."

Gode stepped forward to examine the bow with Hulda, "How do you change the cartridge?" he asked as he studied the intricate design.

"That be easy," Egbert said, reclaiming the bow. He reached down and picked up the extra cartridge from the storage box. "You just slide the empty one backwards in the slot and lift it straight up. Then," he said, demonstrating, "you take the full one, set it straight down on the slot and slide it forward until it locks in place."

He placed the bow back in Hulda's waiting hands. She settled the center brace under her arm, sighted at the target and pulled back the lever. She looked up, surprised by the kick that it gave her. Then, checking her accuracy, she made a small adjustment and ten seconds later, fourteen bolts sprouted from the red circle.

"How many of those little bolts did you make?" asked Gode.

"So far, there be only the thirty you see here." Egbert cocked his head at the group and grinned as he said, "I ran out of time." That got a laugh. He was teasing Cadmon because he knew that he had accomplished an almost impossible task given the timeline that Cadmon had assigned.

In fact, if the group knew, his results were more than amazing. It had been necessary to meticulously craft each piece individually and then assemble them. Everything had to be perfect if there was to be any accuracy in the shooting. For all that, he finished the construction of the bow two days ago, but the catgut string had taken a full forty-eight hours to dry properly.

"We be not planning to leave until the day after tomorrow, so I figured, I could show you people how to make the bolts and you could help me?" The archers in the group nodded in understanding, but Egbert continued for the benefit of the others. "It be the fletching that takes time," he explained. "We have a good store of arrow shafts. I just cut them in half and hammer a metal tip on the end. Then you have to take a feather, split the quill and glue it in place so that the bolt will fly straight. If it be not just right, it won't fly properly at all."

Fleta chimed in, "Each arrow takes about five minutes to fletch so if we all work together, we could get a whole pile ready."

"How many of the narrow-fletched arrows for *The*

Hawk do we have?" Cadmon asked. He was thinking of the ammunition for the short bows.

Fleta replied, "All of the archers have been helping me and so far, we have over five hundred."

"And, how many regular arrows do we have on hand right now?" Cadmon wanted to know.

Hulda answered, "We are continually making arrows around here. There is a stock of about fifteen hundred completed arrows and about the same in shafts in the armoury. I imagine that if we take about three hundred shafts for the bolts we would not be in danger of running low." Her face took on a thoughtful look as she calculated how many arrows could be necessary. "We don't want to leave them short here in case there is some need to defend Halklyen. I'll have some of the archers make more of the long arrows as well."

Flint looked up at that comment. As long as he had lived in the village, there had never been any concern about a direct attack. Studying the faces of the elder *Hawks*, he realized that this was something they had spent some time considering. He looked at Fleta and saw the worry in her eyes.

Fleta deftly flicked her knife down the middle of the last feather. "I have always liked making arrows," she said wearily, "but I am glad to see the end of this job." It was almost midnight and the seven *Talons* chosen to assassinate the King had been fletching arrows for four hours. In that time, they made just over four hundred of the little bolts that the repeating bow required.

Even taking into account the lack of accuracy of the new weapon, Flint could not imagine needing to shoot that many people. He hoped that this planning was overly cautious. He absolutely did not want to be responsible for killing any more guards than necessary to get to the King. Imagine if the four hundred thirty bolts plus the five hundred regular arrows all hit their mark; it would be like wiping out an entire town. They would be as evil as Martokallu.

"Well, the glue should be dry by lunch time tomorrow," said Cadmon. "Let's meet at noon at Egbert's forge and we'll load up *The Hawk*. That way that everything will be ready to go at dawn the next day." He rose from his seat and stretched stiffly.

"There are definite advantages to using a blade," Gode said. "A little time with a whetstone and you're ready to go again. These arrows are finicky little things." He, too, rose and reached up to touch the ceiling of Orma's cottage. "I imagine you hardly ever get them back when you shoot them off in a battle either." He grinned and winked at Cwenhild who smiled back.

Hulda was less pleased with the comparison. She reached forward to put the stopper into the glue bottle. "A well placed arrow can be far more effective than a crashing blade," she said sternly. "Blade fighting is all about the glory, where a bow can accomplish the necessary with very little fanfare."

Orma inserted herself into the discussion. "Both forms of weapons have proven their worth," she said soothingly. "Now, I have some cold ale here. As soon as you clear away these feather trimmings, let's sit down and enjoy a well-earned rest."

Fleta pulled the broom from where it leaned in the corner by the hearth and gently swept up the bits of feather littering the floor around the kitchen table. Cwenhild followed her with a wet cloth to capture any of the floating feathers that eluded the broom. Flint carefully moved the buckets where the bolts sat tip down while the fletching dried.

It had been a long day and when Flint settled in front of the fire with his ale, he found himself struggling to stay awake. Egbert's next words, though, brought him fully conscious.

"Well, Cadmon, I have been busy this last little while," Egbert began and then paused to wait out the laugh that his modest words caused. "But I be wondering about your plans for the defence of Halklyen while we be away on this mission." He raised his eyebrows in inquiry as he spoke.

Flint looked up in interest. Ever since Hulda mentioned the question of leaving enough arrows behind for the defence of Halklyen, Flint had felt a niggling worry in the back of his head. Most of the experienced warriors would be away from the village on one of the two missions.

"Good question," answered Cadmon. "We've been giving this much thought." He appeared to be giving it even more thought as he stared into his mug of ale. Finally, he cleared his throat and looked up at the relaxing *Hawks*. "But it is not something I feel comfortable discussing here." He looked meaningfully at the windows. "This is a subject for the Hawk Hut. All I can tell you now is that Dell will be in charge."

There was silence in the room as each person contemplated the significance of the need to plan a defence for a place that had always seemed so secure.

Flint snuck a look at Orma to see how she felt about this information, but her face revealed nothing. He guessed that she was part of the plan; her shield was the most important feature in their fight against Martokallu.

Chapter 34 - Trickery

It was unbelievably hot inside the belly of *The Hawk*. Flint could feel the sweat running down his back under the linen tunic that protected him from his new chainmail. The armour was far heavier than he had ever imagined.

At noon the day before, when they met to load *The Hawk* with everything they would need for the mission to Kallcunarth, Egbert had surprised Flint and Fleta by handing each of them a very heavy bundle. Unwrapping the linen coverings, which turned out to be new tunics Merylin had sewn for them, they found chainmail armour.

The beauty of the workmanship left them speechless. Egbert had used some of the last skystone to work the chainmail rings and the armoured coats glowed with the same soft light that seemed to come off Cadmon's sword, *The Rising Star*.

After gazing appreciatively at her gift, Fleta threw her arms around Egbert and thanked him with a big kiss planted on his cheek. Flint had added his own thanks in a less exuberant but equally grateful manner.

They proudly wore the armour for the rest of the day.

Cadmon insisted that they practice both shooting and blade fighting while wearing it so that they could become accustomed to the new weight. Flint was astonished to find that even though he felt he could hardly lift the bundled armour, once it was on, he really did not find it difficult to carry the weight.

Flint glanced over his shoulder at Fleta who sat in the chair opposite him. The seats that Egbert had moulded inside *The Hawk* were not designed for taking the bumps out of the road. The fact that the arrow slits were covered by the wooden sides only added to the discomfort. Like him, Fleta had pulled down her chainmail hood and her hair was plastered to her head with sweat.

"By the Fire of Dworgunul, I be thinking that a window might have been a good idea," said Egbert from his seat at the front. It was so dark that they could only vaguely see each other. "You try to think of everything when you design something, but I never considered ventilation."

Hulda smiled as she wiped the sweat from her eyes. "You remembered water," she said, lifting her canteen in a toast. "That's the most important thing."

"I'm thinking those three scallywags on top knew what they were volunteering for when they said they would ride up there," Egbert continued. "Here I be, believing they be taking the big risk by riding out in plain view. Turns out, they be just looking for the comfortable seats."

Sitting in the stifling heat, Flint imagined Gode,

Cadmon and Cwenhild who were seated on the top of the box. The cool air would be blowing through their hair and the sunshine would lend a splendid light to everything.

When they left the village early that morning, everybody had ridden up on top. With the Magnaosseums pulling the heavy *Hawk*, it had been a lumbering trip along the forest path. Eventually everyone except Gode, who had to drive, ended up walking behind the cart rather than endure the bone-rattling ride.

Only when they reached the border of Orma's invisibility cloak had they stopped and prepared themselves for the final approach to Kallcunarth. The three riders on top were dressed like members of a performing troupe.

Hulda took great delight in finding just the right clothes to make Cadmon and Gode appear outlandish yet harmless. Flint had seen the wince that crossed Cadmon's face when he saw what she intended for them to wear.

Gode had been far better natured about it. Putting his costume on, he paraded around to the amusement of all *The Hawks*. Cwenhild dressed in a ridiculous body suit that appeared to have been fashioned from about three hundred scraps of fabric. Anyone who saw them would assume the strange cart and even stranger beasts were all part of the entertainment.

What a passer-by would not see however, were the weapons that each warrior carried. Orma's invisibility potion had been painted onto Gode's axe, Cadmon's

244

sword and the bow Cwenhild wore slung over her shoulder. Flint helped with painting on the potion and he had taken a funny kind of pride in making certain that each arrow in her quiver was fully coated. Remembering his desire to fight an opponent with his invisible blades, he could not help imagining the effect that invisible arrows would have on the enemy.

Before crawling into the belly of *The Hawk*, Fleta and Flint donned their new chainmail. Flint found the combination of the hard metal seat, the unforgiving chainmail and the awkward position he had to sit in because of his double swords in their scabbard, just about unbearable. Every bump the cart hit seemed to jolt right through his spine.

The silence in the small space told Flint that everybody was focused on simply enduring the trip. Suddenly, the sound of the wheels changed and everyone sat up and listened attentively.

Egbert identified the difference. "We be crossing the bridge," he said with some relief. Flint could hear the smile in his voice. "That means we be stopping very soon. Just wait. In a few moments, we be feeling that cool breeze breaking in through the arrow slits."

Only a few turns of the wheels later, his words were proven correct as they bumped to a stop. Faintly, they heard Gode cry out some jest and they knew he was addressing the guards on the wall.

The plan was to act as if everything they did was part of a show so that the guards would not be too suspicious of their strange actions. Back in Vulture Square, Flint had watched while they rehearsed the show.

Now, he could see in his mind's eye what would be happening outside. First, Gode would engage the guards in some chatter in order to distract them. Then Cadmon and Cwenhild would simultaneously do a back flip off the top of the cart and follow it up with a series of acrobatic moves. Gode would keep up his showmanship patter. Flint knew from experience that Gode could easily maintain an entertaining performance for hours.

When the cart shuddered slightly, Flint and Fleta looked at each other and Flint waggled his eyebrows. They knew that Cadmon and Hulda had begun unharnessing the Magnaosseums. A second little jarring told them that the pantomime of lowering the drill into position had begun. Imagining what the guards saw as they watched Cadmon and Hulda struggle with the heavy, yet invisible, drill, Flint could not help smiling.

Egbert had not planned to have the "beak" of his hawk painted with Orma's invisibility potion. He had spent a considerable amount of time making it look as beautiful as possible and had not wanted it hidden. But Flint suggested that the guards would find it less threatening to watch if they thought they were merely watching an entertainment.

He had also been brave enough to offer some suggestions to Cwenhild and a rather surly Cadmon as to how they could make it look more like a pantomime's act. He remembered watching such shows on days when he visited the market as a kitchen boy.

The next jolt informed the sweating occupants of *The*

Hawk that the fake wooden walls of the cart were being removed. They all raised their faces in relief as the first breath of fresh air came in through the slits. The plan was to use the walls to build a shield just in case something went wrong and the three people on the outside suddenly found themselves the targets of the guards on the wall.

So far, everything had gone perfectly. Flint hoped they would not need those shelters, because if that happened, the mission had little chance of success.

Flint recognized a sudden screeching noise as the sound of the wings being lowered into place. More light and air poured in and Flint could see clearly for the first time in over an hour. Peeking out the slit in front of him, Flint saw Cadmon harnessing Os to the front of the wing. Egbert picked up the slack in the reins so that he would be in control of the Magnaosseums.

Through the slit above Egbert's head, Flint glimpsed a group of guards standing casually on the top of the wall. Evidently, Gode had been successful in getting them to relax to the point where they had forgotten their duty.

Flint had a sudden image of the damage that would be inflicted when the shooting began. He hoped the guards would choose to seek shelter rather than directly challenge *The Hawks*. From discussions the previous evening, Flint understood that the plan was to put so many arrows into the air that the guards would have to choose between shielding themselves and shooting back.

He peered at the wall directly in front of *The Hawk*. It did not look any different from the wall to either side of it. The building plans of the palace included measurements for the thickness of the walls surrounding the city. To have such information was even more than Cadmon and Dell had hoped to find when they set out to find the rumoured library. With the new details, they calculated the exact location they would need to drill in order to get inside the small guards' barracks built inside the wall.

Flint glanced over at Fleta. He could see that she studied the wall with just as much interest. She felt his eyes on her and looked up. "Do you think we're lined up in the right place?" she asked him quietly.

"I know they spent a long time on the calculations and seemed pretty confident about hitting the weak spot," he answered. He too kept his voice low but still Egbert overheard their concerns.

"From what I be seeing, I'd say we hit it dead on." He nodded with his head, and asked, "You see that guard tower in front of us?"

"The one on the right?" asked Fleta as she craned her neck to see better.

"Yep. That be the one. The building plans show that the barracks be twelve feet to the left of that. We'll find out soon enough if those plans be accurate. I think things be almost set up out there." Egbert twisted around backwards in his seat to look at Hulda who sat in the chair with the pedals that drove the drill. "Are you ready, lassie?" he asked. "I'm going to set those Magnaosseums in motion the minute those three finish horsing around out there."

248

Hulda flexed her feet on the pedals speculatively. Flint could hear the gears turning. "It feels right," said Hulda. "Can you…"

She never got a chance to finish that sentence because Cadmon suddenly dropped through the top hatch.

Chapter 35 - Surprise

From the instant Cadmon hit the floor inside *The Hawk*, everything suddenly seemed to speed up. He dove to the side just in time to allow Cwenhild to drop in beside him and then, seconds later, Gode jumped down through the opening.

"Go, go, go!" he cried. "Get ready with bows. They are going to get really curious in a moment."

Egbert shook the reins and urged the Magnaosseums forward. In preparation for this moment, they had used the wall of one of the few brick cottages in the village. Gode spent a day driving Mag and Os into the wall and then getting them to maintain the pressure by throwing their weight forward on the harnesses. Strangely, they did not seem to mind pulling hard and going nowhere. To complete their training, Fleta and Flint stood on the rooftop and fired arrows down onto the bony armour that covered the Magnaosseums' entire heads and backs. The massive animals had not even flinched.

Now, they steadfastly pulled *The Hawk* up to the stone wall and held it firmly in place while Hulda kept the drill spinning madly. Cwenhild seized the repeating bow and began to fire at the guards on the wall. No sooner had she emptied one cartridge then Cadmon handed her another. Flint and Fleta were both busy with their short bows. Flint was pleased to note that there was very little return fire. The guards were choosing to stay out of sight.

Gode was seated beside Hulda. The plan required him to change off with her so that the drill could continue to spin at the maximum velocity. A change in the pitch of the drilling noise told Flint that Hulda was already beginning to tire. She relinquished the pedals to Gode who scrambled into her seat and quickly got the drill rotating again.

Inside the metal belly of *The Hawk,* the sound of the drilling was incredibly loud. Flint felt like his head was going to explode from all the noise. Still he kept watching the wall for any sign of guards. Whenever he spotted someone, he would fire off an arrow. Apparently, Cwenhild and Fleta were doing the same thing because there were always at least three arrows in the air every time something moved up there.

At the feel of a hand on his shoulder, he turned to find Cadmon trying to say something to him. The racket was so great that in order to be heard, Cadmon had to shout directly into Flint's ear. "Get yourself forward to the beak," he yelled. "I think it is about to break through."

At these words, Flint felt his stomach clench in a mixture of excitement and fear. He nodded to tell Cadmon that he understood and then pulled up his linen hood, followed by the heavy chainmail. As he felt the weight of it settle on his head, he looked around to see if Fleta was ready to go. Cadmon shouted into her ear, too, and Flint saw her quickly check her daggers and pull up her hoods.

He checked his swords; pulling them free of the scabbards to assure himself that they had not been affected during the bumpy ride. A small smile of satisfaction crossed his lips as he examined the splendid blades. He never tired of looking at them and their smooth brilliance.

Suddenly, the sound of the drill changed. Flint glanced back and saw that Hulda was back in the pedalling chair. Dripping with sweat, she let her legs slow down, and wiped her face in relief. The silence was almost deafening as the drill rattled to a stop.

Flint immediately heard the sound of the repeating bow shooting off a volley of arrows. Someone must have stuck his head out to see what was happening.

By the time Flint turned his attention back to Fleta, her feet were disappearing into the beak. He scrambled past Egbert to follow her. "Good luck, boy. Keep your eyes open," the inventor said quietly.

Flint smiled in appreciation and then dove into the hole. He could see light at the end of the tunnel and assumed that Fleta had already made it through. The chainmail made an awful clattering as he crawled through the tight space. Just as he reached the opening, he saw Fleta stumble backwards when a guard thrust through her defensive stance.

Flint pushed himself out of the chute and catapulted

his body against Fleta's attacker. Springing to his feet, he drew his swords and found himself facing a swordsman who fought more like a practice post than the accomplished sword masters he was used to. A quick parry, followed quickly by an overhand slicing attack, sent his opponent to the ground in a spray of blood.

The sound of a boot on stone alerted Flint that the fight was not yet over. He turned in time to knock aside a blow intended for his head. Again, he was surprised to find the skill level far below that of anyone in *The Hawks*. Neither did these King's Guards compare to *The Followers* that he had fought. He easily slid past the guard's defence and thrust a sword through his chainmail into his stomach. He briefly wondered what the chainmail was made from since his blade sliced through the rings without difficulty.

Quickly surveying the room, Flint saw four guards lying dead on the ground. Two of them had one of Fleta's daggers protruding from their necks. Flint raised his eyebrows at her.

"I took them by surprise," she said with something like regret in her voice. "I got two blades off, but then the other two guards rushed me."

"I expect we've taken everyone by surprise," Flint answered. "Let's try to take advantage of that." He wiped his blades on the trousers of the slain guards and stepped briskly toward the doors. "If I remember correctly, we exit this room and head left down the hallway."

Fleta gathered up her knives and quickly wiped each of them clean before sheathing them. When she was

ready, Flint checked the hallway for any other guards.
"It's clear. Let's go," he said, waving her on.

Fleta moved past him into the point position. Her
throwing blades gave them the advantage when
approaching an enemy. She led him down the dim
hallway and Flint, whose responsibility it was to watch
the rear, found himself swivelling his head back and
forth.

For the last three evenings, Fleta and Flint had sat
with Geir and poured over the blueprints. Geir had
previously been assigned to the palace. He told them
about everything he could think of that might prove
useful on their mission. As well, they had memorized
several different routes which led through to the King's
inner chambers. One thing they did not want was to
have to read a map while trying to keep their eyes open
for guards.

Fleta raised the question of how they would know the
King when they saw him. At first, Geir tried to describe
him but Flint had interrupted. He clearly remembered a
visit Duke Dedrick had received from his cousin, the
King. Flint had spent the evening running back and forth
from the kitchen carrying the heaviest serving plates.
Each time he entered the elaborate dining room, his gaze
had been drawn to the King who seemed to dominate
the room with his presence. Flint knew that recognizing
the man they were there to kill would present no
difficulties.

The biggest challenge with the plan was that the King
had no set routine. The informers in place could not

confirm where he would be at any given time. The plan today was to move with stealth where they were not expected, find, and kill the King.

Wryly, Flint considered how simple and straightforward that plan had seemed when they sat comfortably at Orma's kitchen table. Studying the building plans in the warm light of the coal oil lantern, Flint had imagined that they would move easily through the hidden corridors of the palace, break into the King's sitting room and kill him with a well-placed blade. He had rather grandly told himself that he did not even care whose blade it was; he and Fleta were partners and it would not matter who actually performed the assassination.

Now, however, as he made his way cautiously down the deserted hallway, he could not help thinking about what was happening to the people still sitting in the belly of *The Hawk*. He hoped they were not running out of arrows. At this point, he could not imagine what he was thinking when he judged that they had made too many. Not once had he given any consideration as to how long they might have to wait for him and Fleta to return.

He felt like they should be hurrying, but realized that any carelessness would be a recipe for disaster. They approached a corner that Flint knew would lead them out of the wall corridor into the servant hallways of the palace. At this point, they were as likely to run into a servant, as they were a guard. Flint was not sure he would be able to attack an unarmed person.

Fleta took a moment to use the tiny mirror they had

brought to help see around corners. She gave him a nod to indicate the hall was empty. Then, tucked the mirror away and started warily toward the door that led to the King's bedroom. They were about three steps away from the door when it burst open and two men came out. Flint barely had time to register that the men were obviously body servants. They carried heaps of clothing that looked royal enough to belong to the King.

He dove forward, hooked his left elbow under the chin of the fellow closest to him and brought the pommel of his right sword down on the back of his head, at the edge of his skull. It was as if everything slowed down the moment he began to move. He watched Fleta perform almost exactly the same manoeuver.

Hulda had insisted that they be masters in hand-to-hand combat. This was a favourite technique. Their victims would be unconscious for a while but they would wake up. If they had used the other end of their blades, there would be no coming around.

As he gently let the servant slide down to the floor, he glanced through the still-open door. The room was empty. Perhaps if they did not have a cart full of people waiting for them to return, they could have waited for the King here. Instead, they would need to continue the hunt.

Quickly, they dragged the unconscious men into the bedroom and stuffed them under the enormous bed. Flint figured it would be at least an hour before they woke up, but the need for haste was increasing.

"Too bad we can't ask these two where we might find the King," whispered Fleta.

Flint almost laughed aloud in a release of tension. "It's tempting to wake them up," he joked quietly. "From what I've seen of the King's temper, they might even help us."

"Maybe, but we should probably just keep moving. Cadmon will be wondering what's taking so long." Fleta sheathed one blade and pulled out the mirror again. She checked the hallway and then, lapsing back into hand signals, motioned him forward and led the way back into the hall.

They crept past three doorways without encountering anyone. Nor did they hear any sign of the rooms being inhabited. At the fourth door, Fleta paused and listened carefully when she heard voices within the room. At first, it was difficult to figure out what was being said, and then Flint recognized the words, "Your Highness." He stiffened and looked at Fleta. She had heard it too. She waggled her eyebrows at him and Flint stepped forward to open the door.

Chapter 36 - Assassination

Paal rushed toward the front entrance of the throne room. He had just come from the wall where he tried to figure out what was happening. When he stuck his head out from behind the tower to see the source of all the arrows, he had to pull back almost immediately to avoid being hit. As far as he could judge, the odd-looking conveyance sat about two metres from the wall and its occupants were firing arrows at a ridiculous pace.

Two massive beasts were harnessed to the metal bird-shaped cart. The animals simply stood passively with their long horns practically touching the wall. In the quick glimpse he managed to get, he could not see anything else happening. No doubt, it was some addle-pated king-hater who had decided to launch an attack.

As Supreme Commander of the King's Guard, it was Paal's duty to report to the King. He decided that the King would wish to be informed of the disturbance. Knowing him, he might even want to come and see it for himself.

As usual, Paal wore full armour and carried both his huge kite shield, which bore the King's Insignia, and his long steel broadsword. The elegantly simple blade's only adornment was a ruby embedded in the hilt. Paal's armour was much more ostentatious than his sword. The breastplate, like the shield, was emblazoned with the King's Insignia; every ridge of the plate metal trimmed with gold. Even the chainmail covering his arms and upper legs was made from such high quality steel that the rings glinted and sparkled in the light.

Paal found it useful to be easily identified in a crowd. His massive build and height aided that goal, as did the splendid armour, but it was the helmet that made him most distinctive. Made of the same superior steel, the full-visor helmet featured more of the elegant gold trim. He rarely removed it to display his cleanly shaven head and many people would not even recognize him without it.

As he hurried down the staircase that led from the top of the wall to the palace courtyard, he contemplated how exactly he would describe this latest attack to the King. He scowled as he imagined his ruler's reaction. Lately, there had been too many unsatisfied citizens who tried to mount a protest. Even the brutal retaliations the King ordered each time had done nothing to slow down the outbreaks.

Thrusting open the throne room door, he swept into a deep bow. "Your Highness," he greeted the King who sat in a large throne facing the entrance.

King Abelard looked up from the manuscript he had been examining. His pale blue eyes squinted as he peered near-sightedly at his Supreme Commander. "Paal. I take it by your sudden entry that you have important news for me," the King spoke in a drawling, sarcastic tone.

Abelard's tall, muscular form rested easily in the padded throne. His elaborate robes were in his favourite hues of gold and purple. Sometimes, people made the mistake of underestimating him because he fancied himself as a fashion setter, but it was a mistake that they made only once. After assuming the throne from his father when he was only fifteen years old, Abelard had demonstrated himself to be a hardnosed, autocratic leader.

It was his desire for ever-greater power that had led him directly into Martokallu's influence. Almost twenty-five years ago, when he was a young King struggling to establish his authority, Lorund had approached him and offered an easy route to that power. Abelard recalled listening in shock as the repulsive *Follower* told him about the agreement that Martokallu had held between both Abelard's father and grandfather.

For Abelard, the greatest surprise came when he learned that Martokallu was real, not some fairy-tale invented to scare little children. Once he came to terms with that idea, it had not seemed that Martokallu demanded too much. All he asked was to be able to command the army through Abelard. In return, he offered the advantage of omniscient vision that would let Abelard know about anything that happened anywhere in his kingdom.

Abelard figured that he would be able to handle the demands that were put upon his army. Obviously, both his father and grandfather felt it was worth it. The benefits of having *The Followers* and Martokallu on his side were sufficient to convince him to take the vow of cooperation that Martokallu demanded.

There had only been a few moments during his reign when he had doubted the wisdom of that decision. Occasionally, the actions of *The Followers* were too grisly even for Abelard's ruthless nature.

Paal snapped to attention. "Your Highness," he repeated. "There is a disturbance at the wall. It is difficult to describe exactly…"

He cut himself off as he saw the servants' door at the back of the throne room swing open. Paal just had time to glimpse a young man wearing chainmail. The boy ducked down to reveal a similarly dressed girl right behind him. Before Paal could react, she threw a dagger at him. Paal felt it bounce off his armour. The force of the blow surprised him and he was grateful for the quality of his steel.

Once again, his reaction time was slightly behind the boy's speed. Immediately after ducking so that the girl could throw her dagger, the boy flung himself toward the King in a low forward roll. Springing to his feet the boy threw his sword straight into the King's neck. The rush of blood almost stopped Paal cold, but he forced himself across the room to reach the young attacker.

The boy shifted his stance and Paal realized that he still held a sword. A double-sword bearer? He raised his own blade in preparation for a killing blow. Across the room, he saw the girl rush forward and with a few quick swipes of her daggers both guards who had been assigned to the King's safety, dropped heavily to the floor.

Paal struck hard at the boy. When his blade met by defensive blow, he swung wildly with his heavy shield. The boy maintained his balance and took a step closer to the throne.

The King made a horrible sucking sound through the hole in his neck but he could not move. The sword had gone right through his flesh into the throne itself. The boy reached out and wrenched the sword free in a gout of blood. The King gasped and Paal attacked again. For a moment he was distracted when he saw the girl dash across the room to the King. She reached forward and ended his life with an expert crack of his neck.

Flint felt better with his second sword back in his hand and he turned more confidently to face the huge armoured man charging at him with a raised blade. He could almost hear Cadmon's voice in his head as he settled into a defensive stance. *Use the force of a bigger man against him. Stay balanced, defend yourself but look for any openings he may leave.*

Suddenly, there it was. Something over Flint's shoulder caught the man's eye and Flint had to react quickly to take advantage of his distraction. He stepped inside the long sword's reach and slid his left blade down the length of the long sword until he felt the cross guards lock. Flint struggled to hold the powerful man away. He felt the weight of the huge kite shield pound against his chest and reached out with his right hand.

Knowing that he would not be able to hold him off very long, Flint mustered all his strength and hammered his sword into the elegant helmet. He felt the jarring right through his arm but it had an immediate effect. The pressure on his left arm and the push on his chest disappeared. Flint saw the man's eyes roll back into his head and he went down like a tree.

For a moment, Flint could do nothing but stand gasping for breath. Then, he turned and met Fleta's eyes. Unable to read the play of emotion he met there, he glanced away and saw three dead bodies. The huge warrior lay senseless at his feet, a sharp edged dent in his helmet where Flint's sword had hit. The helmet was beautiful but evidently, it was no match for the hardened metal Egbert produced.

"Well," he said, unconsciously mimicking Cadmon, "we should get out of here."

The King was dead, and so far, no alarm had been raised. They should be able to slide out the same way they had arrived. Fleta quickly stepped past Flint and he watched as she demonstrated more of her practical thinking. Grabbing the long sword lying beside the unconscious commander, she hurried across the room and thrust the blade between the two door handles. The cross guard snagged in the latch and she gave it a wiggle to see that it was secure.

"That might buy us a few minutes," she said as she turned and hurried to the servants' entrance.

Chapter 37 - Escape

Fleta hesitated when she reached the door leading to the servants' hallway. She felt an exhilaration that seemed to sharpen every sense. Before taking hold of the door handle to pull it open, she looked at Flint to see that he was prepared. He had taken a moment to wipe the worst of the King's blood from his blade, but it still had long ugly streaks of brown on it.

When she met his eyes, she saw the same blazing excitement she felt. He gave her a confident nod and after a quick check of the daggers in her belt, as well as the one in her hand, she threw the door wide and stepped through it.

Fleta thought she was prepared to fight, but when she saw the two small servant girls hurrying through the passageway, she could not bring herself to attack. Flint noticed her indecision and stepped cautiously into the hallway to see the problem.

When he spotted the servant girls, he reacted immediately. His time as a servant in hallways just like this one, told him that that these girls did not have to be a danger to them.

Flint took three quick steps to where the girls had stopped to stare at the intruders and went down on one knee in front of them. "I know you will have trouble believing this," he began, "but we are here to save you." He smiled gently as he saw the hope in the smaller girl's eyes. "The King is dead, and soon there will be a new King who will work hard to make a better life for everyone."

This announcement brought a look of shock to both small faces. After a moment, the older girl found the courage to speak, "A King is a King. To such as us, it makes no difference who's in charge. We still have work to do."

Flint maintained his gentle smile and his eyes softened in recognition of the truth of her statement. "Of course, you are right," he said. "There is always work. But, it doesn't have to be done for a cruel master." He watched the reactions of the girls as they digested this thought. After a moment, he said, "You haven't seen us. We never came this way."

Flint waited with bated breath for their response. It came quickly. The two girls looked at each other and then back at Flint. They both gave identical but determined nods. He smiled at them once more then turned and fled down the hallway back the way they had come.

He could hear Fleta's boots tapping lightly behind him and he slowed as he approached a corner. It would not do to fly around a corner and crash into a group of armed guards. He stopped and held his breath so that he could hear better. There was no sound and Fleta, who had stopped beside him, used her mirror to see around the corner. The entire route was empty. This was good news. Everyone must still be involved in the attack on the wall.

Suddenly, Flint realized that they had really only been gone for about ten minutes. It seemed like a lifetime. They hurried down the deserted hallway and turned into the room where they had entered the palace. The four bodies of the men they killed still lay on the floor. More good news, despite the unpleasant odour coming from the corpses. No one had discovered their entrance yet.

He dove into the hole and scrambled through the tunnel. He could feel Fleta right behind him and he hurried to crawl the length of the chute. The noise of their chainmail rattling against the metal walls alerted the occupants of *The Hawk* that someone was coming. Flint heard Egbert call out a warning. Guessing that if he made his entrance unannounced, he would no doubt lose his head, Flint called out a greeting, "Hold up. We're back. We're coming in."

With that, he pushed himself through the last few feet of the tunnel and tumbled into the belly of *The Hawk*. Immediately, he rolled to one side and Fleta dropped in after him. Flint raised his head and met Cadmon's eyes.

"Success?" he asked urgently. The question was brief but Flint could feel everyone in the enclosed space holding their breath as they waited for the answer.

Both Flint and Fleta answered at the same time, "Success." They looked at each other and smiled.

Flint continued, "Right now, no one is chasing us, but I think it might be a good time to get out of here."

"That might just be the best idea I be hearing in a long time," declared Egbert. "Fleta, will you take care of the beak, please?"

Fleta turned herself around in the tight space and stuck her head inside the tunnel again. She saw with relief that there were still no pursuers. Reaching out with her left hand, she found the clip and unfastened the latch holding the beak in place.

On the way there, it had already been fastened together. Egbert designed the beak so that it tilted upwards out of the way, allowing the Magnaosseums room to move. From that position, it could easily be lowered into drilling position. The latch arrangement allowed the occupants of *The Hawk* to fold it up without actually needing to go outside. As soon as she flipped the latch, Fleta began pulling in the sections of the beak rather like a telescope. The outside shell moved easily and she pulled in two levels of it before it was necessary to shift the drill.

This turned out to be far more difficult. When they practiced it back in Halklyen, Fleta had been able to pull the drill in alone. Now however, she found it stuck fast. In her cramped position, she could not get a strong enough grip. No matter how she wiggled it, she was unable to budge it more than a few inches. It must have been jammed on the rock.

"Flint," Fleta called. "I can't get the drill loose. Can you pull on my legs? She felt him grab her just above the knees and start to haul. At first, nothing happened, and she struggled to maintain a grip on the drill. Then, whatever had been caught, suddenly released. Before Flint could react, he yanked both Fleta and the drill into the belly.

Egbert's design worked perfectly and the rest of the chute telescoped completely out of the way. Fleta untangled herself and wiggled forward once more to close the hatch. Egbert immediately began bringing the Magnaosseums around from their stance up against the wall.

The first sign of motion in over half an hour brought about a flurry of activity on the top of the wall. Cadmon hurried to refill the cartridge for the repeating bow as Hulda kept the air thick with the dangerous bolts. Cwenhild moved herself to the seat that Flint had previously occupied and made good use of one of the short bows. While Flint watched, two of the guards on top of the wall ducked behind the tower just in time to avoid being hit.

Egbert guided the Magnaosseums around in a wide circle and then shook the reins to let them know it was time to run. Flint made his way unsteadily to the one remaining chair. Fleta had chosen to sit up front in the chair beside Egbert.

The uneven ground had the vehicle rocking and bumping just as it had on the way there, but now it was a hundred times worse as Egbert encouraged the beasts to give their maximum speed.

This part of the plan was the most uncertain. It all

depended on how quickly the guards decided to pursue and whether they had thought about preparing a troop of riders with ready horses. In his rear seat, Flint peered back to gauge the pursuit. So far, nothing was visible.

In a flash of insight, Flint understood that the man he had left wounded on the floor of the throne room was the commander of the guards. Without him to give the order, there would almost certainly be a delay before anyone took the initiative and organized a chase. Already, they were out of bowshot and still the gates had not opened.

They would have to stop soon in order to fold the wings up and re-harness the Magnaosseums. The road would not accommodate a load as wide as *The Hawk* at its full wingspan. The idea was that they would race full speed across this field but as soon as they reached the beginnings of the forest, four people would jump out and make the adjustments as fast as possible.

"Get ready," called Cadmon. "We'll stop just past this first tree."

Egbert hauled on the reins and slowed the team to a walk before bringing them to a halt.

No orders were necessary. This too, had been practiced back in the village. Working in pairs, Fleta and Hulda ran to Os on the right side while Cadmon and Flint unhooked Mag from the left. Amazingly, the Magnaosseums did not even appear to be winded. In a matter of moments, all of the chains had been reattached to the front of *The Hawk* and each team rushed to fold up the wing on their side. This was a little trickier.

The length and weight of each wing made them cumbersome to move. As soon as they got it flipped up in the air, Fleta and Flint clambered up the steps on the back of *The Hawk* while Cadmon and Hulda held their sides in place. A strap to hold each wing upright hung from the top and Flint got his clipped into place without falling off the vehicle. He glanced over and saw that Fleta was struggling to get hers fastened. Just as she seemed to lose her balance, Flint grabbed her arm and pulled her back aboard.

In the meantime, Cadmon climbed up top, and taking advantage of his longer reach, stretched out and fastened the strap in place. As soon as she saw it was done, Fleta dropped through the hatch, followed quickly by Flint. They moved out of the way, onto their chairs and waited for Hulda and Cadmon to make their entrance.

Seconds ticked by while everyone stared anxiously at the hole in the ceiling. Suddenly, Hulda dropped down with Cadmon right behind her. "Let's go! Go! Go! Go!" shouted Cadmon. For a moment, he lost his customary calm. Egbert whipped the Magnaosseums up to speed and then turned in his chair with a raised eyebrow. Cadmon shrugged sheepishly and said simply, "We may have a problem."

Chapter 38 - Ambush

Kjell felt a rush of satisfaction. While that bootlicking Paal had scurried off to inform the King of the attack on the wall, he had taken a troop of mounted soldiers out the back gate. Moving in a wide circle, back to the road where the odd-looking cart had first been spotted, he settled his soldiers and waited. He knew the attackers would have to leave at some point and now he was in place to cut off their retreat.

Just out of sight of the city walls, concealed in the woods at the side of the road, Kjell set up his ambush. Not an ideal situation, perhaps, given that his troop, was made up of mere humans. But he had been living in the capital for a long time and was accustomed to their weaknesses. For one thing, he knew they would follow every command he gave. These brave warriors could hardly even bear to look at him.

It was funny to remember that before he gained his current strength and powers, he too had once been a puny, weak human. Thin, yet well-muscled, Kjell's light grey skin was just beginning to show a few cracks where pulsing blue veins of light were visible.

In place of a helmet, he wore a black cowl over his head. In the distant past, his shirt had shredded away, but he continued to wear the thick, black, leather trousers and pointy metal boots that had made up his uniform so long ago. The charred yew bow he carried barely looked serviceable, yet any arrow he shot would instantly ignite with a magical fire that made his attacks deadly.

Sometimes, to entertain himself, Kjell performed little charades that seemed to frighten the humans even more than usual. That always gave him a chuckle and reminded him of the old days before he became a *Follower of Martokallu*. In his memory, life had been fun then, not the grim existence he now inhabited.

For two generations, Kjell had received the messages in Kallcunarth whenever Martokallu had something he felt the King should know. It was his role to tell the King what Martokallu wanted to happen. Over time, the King, and his father before him, had come to rely heavily upon the advantages such information provided.

However, it was not a position he relished. Loneliness and boredom were his only companions, especially since Lorund left. However, that was unimportant compared to the fact that he had so few opportunities to use his fighting skills. For a long time, his political skills had been more useful. Maintaining the reins for Martokallu in the face of the King's greed and the resistance of that toady, Paal, was difficult and rarely rewarding.

Today, Paal had been more concerned with rushing off to tell the King of the attack than he had been in actually dealing with the problem. While he would never dare to order Kjell to do anything, the course of action he proposed involved nothing more than sitting and waiting until the attackers ran out of arrows.

Of course, Kjell did not know what the attackers planned to accomplish with that little performance, but he was certain they would try to escape before the ammunition ran out. Such an elaborate setup suggested some real long term planning. Unfortunately, Kjell could not quite figure out what the plan might actually be.

What could be the purpose of driving that pair of matched Magnaosseums straight up to the wall? Where did they get the Magnaosseums anyhow? They were not often seen in Abbarkon. Also, what exactly was the purpose of the iron bird-cart? Surely, they must have had something more in mind than simply shooting at the King's Guards who happened to be on wall patrol.

Now here it came, barrelling across the open meadow heading straight toward the ambush Kjell had arranged. He saw them stop. Four people dived out and did some alterations to the outside of the armoured cart. What the purpose did those long wings serve and why re-harness the Magnaosseums?

As Kjell watched from his hiding spot, he considered mounting an attack while they worked outside the armour. However they moved so quickly he judged that he and his soldiers would not be able to get there before the strangers had time to get safely back inside. If he were patient, his ambush would be much more likely for success.

When he led his troop from the castle, Kjell briefed his mounted guards while he jogged beside the horses. Everything was dependent on the soldiers' will to stop the armoured cart, but Kjell was confident that their fear of him was greater than their fear of whoever was inside.

Suddenly, Kjell grabbed his head in pain. He was accustomed to receiving messages from Martokallu, but rarely was there this level of anger involved. His head felt like it would tear apart as he received both the emotion and the message. It came through as a growl. *The King is dead. Involved are the same people who have been ruining our work all over Abbarkon.* Kjell shuddered under the weight of the rage.

Martokallu began to project the images of just how the assassination had occurred. It was confusing to see the hole being bored through the stone wall. There was no sign of how it was being done. Then he saw two people crawl out of the armoured cart and somehow, through the air, into the hole. It was ridiculous. It did not look possible.

Kjell stood frozen as he received the whole story right up to the point where the armoured cart charged across the meadow. Martokallu finished the communication with one hissed command, *This ends now. Take care of it.*

Flint craned his neck to see what had caused Cadmon to lose his calm. He rarely saw the man show any sort of emotion so he knew it must be serious. From his seat in the rear, he caught a glimpse of what might be termed, "a problem". A troop of about fifty mounted men charged across the open field.

Now that the Magnaosseums were moving again, the horses were certainly not gaining, but this did present a problem. Their escape route had always been the weak part of the plan. If they had been able to get away before a force was sent after them, they planned to get off the road into the woods as soon as they crossed the bridge. However, it looked very unlikely that they would be able to disappear under Orma's shield with fifty people watching.

"Watch out," Fleta screamed. Flint felt himself thrown sideways in his seat and he twisted around to see what had happened. They slowed, and then came a terrible, wrenching noise, audible even over the racket of the rattling cart. After a few faltering steps, Flint felt the Magnaosseums resume their speed.

Up front, Egbert whooped and shook the reins to encourage the Magnaosseums to an even faster pace. Beside him, Fleta and Cwenhild had also seen what caused the great beasts to slow. Cwenhild turned in her seat and yelled back, "There was a chain across the road!" She was as exhilarated as Egbert. "The Magnaosseums! They ripped two trees right out of the ground!"

Cadmon immediately recognized the implications of the chain. "It's an ambush!" he shouted. He spun in his seat, trying to see through all of the arrow slots at once. "Where are the attackers? I can't see anyone!"

Suddenly, the top hatch opened and Flint looked up

to see the frightened face of a King's Guard peering in at them. The man appeared to be hanging on for dear life and he was obviously fighting against his fear. He cleared his throat and attempted to speak, but no sound came out. When none of the occupants of the rocking vehicle made a move to shoot him, he tried again, "Kjell orders you to stop."

His voice was barely audible over the sound of the crashing hooves and the rattling cart. Cadmon tore his eyes away from the arrow slits to examine the face of the messenger. "Who orders us to stop?" he demanded incredulously.

The man seemed to find his courage and he spoke more firmly, "Kjell. Kjell orders you to stop."

Hulda spoke sardonically from her seat at the back of *The Hawk*. "That wouldn't be the fellow jogging behind us? The one with the huge bow?"

The man lifted his head, and when he saw who followed, an expression of terror overtook his face once again. Flint watched the man, who could only be one of *The Followers of Martokallu,* raise his bow, and without missing a stride, notch an arrow, and fire.

In this case, the arrow literally "fired". The instant that the arrow left the bowstring, it ignited into a blaze so bright that Flint had to close his eyes. When the arrow struck *The Hawk,* the entire shell was immediately engulfed in flame. The man perched on top disappeared and Flint heard him screaming as he fell.

As quickly as the flames had enveloped the metal vehicle, they disappeared. The temperature rose perceptibly inside the belly, but there was nothing to burn so the flames extinguished themselves.

In the meantime, Hulda raised the repeating bow, aimed it through her arrow slot and fired the entire cartridge into the bare chest of the chasing *Follower*.

Chapter 39 - Pursuit

As soon as *The Follower* collapsed to the road, all thought of pursuit vanished. The mounted King's Guards pulled up and silently gathered around their dead commander. No one was sure whether he could truly be dead. Did *Followers* die? However, no one wanted to be the one to check to find out either. They sat on their nervous horses and watched the glowing blue blood flow out onto the dusty road.

Many of the men had been part of the King's Guards force in Kallcunarth for their entire careers and they were very cautious of the powerful *Followers*. It was rumoured, that they could communicate directly with Martokallu. What if Martokallu was watching them right now?

The circle broke up at the sound of a groan coming from the side of the road. The men shifted uneasily and turned to see the source of the sound. Crawling painfully out of the ditch was the unfortunate man who Kjell had ordered to climb the tree that hung over the road. He was supposed to drop down on the cart and then when the Magnaosseums ran into the chain and the cart stopped, point his bow at them and order them to lay down their weapons.

Of course, it had not actually worked out that way. He had dropped down on the cart as it raced underneath him and barely managed to grab onto something before it was wrenched violently sideways. His bow had been thrown off and he was left without a weapon. Then before he knew what was happening, the cart began to accelerate again.

When they first spotted the crawling man, none of the guards recognized him as one of their own because he and his uniform were so battered. For a group of soldiers they were ridiculously slow to react. Finally, one of his friends recognized the apparition and rushed to his side. "Niek," he said reaching down to pull the injured man to his feet. "I thought you were dead! What happened?"

Niek swayed unsteadily as if he still rode on the rocking cart. "I tried to tell the people inside that contraption, that they needed to stop." He wiped his brow at the memory of his terror, and continued in a shaky voice, "They just ignored the order and kept on going. When I saw Kjell notching his bow, I figured I better get off." He nodded with his scraped chin and smiled wryly as he said, "I jumped for that big clump of gorse. I hoped it might cushion my fall."

The others nodded sombrely. No doubt, his quick thinking had saved him from some terrible burns. Everyone knew that to be touched by one of Kjell's burning arrows was to face months of agony.

At the reminder of their dead commander, the soldiers turned back to the body on the road. Niek saw what they were looking at and asked incredulously, "He's dead?"

The friend who had come to his aid nodded, "We think so."

The guards went back to their silent contemplation of the body. Finally, one of them asked the question they were all thinking, "What are we going to do with him?"

No one seemed willing to risk an answer, but eventually, one man, brave enough to offer a solution, said, "Why don't we move him to the side of the road and ride back to the city to get a cart so we can carry him back for a proper burial." As soon as he spoke, the man peered around with a questioning look on his face. There was no doubt he hoped that Martokallu would approve of his suggestion if he was watching.

With no one actually wanting to touch the body, it was an awkward process to move it off the road. Using a system of poles to shift him along, they managed to get him out of the way of any passing traffic. When faced with the question of what to do with the bow, one man stepped forward boldly and declared, "We should take it. A bow like that would be useful."

No one replied to his brave statement, so he walked over to the spot in the road where the bow lay beside the muddy mess left by Kjell's blood. He stood for a moment looking at the charred wood before reaching down to grasp it. Moments later, the bow clattered to the ground again as the man who had claimed it crouched, gasping in pain. Raising his hand, the others saw that he had been horribly burned in the second he held the bow.

Apparently, this was not a weapon that could be wielded by anyone other than Kjell himself.

"Be there anyone behind us?" yelled Egbert over the clatter of the wheels on the road.

Flint and Hulda had been watching their back trail ever since *The Follower* dropped to the road with a chest full of Hulda's arrows. Since then, there had been no sign of pursuit at all.

"I think it's clear," called Hulda. "We haven't seen anyone since the ambush."

Flint felt *The Hawk* begin to slow as Egbert pulled back on the reins. He had been surprised several times when they passed places where he expected to have Egbert guide them off the road into the woods. Now here they were practically at the front gates to Fasnul.

It had been far too loud inside *The Hawk* to ask questions, but now in the sudden silence, Flint's anxieties flooded out, "Why are we here? Shouldn't we be heading back to Halklyen? What if they somehow find out how to get through Orma's cloak? Shouldn't we be there to help?"

Flint had more questions but he stopped at the look from Cadmon who stood by the ladder. Cadmon had never appreciated his questions. Then Cadmon smiled and said, "Flint, you and Fleta did well. It went exactly according to the plan."

Flint looked down at the unexpected praise and Fleta found herself blushing.

"But," continued Cadmon solemnly, "it's not over yet. Remember that I told you that the defense of Halklyen was in Dell's hands?"

Flint found himself nodding as he waited to hear what Cadmon would say.

"As soon as we left this morning, Dell started evacuating everyone to Fasnul. Orma planned to try to throw a cloak over their route so that Martokallu couldn't see." Cadmon stopped and looked around at the six faces studying him. "We are expecting an attack and this is where we are going to hold off *The Followers.*"

Hain ran at the head of a column of forty *Followers.* After his recovery from the poisoned arrow, Martokallu had sent him back to complete the fight. Now that they knew who was behind the rebellious acts that kept popping up throughout the kingdom, Hain knew exactly where to go.

Martokallu was frustrated by the problems he had been having with his vision. It seemed that every time he followed the rebels, something would go wrong and he would lose them. Hain wondered if Martokallu was losing his power and he suspected that *The Master* had his own doubts as well.

When Martokallu finally figured it out, the explosion of rage in Hain's brain had been almost overwhelming. The realization that there was a cloak over an entire area just outside the capital city was shocking. What sorcerer was powerful enough to maintain such magic?

Martokallu was watching the area carefully now and kept Hain apprised of any comings and goings. The most recent vision showed an ungainly cart being pulled by the Magnaosseums, heading toward Kallcunarth. He could not imagine what they had in mind, but he was certain that Martokallu would not be pleased.

Hain would have liked to be able to intercept the vehicle but he was still too far away. It did not matter now anyway. Their secret was out. The rebels would not be hiding anymore.

He calculated in his head. At this rate, they could arrive at the cloaked woods within fifteen hours. Hain felt a rush of pleasure at the thought that they would finally be able to crush the troublesome rebellion.

Suddenly, Martokallu was inside his head again. He could feel the rage pouring through the link. When he received the vision, he felt his own bolt of fury. The interfering rebels had killed the King. Not that the loss of that snivelling and greedy man would make much difference in the long run, but the thought that the rebels were able to penetrate their defences so easily was alarming.

Hain glanced back at the column behind him and increased his pace slightly.

The entire population of Halklyen was easily aborbed within the walls of Fasnul. Duke Sebastien had arranged for people to move into the homes of residents so very little evidence of the increased numbers was evident.

There were still some concerns about informers working within the walls of Fasnul, but as Dell pointed out, it was no longer as important to maintain the veil of secrecy.

Martokallu would have seen the attack on the King and he would have watched as *The Hawk* drove straight to Fasnul. It was only a question of how long it would be before the attack came.

Duke Sebastien was the next in line for the throne and as far as Fleta was concerned, he was as good as crowned already. In the war meetings, she and Flint sat and listened while plans were laid for defending the town.

Dell had obviously been preparing for this eventuality. Bales of arrows, casks of his favoured explosives, and food enough to feed the town for close to a year stood everywhere. Flint hoped it would not take that long to defeat *The Followers* and place Sebastien on the throne.

He and Fleta had been billeted with a family that had also taken in Orma. They were supposed to report for duty in eight hours and hoped to get a few hours of sleep before that time. Flint felt exhausted, but his mind ran wildly in circles as they strolled toward their assigned house.

"Remember when Hulda shot *The Follower?*" he asked quietly. "Why do you suppose the guards quit following us then? They were on horses but they could have kept up. The Magnaosseums were pulling *The Hawk.*"

"Do you suppose they knew that the King was dead? Maybe without *The Followers*, the King's Guards will be on our side," Fleta suggested hopefully.

This was an interesting idea and they walked in silence while they considered it. They were at the cottage door before Flint finally answered, "Maybe."

Chapter 40 - Rivals

Paal woke up to a room filled with noise and confusion. His head throbbed terribly and when he tried to sit up, he sank back down with a groan. He made another effort, but this time, he merely turned his head toward the spot where all the activity was taking place.

A group of the King's advisors huddled around the throne and spoke in frantic whispers. One of them stepped back and Paal had a clear view of what had upset them. The King sat slumped in his throne; bloodied and limp, with his head twisted at an unnatural angle that left no doubt he was dead.

Reaching up to feel the source of his pain, Paal discovered still wore his helmet, a deep dent creased just above his ear. He struggled to pull it off and immediately felt somewhat better.

One of the advisors noticed he was conscious and moved to his side. "Commander Paal, what happened here? It looks as if a whole force of assassins managed to get past the defences."

Paal's mind felt slow and he made a great effort to recall exactly what had happened. Letting his eyes slide around the room, he saw the two dead guards, the dead King and the servants' entrance behind the throne.

Suddenly it all flooded back to him: the girl with the daggers, the boy with his double swords, the girl wringing the King's neck and then, nothing.

He forced himself upright, ignoring the protest in his head. "It was that crazy bird-cart with the performers. They must have had some way into the city. That's what they were doing. No wonder they just kept up that hail of arrows. It was a distraction."

The advisor started to demand more explanation but Paal held up an imperious finger and the man halted midsentence. Paal thought for a minute then carefully got to his feet. When he found he was able to stand and that the pain in his head had lessened, he turned and headed for the door.

"I will assume command until the next in line to the throne can be brought to Kallcunarth," he stated as he strode forward as quickly as he was able. "Right now, I am taking a force and we will track that cart to wherever they are hiding. I will also send a messenger to Duke Sebastien to let him know that the King is dead." Almost as an afterthought, he added, "Long live the King."

Kjell looked down at his stomach. It was a pincushion of arrows. He plucked one free and examined it with interest. Shorter than usual it looked to be about half the length of a regular arrow. Its tip was not barbed so it pulled out cleanly. As he casually worked to remove the fifteen bolts from his stomach, he realized two strange things. One, he was not dead. And, two, he could not feel the pull of Martokallu's mind.

For almost three centuries, he had known the power of Martokallu through the link that was there even if it was not active. Now, he searched his consciousness, but discovered none of the evil that had been a part of his being for so long. With the removal of the last arrow, he stood up and seeing his bow nearby, bent down and picked it up.

It was the same bow he had carried as a young cavalier in the King's Army. Martokallu had enchanted the bow so that his weapon would be as feared as Hain's blades. Over the years, it had gained its charred exterior from the centuries of firing flaming arrows. Out of curiosity, he drew an arrow from the quiver on his back, nocked and fired it. As it left the bowstring, it immediately burst into flames. It was strange that even though he could no longer feel his connection with *The Master*, his bow maintained its power.

Kjell stood in the middle of the road and glanced back toward the capital before making the decision to head in the opposite direction.

Hain was impatient. He had called a halt to allow a brief rest, but already he regretted it. The last vision Martokallu had sent showed that the strange vehicle which the Magnaosseums were pulling, had gone straight to Fasnul. That was interesting. Why would they be heading to a place not under the cover of their magician's cloak?

He had also received information about the King's Guard out of Kallcunarth. He had watched Kjell being killed and seen the way the human soldiers had given up the chase. And now, that worthless Paal was taking the Guard out of the capital and making double time along the road to Fasnul.

What was his plan? Without a *Follower* travelling with Paal's army, Hain had no direct source of communication. He felt exposed and unprepared. He knew that the best solution was to get his force in place at Fasnul before Paal got there.

It was time to get moving again.

During the night, Kjell heard a large force approaching on the road. He was not sure what made him decide to hide, but before he knew it, he was concealed in the woods. Watching from his comfortable position, reclining on the soft forest undergrowth, he alternately counted the size of the force passing in front of him and casually inspected the rapidly healing wound in his stomach.

Kjell felt oddly disconnected from the army that he had commanded for the last two hundred years. The ant crawling across his leg was far more interesting. Without the driving anger that he had always felt from Martokallu, he had no desire to fight. He did vaguely wonder where the army was headed. It was a large force.

He was not even particularly interested in the fact that the grovelling Paal led the way.

Paal, always tried to prove that he was the real leader of the King's Guard. Kjell had let him believe it when it suited his purposes, but he knew that when push came to shove, *A Follower of Martokallu* is always more powerful than a mere human. Now watching Paal ride purposely past his hiding spot, he wondered whether Paal would still be fighting for Martokallu.

Impulsively, Kjell rose from the forest floor as the last soldier passed, and fell in behind the army. Perhaps he would go to see what had brought Paal out in the middle of the night.

Flint could not stop yawning. Orma had tried to awaken him, but only when Fleta dragged him out of bed, did he actually rouse. The night before, when he and Fleta arrived at the home where they were to be billeted, Orma greeted them and asked to hear the whole story. Flint noticed that she looked particularly tired but he recognized her need to know what had happened. Selfishly, he also recognized that he would feel better if he told her about it.

When they headed off to bed, he struggled to fall asleep as his mind repeatedly replayed the scene in the throne room. He kept seeing the bright blood pumping from the King's throat when he tore his sword free. As well, he could not help wondering about the huge armoured warrior who he had left lying on the floor.

Was he dead?

It had been close to dawn before he finally drifted off and it felt like he had only slept for a few moments before Fleta tumbled him to the floor.

Fleta did not seem to share his fatigue; she practically danced with excitement. "Do you think the King's Army will arrive today?" she asked. Then without waiting for an answer, she continued, "What if the King's Guards are on our side? Maybe we won't even fight. Maybe Duke Sebastien will step up and the Guards will just take their oath to him and everything will be alright."

Flint did not feel the same level of optimism. He grunted, "Maybe." After a few more steps, he continued, "Or maybe, Martokallu will send a whole force of angry *Followers* and we'll end up in a fight for our lives." He was beginning to wake up.

Thinking back to their conversation with Orma, he said, "Orma only wanted to talk about our mission, but did you notice how tired she looked? I bet she covered the entire escape. Maybe *The Followers* won't show up," he added hopefully. "Maybe they don't know where we are."

As they walked along, he started to imagine that they would have no need to defend the town; that the people of Abbarkon would recognize Duke Sebastien as their rightful ruler; that Orma's shield had been so effective that Martokallu had no idea what preparations had been made for war.

His images of the future had become so real that he was completely unprepared for the vision that met his eyes when they reached the top of the stairs. Stretched across the open meadow just out of bow range were about three hundred armoured soldiers and a whole contingent of *Followers*.

Beside him, he heard Fleta let out a long low whistle.

Chapter 41 - Allies

From his position on the top of a small hill outside of Fasnul, Hain watched Paal lead his army into the great open area. He noticed that they stayed carefully out of bow range of the town walls and felt somewhat reassured that the King's Guard still appeared to be allied with Martokallu. Sometimes humans could be unpredictable. Even after all this time, he never felt comfortable working with them.

Evidently it had been a forced march because the men collapsed in groups and no one made any effort to start cooking fires or set up tents. Hain viewed the sloppy preparations with disdain. His own army had been allowed to sit down to rest, but weapons were ready and sentries had been posted.

Judging by the lack of purpose in Paal's force, Hain decided that an immediate visit was necessary. He descended from the hill and stopped for a brief conference with his new second-in-command.

Antal was not an ancient *Follower*. His armour and weapons still had some shine to them, but the number of more experienced warriors had shrunk lately after all the attacks. Hain felt a rumble of rage rush through his body.

He did not remember any *Followers* ever dying before. This rebellion must be crushed.

"Keep the men ready for immediate combat," he ordered. "They may pair off for rests, but one man must remain alert at all times." Hain expected that Antal would have no trouble with these simple commands. It was no more than soldiers of Martokallu were trained to do.

Having taken care of that responsibility, Hain headed briskly for the command post Paal was arranging. He had taken control of the highest point on that side of the field and watched four fatigued soldiers struggle to set up a tent. Hain did not deign to return any of the worried stares he received from the men resting on the ground. Looking neither left nor right, he strode directly toward Paal.

The commander's attention was so taken up with the incompetent fumblings of his underlings that he did not immediately realize who had arrived. When he did turn to look at Hain, he struggled to maintain his composure.

Rather than alarm the human commander, Hain merely nodded. Paal returned the greeting mutely. Seeing that the soldiers had finally managed to get the tent erected, Hain made a decision to appear cooperative. "Welcome Paal," he said smoothly. His voice was a low rumbling. "I am Hain. I too have just arrived. Perhaps we could talk in your tent."

Paal looked surprised at the courteous language. His experience with the insolent Kjell and the belligerent Lorund had led him to expect rude behaviour from all

Followers. He managed a small bow in return and gestured for Hain to precede him into the tent. Meeting up with another *Follower* was not part of his plan.

Paal was not so naïve as to believe that he could just march his army up to the gates of Fasnul and demand entrance. However, he did expect that Duke Sebastien would be pleased with the news he brought. He chose the cautious approach because his trackers assured him that the bird-like vehicle had come straight here. If the rebels were working with the Duke, Paal knew that he would have to be careful.

Now, as the tent flap fell into place behind him, he straightened to his full height, which still left him looking up at the huge *Follower* who stood slightly hunched over in the large tent. Paal steeled himself for the confrontation he knew was coming. Often enough, he had watched the arrogant Kjell casually direct the King's actions. He had always resented it and did not plan to follow that example.

With that in mind, he decided to take the lead in this meeting, "I believe I have heard of you," he said, eyeing the ancient warrior. "Hain, you said?

Hain let a disdainful smile twist his lips as he answered, "I did. And you are Paal, the Supreme Commander of the King's Guard."

Paal's eyes widened. Surely, Hain knew the King had been assassinated. Kjell had made it perfectly clear that *Followers* know everything. "The King is dead," he said slowly.

"Of course he is," answered Hain scornfully. "And

now we have to decide who will be the next King."

"Decide? But Duke Sebastien is the next in line." Paal prepared to argue the rights of succession but before he could continue, Hain stepped closer.

Lifting his hand, Hain struck. Suddenly Paal could not breathe. He looked down and saw with horror that Hain's fingers had penetrated his chest. "Your heart now belongs to Martokallu," Hain intoned. "Everything you do is done to increase the power of *The Master*." Hain squeezed the heart he held in his hand and directed his yellow eyes at Paal.

Paal felt his mind drowning in the power of Hain's gaze. All thoughts of manipulating the situation for his own benefit were gone. Paal knew only that all his efforts would be made for Martokallu.

On top of the town walls, a large group gathered to inspect the two armies camped in the cleared area surrounding the town. Duke Sebastien shook his head and said thoughtfully, "I can understand why the King's Guard followed you here from Kallcunarth, but I hoped that we wouldn't see *The Followers* for a while." Checking to see who was standing within earshot to him, he lowered his voice and muttered a question to Cadmon, "Does this mean Orma's shield was ineffective?"

Cadmon's answer was no more than a slight lifting of his shoulders. He was watching a tall figure make its way from the hillside where *The Followers* had settled, over to the smaller hill that the King's Guard had claimed. The

296

distance made it difficult to be sure, but he thought he recognized the monster from whom he had run after the fight by the waterfall. Apparently, the poison had not killed him.

Surveying the two separate armies, Flint could not resist asking the question that kept running through his head, "Do we have a plan?"

He had not really expected an answer, so he was surprised when Cadmon looked Flint in the eye and replied quietly, "Yes." The big man gave him a reassuring nod and then turned to look at the crowd that had assembled in the square inside the town walls. Raising his voice, he called, "Duke Sebastien, will you be taking command of the town defences?"

The Duke drew himself to his full height as he too scanned the crowd. Speaking loudly enough so that everyone would hear, he declared, "I will not." He continued before the collective intake of breath from the crowd could become a rumble. "I would like to formally pass the defense of Fasnul over to Cadmon of *The Hawks*. From now on, look to him for leadership in all matters related to the protection of the citizens of our town."

Flint expected the assembled people to be surprised at such an announcement, but the reaction he saw was one of relief. He realized that everyone had come to trust that *The Hawks* could protect them from Martokallu and his *Followers*. Watching Cadmon, he also saw the look of agreement that passed between him and Sebastien and he realized that this must be the first part of the plan.

Cadmon then turned to the Captain of the King's Guard, and ordered, "Assemble your men in the Market Square." With a sweeping gesture, he indicated the army straggling over the hill outside the town walls and said, "The troops sitting out there are tired and will be wanting to rest. We will not give them that opportunity."

"Yes, sir," the Captain answered. Without hesitation, he saluted sharply and hurried away.

Cadmon turned to the crowd once again. "Pass the word," he declared in a voice meant to carry. "Arm yourselves and meet in the Market. We will take the fight outside the walls."

Chapter 42 - Preparations

When Flint and Fleta arrived in Market Square, it was already crowded with assembled troops. Immediately after Cadmon had given his order, the two young *Hawks* raced back to the billet where Orma waited. In the morning when they left for the wall, neither of them had anticipated that there would be fighting. "I can't believe we didn't put on our chainmail," Fleta said anxiously.

"I know," Flint agreed. "It makes us look like amateurs. Did you see the other *Hawks*?"

"I did," she puffed. Although they sprinted, they still managed to continue the conversation. "Armed to the teeth, and ready for war in a moment."

At the cottage, they hurriedly slipped into their chainmail; helping each other to fasten the heavy coats. Then they armed themselves with their blades and both of them took the short bows they had used inside *The Hawk*. Flint had figured out a way to wear the quiver on his back so that it did not impede access to his blades.

In their rush to don their armour, neither of them spared a glance for Orma who sat slumped in a chair. As they prepared to dash off again, she called them over.

"Before you go," she called weakly, "take a message to Cadmon for me." Fleta slid to her side and put an arm around the old woman's shoulders.

Never before had Flint thought of Orma as old, but now she sagged wearily in the chair and her voice sounded unsteady and weak. "Tell Cadmon that Martokallu is pounding away at my shield." Almost inaudible, she continued, "I'm not sure how much longer I can hold it."

Fleta wrapped her arms more tightly around Orma, and said, "I'll stay with you. Flint, you go tell Cadmon."

"No," for a moment the strength returned to Orma's voice. "You both go. If I need anything, our host here can help me." Flint and Fleta both looked up at the woman whose cottage they had invaded.

She nodded confidently and moved to Orma's side. Flint and Fleta hesitated a moment longer and then remembering Cadmon's orders, ran off toward the square.

Now they hurried to the spot where Cadmon stood talking with Dell. Both men looked up as Flint and Fleta approached. Fleta covered the last few steps in a rush. She spoke in a hushed voice that would not carry to the nearby crowd, "Cadmon, we just talked to Orma. She wanted you to know that Martokallu is attacking her shield. She's not sure how much longer she can hold on." She paused and looked at Flint, then added, "She looks exhausted. It's taking all of her energy."

Cadmon nodded abruptly and said, "Well, that settles it. We will attack immediately." He leapt up onto a barrel and, clearing his throat, addressed his assembled army.

"Citizens of Abbarkon," he called, and then paused while the soldiers silenced themselves and turned their attention toward him. Cadmon began again, "Citizens of Abbarkon, we have been called upon to face an enemy that fights for the side of evil. For sixteen years, *The Hawks* have stayed in the shadows and tried to work for the side of good. We have watched from the sidelines and prepared for a day when we could make a difference. When we have seen evil, we have tried to stamp it out. Today, we stand up for all that is good in our world.

"Today, we face two armies. One we know is evil. The other, although it has set itself up against us, may be on the side of good. Some of us know people out there in the King's Guard who are good people. Some of us have brothers or sisters, cousins and friends; people we would never want to fight. This does not have to be a war against those people.

"Let us go beyond the safety of these walls and take the fight to the real face of evil in Abbarkon. Let us turn our attack on *The Followers of Martokallu*. There is an army of monsters just beyond these walls and we are going to destroy them. But, we are going to do it without destroying ourselves."

Kjell started to feel even better as he strolled along behind the army. He was enjoying his view of the stars and the sliver of moon kept drawing his eye. When was the last time he had noticed such beauty? As the night passed, he allowed himself to drop further and further behind the King's Guard. There were just too many things to see and think about.

By the time he arrived at the open field in front of Fasnul, Paal had already settled his Guards on a small rise. Across the meadow on a much bigger hill, he could see a second force camped. He was surprised that he could not make out who was in the camp. *A Follower of Martokallu* could usually see clearly across great distances.

It looked as if everyone were resting, so he too settled down to wait.

After his speech, Cadmon handed a small package to Flint and told him to get Geir and head for the gate. Dell would meet them there.

Flint leapt up onto the barrel that Cadmon had just abandoned and scanned the crowd looking for Geir's red head. He easily spotted the big man who stood out from the men surrounding him. Jumping down, he threaded his way through the crowd toward Geir and quickly explained the assignment to him.

Together, they hurried toward the gates. When they arrived, Dell was speaking with the gate guards. As soon as he saw them, he immediately left the conversation and led Flint and Geir into a small guardroom normally used as a shelter in cold weather. There, Flint handed over the package and Dell explained the first part of the plan.

Geir had a brother named Gar; a lieutenant with the King's Guard stationed in Kallcunarth. If Geir could slip unnoticed into the armed camp, he could speak with Gar and explain that no one in Fasnul wanted to fight the King's Guard. Duke Sebastien was next in line for the throne and as far as he and *The Hawks* were concerned, the only enemies were *The Followers*.

The added strength of the Kallcunarth regiment would help in the fight. Geir's brother would have to spread the word quietly and if Orma's shield were failing, they would have to act quickly.

Inside the guardroom, Flint unwrapped the package that Cadmon had sent and was surprised to find that there was nothing visible under the wrappings.

Dell knew what it was though. Delicately, he made as if to pick something up and gave it a shake. "No one will notice you when you are wearing this cloak," he said. Careful not to touch the fabric with his gauntleted hand, he helped Geir find the opening. "You just have to close your eyes and pretend you are putting on a shirt in the dark."

Geir slipped the cloak on over his head. As he did so, he disappeared from the attention of everyone in the room. Flint forced himself to look where he had last seen Geir. He thought he could just make out a vague disturbance of the air in that spot.

When Geir suddenly appeared directly in front of him, Flint nearly jumped out of his skin. Geir gave a short laugh and dropped the cloak back over his head, saying, "It works. I couldn't even see me. What is this thing?"

Dell chuckled as well, and Flint looked at him in

surprise. It was unusual to hear the forbidding man laugh. "We call it the *Cloak of Nothing*," he answered and Flint thought he saw his eyes crinkle in a smile. "Orma made it with magic similar to her invisible paint. The beauty of this cloak, however, is that somehow she managed to make the invisibility permanent. Not like the paint Flint used on his swords that loses its power after a couple of days. The cloak is a well-guarded *Hawk* secret," he added with pride. Nodding thoughtfully, he said, "It has certainly come in handy on more than one occasion over the last few years."

Turning his attention back to the business at hand, Dell asked abruptly, "So, you understand the plan? I will be standing on the top of the wall with eagle eye Flint here, and we will watch for your signal. When you have passed the message to every one of the King's Guards, shoot this arrow into the air." Dell passed over an arrow that looked a little top heavy. "It will explode in a flash of bright light. That will be our signal to start the attack on *The Followers of Martokallu*."

Geir took it cautiously. "It will explode?" he asked nervously.

"Only after you stick it in the fire and shoot it into the air," Dell answered nonchalantly. The man always found a way to make use of fireworks. Flint found it odd that someone who had been so badly burned would be so attracted to blowing things up.

Gingerly, Geir slid the arrow into his quiver and checked the blade in his scabbard. He let the cloak drop around him and asked, "How do I look?"

Flint laughed and answered, "I don't know."

Dell inspected him carefully, nodded in approval and opened the door. Flint felt a rush of air sweep past him and knew that Geir was moving. Dell strolled over to the gate guards and asked quietly for the gate to be opened slightly.

The guards looked at him in surprise, but recognizing Dell as one of *The Hawks* and taking note of the sharpened blades of his gauntlet, they did as they were asked. When Dell simply stood in the opening for a moment, and then stepped inside and pulled the gate closed again, the guards looked even more baffled.

Chapter 43 - Agreements

Paal looked at his soldiers and saw them for what they were: weak and pathetic. He revelled in the newfound power he could feel coursing through his muscles. Before Hain left the tent after their meeting, he instructed Paal to immediately prepare his soldiers for fighting.

It was easy to see that Hain was right. They needed to take the fight right up to the walls of Fasnul. It was useless to wait and see if an agreement could be negotiated.

He could see now that his initial plan had been weak and pathetic. There was no point trying to make contact with Duke Sebastien and offering to escort him to the capital to claim his crown. It was certainly not enough to demand that the people who had killed the King be taken prisoner and set to stand trial.

He scowled as he thought of the young girl and boy who had broken through all the defenses and assassinated the King. He shied away from remembering that the boy had also defeated him in combat.

Noticing the complete lack of discipline and order on the field in front of him, Paal realized that something needed to be done. He strode brusquely to the nearest campfire and addressed the men reclining there. "Rest time is over," he declared. "Prepare yourself for fighting. I want to see this entire force ready to face an enemy before the hour has passed."

He let his eyes pass slowly across the faces of the men and enjoyed the thrill of authority as he watched each man drop his gaze. He gestured impatiently to one of the men. "You there," he said. "Pass the word through the camp. Tell the soldiers to prepare themselves." When the man did not move quickly enough, he barked, "Go!"

With that, the man scrambled to his feet and took off in the direction of the nearest fire. Paal watched with satisfaction. What he did not realize was that his eyes had taken on the telltale signs of a *Follower of Martokallu*. When the men saw the weird glowing colour in his eyes, they knew that he had been possessed and feared for their lives.

Geir might have enjoyed the stroll across the open field as he made his way toward the camp of the King's Guards but he could not quite believe that no one could see him. He kept expecting an attack at any second. He also worried about how he would find his brother. And, when he did find him, how he would announce his presence? He could not just walk up to him, whip off the *Cloak of Nothing* and say hello.

As he approached, he noticed more activity in the camp than there had been a few moments before.

Something was happening. He had best hurry if this plan was to work at all. He jogged the last couple of hundred yards and only slowed to walk quietly past the first guards. They did not even look up from their preparations. Apparently, they were getting ready to move out.

Deciding he better take advantage of all the noise people were making as they saddled horses, checked weapons and settled armour, Geir picked up his pace to a jog and began to search in earnest for Gar. Fortunately, his brother shared Geir's noticeable height and colouring. Before too long, Geir spotted the big man talking to a group of soldiers.

A tent stood nearby and Geir ducked into it hoping that no one was inside. Luck was with him. Wiggling free from the *Cloak of Nothing*, he folded it as small as it would go and stuck it inside his tunic.

Now, was the difficult part. He needed to approach a brother he had not seen in almost a year without creating a scene. Evidently, he would have to do it in plain sight since Gar did not seem to be moving from his group of friends.

If Dell had not made it clear that he needed to do this quickly, Geir might have been tempted to wait for a better moment. After watching briefly, he decided a straightforward approach might be the best.

He pushed the tent flap wide, stood to his full height and headed directly toward Gar. Before he had taken three steps, one of the soldiers in the group noticed him and said something to his brother. Turning to look, the tall, redheaded man's eyes widened in surprise when he saw Geir.

Quickening his pace, Geir covered the ground between them in four more steps. "Don't say anything to give me away. Just nod and listen," Geir spoke quietly before his brother could say anything. "There is going to be an attack very soon and the people inside those walls," he nodded toward Fasnul with his chin, "do not want to be fighting against other people."

Geir saw the looks of confusion that crossed the faces of all the listening men. "There are too many people on both sides of the wall who know each other," he explained. "This is not a war between us. This is a war on *The Followers of Martokallu*." He lowered his voice as he spoke the last words and saw the confusion change to understanding. "I don't know if you have heard of a rebel group known as *The Hawks?*"

One of the men answered, "I heard it was them what killed the King."

Geir nodded and said, "The King was in thrall to Martokallu. In order to bring Abbarkon out from under the influence of evil, the King had to die." He stopped and waited to see what the reaction of the men would be. This was the deciding moment.

His brother ended the brief silence. "I am for the side of good," he said vehemently "What do you want us to do?" He looked at the soldiers beside him and each one of them added their agreement.

Geir felt a wave of relief. "I need you to get the word out to every human soldier in your camp," he said. "We are going to attack *The Followers*. They are so much stronger than we are that they are difficult to kill, but if we work together, we can wipe them out and leave Martokallu without his army."

The men in the small circle looked shocked as Geir outlined the plan. When they began to understand what he was saying, the faces relaxed. One of them spoke up, "We will not waste our lives fighting our friends and brothers on the orders of a mad man. We will fight for the good in Abbarkon."

"You understand. Thank you." Geir felt a burden slide from his shoulders. "Now, how quickly can you pass the word to the rest of your soldiers? As soon as everyone knows, I will fire an exploding arrow and that will signal the start of the attack. We have to hurry, though. Time is short."

Flint kept watch impatiently. Dell had left him standing on the top of the wall with instructions to strike the gong as soon as he saw the exploding arrow. He stared at the field, trying to spot Geir's progress. There was nothing to see and he began to study the camp on the hill trying to catch the moment when Geir showed himself.

As he watched, Flint realized there suddenly seemed to be more activity in the camp. Perhaps Geir had already managed to pass along the message. He studied the action for any clues about what was happening. Frustrated, he realized it was just too far away to distinguish properly what he was seeing.

With a groan of impatience, Flint gave up his intense scrutiny of the King's Guard and turned his attention to the camp of *Followers*. There did not seem to be any new action there. Everything sat in the same precise lines that had been established the moment they arrived.

Suddenly, recognizing that he had let his attention wander from his assigned task, he returned to studying the camp of the King's Guards. Long minutes dragged on while he conscientiously kept his eyes moving around the camp.

When the signal came, he realized that he could have been looking almost anywhere and he still would have seen it. A bright orange fire lit the air, accompanied by the sound of several sharp explosions. Everyone on the wall turned at the noise. Flint grabbed the hammer and struck the gong as loudly as he could.

From that moment on, an element of organized confusion took over the town. Cadmon had ordered a squadron of archers to stay on the wall, but almost everyone else funnelled through the open gate. The first soldiers out into the meadow waited only long enough for their squadron to join them before setting off toward *The Followers'* camp.

Soon, twenty squadrons of ten men each, marched rapidly in the same direction. Flint continued to watch from his vantage point for a few minutes; long enough to see the soldiers in the King's Guard camp also begin to head toward *The Followers*.

They were hurrying and he wondered at their haste.

One man hustled to the front of the disorganized throng and within minutes, they too, had arranged themselves into squadrons of ten. As the soldiers from Fasnul drew even with them, the men from Kallcunarth began to move forward again. Flint wondered which squadron held Geir.

With a jolt, Flint saw that the last of the soldiers had passed through the gates. He would be left behind if he did not hurry.

Chapter 44 - Battle

Geir led the way across the field. Somehow, he had become the commander of the King's Guard from Kallcunarth. He had just survived his first real battle still felt the excitement of the fight. Up to this point, most of his fighting had been done in training. To face a *Follower* as his first real opponent had been terrifying.

Of course, he did not have to face the monster alone. His brother had been right there by his side. Once Gar got over the shock of seeing him, he had immediately understood the wisdom of Cadmon's plan and used his influence to convince the other soldiers in the regiment.

As soon as he saw that people were on his side, Geir carefully drew the exploding arrow from his quiver. Under the questioning gaze of his brother, he quickly stuck the heavy end of the arrow into a nearby fire and without wasting any extra seconds, nocked and fired in one smooth motion. The arrow travelled straight up into the air and just when Geir began to believe that the signal would not work, it crackled to life in a blaze of orange light.

Moments later, Geir spotted a man shouldering his

way through the stunned crowd. Gar stepped forward when he recognized the man, and introduced him to his brother. Reaching out a big hand, Geir said, "Greetings of the day." He spoke politely, but was distracted by the need to get the army moving.

Gar's friend looked around furtively, stepped closer to Geir and said, "I've just seen something I think maybe I should tell you about." He spoke quietly and Gar leaned in to hear. "A big *Follower* was just here and he took Commander Paal into the tent." With a nod of his head, he indicated the command post on the crest of the hill.

Geir lifted his eyebrows in inquiry. Suddenly, the man had his full attention. "When the Commander stepped out, he acted purely strange." Another cautious look let him know no one else was listening so he continued, "I think, maybe, the Commander has been…" He hesitated before almost whispering his fear, "enthralled."

Geir's head shot up as he realized their first target was right here in camp. Looking at his brother, he said, "Get a group of your best men, and let's find this Commander of yours."

It seemed to take too long as they hurried from one group of soldiers to another. Everyone had just seen Commander Paal. When they finally came face to face, with the *Follower*, Geir had been unprepared for the level of hatred he felt pouring out of the man.

Gar tried talking to his Commander, but Paal had simply ignored him. That alone was enough to alert his soldiers that something was wrong. Paal was usually happy to stop and chat. However, the thing that really convinced the King's Guards that their Commander had been turned to the side of evil was the crazed look in his glowing red eyes. There could be no doubt that he was no longer human.

Geir knew that the biggest reason for his victory against *The Follower* was the fact that Paal had been completely unprepared for an attack from his own men. As soon as Geir judged that Paal really was a *Follower,* he did not hesitate to act. After a quick check to see that his brother understood what he planned, he drew his sword and swung hard at Paal's head.

Paal had been standing with his sword unsheathed as he barked orders for his soldiers to prepare an attack. Somehow, when he saw Geir begin his swing, he moved his blade up to protect his neck. Geir was shocked at the power of his block. It was unlike anything he had ever experienced before. He knew he was in trouble when he saw the wicked smile take over Paal's face.

His brother and two other swordsmen jumped in at that point. Although Paal's reactions were lightning fast, the four of them did not allow him any time to press an attack. Eventually, an opportunity opened up and Gar had swung a heavy blow at Paal's side. Paal barely managed to counter it. Seizing the chance, Geir slipped his blade under Paal's arm and pushed until he felt the tip stab right through to the heart. Giving the sword a savage twist, he ripped it clear and stepped back.

For a moment, everyone froze as they watched their Commander. Paal took one last shuddering breath and collapsed on the ground. Initially, no reaction came from the soldiers. Then one of them cried, "That's the first one down. Let's go get the rest of them. For Abbarkon!" With that, the crowd let out a blood curdling shout and started across the meadow on a dead run.

Geir's first thought was to let them go, but he realized that they would all die if they attacked without some sort of organization. He did not hesitate. Sprinting to the front of the pack he summoned all of his strength and shouted, "Stop!" Somehow, the excited soldiers heard the authority in the voice and recalling themselves, came to an abrupt halt.

Surprised at his success, Geir had been uncertain about what to say next. He let his eyes sweep slowly over the faces of the King's Guards and allowed his gaze to calm them. He knew they were waiting for orders because that is what soldiers did. "Muster up in your cohorts," he had shouted. Then he waited while the men sorted themselves out. Shortly, they stood at attention waiting for his next order.

"We are going to do this with as few casualties as possible," he began. Geir was surprised at the looks of relief he saw. He thought they had turned into a mob, but most of them retained their sense. "The plan is to try to isolate each *Follower* so that we have at least ten men taking on one. You saw what happened when four of us fought Paal. We can do this if we work together."

By this time, the cohorts streaming out of the open gates of Fasnul had almost made it to where Geir stood with his soldiers. He watched them come for a moment and then turned his attention back to the men in front of

316

him. "Two armies will fight side by side, and we will win!" The last three words he shouted and the men roared in approval. Geir was not certain where the words were coming from, but he knew that they were true.

As the soldiers from Fasnul drew even with the King's Guard from Kallcunarth, Geir turned and began to lead the way toward the camp on the hill.

Igon had been one of the first men through the gates. At his back, he led a cohort of fighters who he had just met that morning not long after he arrived in Fasnul from the library at Oruk. He and Dagur left the guard duty to the replacements as soon as they arrived. Halvor had briefly considered accompanying them, but the draw of the books was too powerful.

The soldiers behind him seemed like good types but he knew that he would be the one to engage whatever *Follower* they ended up fighting. He just hoped they would be there to back him up if he ran into trouble. In anticipation, he tightened his grips on the flails he carried in each hand. His head still pained him on occasion after his run-in with the huge *Follower* by the waterfall. Today, he would get his revenge.

Marching steadfastly across the field, Igon divided his attention between *The Followers* on the top of the hill in front of him and what was happening in the King's Guards' camp. He had expected that when Cadmon ordered him forward, the King's Guards from Kallcunarth would be ready to move.

However, so far, all he could see was some sort of commotion at the highest point of the camp. Even as he watched, however, the crowd of soldiers broke up and began to run toward *The Followers'* hill.

Igon saw a very tall, redheaded man dash to the front of the mob and shout them to a standstill. Recognizing Geir, he watched with interest as the man urged the men into some semblance of order. When Igon and his men drew abreast, Geir commanded his army to move forward and just like that, all signs of the undisciplined horde that had charged across the meadow were gone.

Kjell sat up from where he had been watching the light play across the leaves. Incredibly, it had been years since he looked at anything worthwhile. Glancing around he saw Paal's army move out.

Feeling curious, he rose to his feet and followed. As he strolled through the camp the soldiers had just left, he was struck by the lack of order. In his experience, army camps were always set up on a perfect grid. This seemed to be rather disorganized. He found he was in no rush to catch up to the departing army.

Suddenly, he stopped short. Paal lay in a puddle of glowing blood. Kjell studied the scene with interest. He knew the significance of the blood immediately. For over two hundred years, whenever he cut himself, the resulting wound always bled with blood that held a life of its own. What had happened here? Who had turned Paal? And, more intriguing, who had defeated him in battle so soon after he gained his powers?

Kjell stepped away from the body and looked out across the meadow. He saw the force from Fasnul meet up with the King's Guard and together, they continued toward the distant camp. Suddenly, he understood. They would not be fighting each other. The humans had joined forces to battle *The Followers of Martokallu*.

Thoughtfully, Kjell watched the advancing army. He felt something inside him working to make a decision. For so long he had been a *Follower of Martokallu* and he had not had a thought of his own. Everything had been tainted by the evil that was Martokallu. Now, however, he was a man again. Men should fight against evil. He would join the fight against *The Followers*.

Igon nodded at Geir from his position at the front of the King's Guard out of Fasnul. Geir lifted a hand in reply and gave a bemused smile in return. The two armies merged and continued to advance until they were just outside bowshot of *The Followers* on the hill. Igon raised a hand to halt the squadrons and Geir repeated the gesture for the men who followed him. They needed to get set up for the attack.

It appeared as if *The Followers* were in on the plan as well. They had lined themselves up in a single row, facing the soldiers with weapons drawn. This would make it easier to send squadrons in with specific targets.

Turning, Geir shouted an order for the squadrons to line up. Gar had done a fine job of ensuring that each squadron had someone who understood what to do. Geir watched the line spread out to mirror the formation of *The Followers*. Beside him, the squadrons from Fasnul did the same thing. Geir could see at least one *Hawk* in every squadron. That made sense. No one trained with the intensity of *The Hawks*.

As soon as enough squadrons in moved into place to offer every *Follower* an opponent, Igon raised his flails, and shouted, "Forward!"

The entire line began to advance at a slow walk. The soldiers all knew that they needed to pace themselves if they wanted to be able to fight when they got to the top of the hill. Geir fought his urge to break into a run. Patience would get them there.

Chapter 45 - War

Hain watched the two armies draw together and then without even slowing, head straight toward his camp. What were they doing? He had left Paal in charge, with very clear orders that he was to attack Fasnul immediately. He had been surprised to see the gates of Fasnul open just when it appeared that the King's Guard were prepared to mobilize.

Watching the soldiers' determined progress across the field, he suddenly understood that somehow the two forces had formed a pact to unite. In his confusion, his first thought was to contact Martokallu. However, since his arrival at Fasnul, he had been unable to feel the mind of *The Master*. It was yet another thing that had been bothering him.

He turned his attention to *The Followers* who stood by his side. They too watched the progress of the armies. He could see that they eagerly anticipated the fight to come. If he gave the order, he knew they would charge down the hill to attack. Only their years of discipline held them in their positions at the top of the hill.

For a moment, he considered unleashing his force on

the advancing army but he waited. If he made the men climb the hill, they would be tired. Then as he watched, he realized that it did not matter. These were mere humans. He and *The Followers* were members of an elite force, with enhanced powers. The humans did not have a chance. With that thought, he raised his arm and ordered his fighters forward.

Igon saw *The Followers* start their charge. He felt a flash of fear and then reassured himself that he had seen enough *Followers* killed to know that it was possible.

Geir had counted off *The Followers* and assigned each squadron a target. Igon headed directly toward a monstrously large troll-like creature hurtling down the hill. *The Follower* carried a huge axe on his back and although he held no weapon, the backs of his hands and forearms were covered in wicked looking barbs.

Igon planted his feet and started his flails spinning. Out of the corners of his eyes, he could see his squadron moving into position as well.

No sooner had he found his rhythm than the monster crashed into him. The impact almost knocked him off his feet and he felt a pain in his cheek as the barbs raked his face. *The Follower* used his force to grab the swirling chains of the flails. Regaining his balance, Igon turned the handles of his weapons to expose the blades embedded there.

Although limited by the length of chain held in *The Follower's* powerful grip, he jabbed both blades up into its stomach and ripped sideways. His first thrust somehow broke through the old chainmail. Gritting his teeth, he tore in opposite directions. The armour gave away like a threadbare piece of cloth. The resulting wound exposed *The Follower's* guts which spilled brightly glowing gore onto the field.

While Igon stood caught in the twisted grasp of *The Follower*, one of his squad mates stepped closer. Igon saw the man raise his sword and ducked. The blade came sweeping down and *The Follower's* head bounced to the ground.

Flint joined the last squadron through the gates, which turned out to be captained by Cwenhild. She explained that they were a reserve squad assigned the responsibility of watching for points along the line where another squad might have been overrun.

Except for Flint and one tall member of the King's Guard, all of the people in the last squadron were archers. Flint could see the logic in that. An archer can make a difference from a distance. He wondered if he had missed his chance to be a part of the battle by waiting too long.

By the time they got close to *The Followers'* camp, the fighting was well under way. Flint spotted Igon struggling with a huge opponent. For a minute, he thought the big man was lost. Then, unexpectedly, it was *The Follower* whose body sagged sideways as his head went flying.

Everywhere he looked, Flint saw teams of humans battling against the tireless *Followers*. He tried desperately to spot Fleta in the field. His heart dropped when he finally caught sight of her. Standing with Hulda, a little way back from anyone engaged in the fighting, she held a throwing dagger in each hand. Suddenly, *The Follower* challenging her squadron broke through his opponent and charged directly toward the two women.

Both Fleta and Hulda threw their daggers at the speeding target. Four daggers struck home, but did nothing to slow the advance. Flint started forward, but before he took two steps, a flaming arrow whizzed past his head and with a sickening thud, found its mark in the belly of the attacking *Follower*.

Flint turned to see the source of the rescue and saw the strangest sight. The man wore neither the flashy blue and white uniform of the King's Guard, nor the black of *The Hawks*. In fact, he wore no shirt at all and his stomach was a vivid scar of mottled tissue. His trousers appeared to be of much-scuffed leather and the bow he held looked to have been charred in a fire.

Despite his ragged appearance, Flint knew that the man had saved the life of both Hulda and Fleta. He saw the man give a small, satisfied smile as he watched the body of *The Follower* burn.

From the moment Cadmon passed through the gates of Fasnul, he kept the big *Follower* in his sights. It had to be the one known as Hain; the one he had run away from in the valley of the waterfall. Never before, had Cadmon turned from a fight. This time, he was determined he would triumph.

Making his way across the field, he kept his attention on his enemy and ensured that his squadron stayed in the right position for an attack.

When he saw *The Follower* raise his hand to order a charge, Cadmon felt a rush of adrenalin that left him with a sense of power. He stopped his squadron right where they were rather than continue the charge up the hill.

As he watched, his enemy drew the two swords he remembered. With speed greater than Cadmon would have imagined possible, the monster was suddenly on top of him. He barely had time to get the *Rising Star* around to defend against the double blows delivered in quick succession.

Somehow, Cadmon still had time to think of the training he had done with Flint and to mentally thank the boy for teaching him the tricks of a two-handed swordsman. He twisted under the attack and swung around to bring himself into position to attack, but again, his opponent was faster. Just like the fight by the waterfall, no matter what he did, the monster seemed to anticipate his moves and to counter easily.

Hain raised his sword and brought it down hard. Cadmon's arm went numb under the power of the blow Somehow *Rising Star* tumbled from his grip. He lost his balance. The next thing he knew, the flat of a sword smashed into his ribs and the ground rushed up at him.

Desperately, he rolled to his back and brought his feet up to fend off his attacker. *The Follower* casually sheathed one sword and reaching down, used that hand to punch Cadmon a punishing blow in the ribs. Cadmon felt his ribs break and suddenly he was unable to breathe.

It appeared as if Hain wanted to enjoy the pleasure of killing Cadmon with his bare hands. He dealt another mighty blow to Cadmon's ribs and a trickle of blood ran out of Cadmon's mouth.

But then, Dell was there. He leapt upon the back of the attacker and plunged a dagger deep into his throat. Tearing sideways with his right hand, he opened up a wound that sent bright blood flooding over Cadmon. With his gauntleted left hand, Dell grabbed the back of *The Follower's* neck and ripped the spinal cord free with a savage cry of triumph.

Shoving the suddenly powerless body away from Cadmon, Dell rose to survey the battlefield. At that moment, a blinding light flashed near the crest of the hill. Everyone looked up to see a huge dark figure appear from out of nowhere. Fighting stopped while the warriors on both sides stared at the newcomer.

Flint gaped at the hooded monster directly above him on the hill. In a flash, he understood that he faced Martokallu. An icicle of dread stabbed him in the stomach and he stood frozen in place. Those eyes felt like two black vortexes draining the life out of the world.

The robe he wore was covered in intricate yellow symbols that seemed to move even as Flint tried to make out what they were. There were also flecks of yellow light on the grey plate armour that covered part of the robe. Somehow, the carefully shaped metal sent shivers through anyone who looked upon it. His conical helmet, worn over a hood, did not cover his entire face. A long strip of metal down the middle, meant to protect his nose, served to draw any opponent's gaze to the eyes that could suck all will from a human.

Flint covered his eyes as another flash of light ripped through the air. When he looked again, the figure held a giant golden sword in one hand and a large staff in the other. Those horrible eyes scanned over the entire battlefield and came to rest on Flint again.

The terror Flint felt washing over him was worse than any nightmare but he had no hope that waking up would make the monster disappear.

As the creature took a slow step forward, all of his training left him and Flint stood rooted to the spot. His mind was numb in the face of the power directed his way. Until, out of the corner of his eye, he caught a flash of movement.

Fleta moved up beside him. Suddenly a dagger was sticking into Martokallu's helmet. It did not appear to penetrate the metal very deeply and after hanging precariously for a moment, it clattered to the ground. But, it was enough to break the spell that held Flint rooted where he stood.

Distracted, the monster briefly halted his progress toward Flint. With Fleta at his side, Flint was finally able to shake the torpor that had taken over his mind. A movement off to the side caught Martokallu's attention and he turned just in time to catch Dell's charge. Almost indifferently, Martokallu tossed the man across the field. When Martokallu stood up again to assess the situation, he caught sight of Hain's body lying beside Cadmon.

In the blink of an eye, he stood over Cadmon who still struggled to breathe. Martokallu regarded the body of his second-in-command, rage visibly pouring out of him in streams of ugly yellow light. The golden sword flashed in the sun before embedding itself in Cadmon's chest.

With a cry, Flint launched himself at Martokallu. His first blade ripped through the ancient armour. Martokallu screamed in agony and the entire world shuddered, sending everyone tumbling to their knees. Raising his head, Flint saw that Martokallu had grown to an immense size so that he towered over the battlefield.

The gaze of those piercing eyes held Flint pinned to the ground. For an instant, he dared to hope that he had accomplished the ultimate goal in the fight against evil. But then Martokallu's massive mouth opened and a terrifying voice grated, "This is not over."

In a final burst of light, Martokallu vanished, taking Flint's sword with him. At the disappearance of their leader, *The Followers* who had all watched the drama with as much interest as the humans, sheathed their weapons, turned south and began to run.

Chapter 46 - Aftermath

Flint scrambled to Cadmon's side. He still breathed but it was a weak and raspy sound. "Flint," he whispered on a shaky exhalation. "Find the *Rising Star*. Bring her to me."

The sword lay a few feet away from Cadmon's outstretched hand. From his knees, Flint stretched out and grasped the hilt. Crawling back to Cadmon, he tried to put the sword in the injured man's hand, but Cadmon was not finished. Struggling to speak, he said, "She is yours now. Take good care of her."

Flint protested, "Cadmon, no. Orma will…"

The dying man interrupted, "My time is over." He drew another slow painful breath and began to cough. More blood bubbled to his lips. He tried to speak again, "Gode will help you…" The rest of the breath sighed out of him and he ceased to breathe.

Flint felt a tear roll down his cheek and he looked up to find a circle of concerned faces surrounding him and Cadmon.

Fleta dropped down beside him. "He has passed over," she said gently, reaching out and closing Cadmon's staring eyes. They all stayed in silence beside the body for a long while.

It was horrible moment. It was an impossible moment. Impossible that Cadmon could have died when they were so close to their goal. Finally, wiping his tears with the back of grubby hand, Flint rose, holding the *Rising Star* in his hand.

He gazed around at the body strewn battlefield. There did not appear to be very many human casualties but at regular intervals the mutilated remains of the slaughtered *Followers* lay where they had fallen. Flint spotted the body of a man he had talked to on the wall earlier that day. Was that really just this morning?

Looking around at the soldiers who stood watching him uncertainly, he felt something needed to be said.

Raising Cadmon's meteorite sword high, Flint called out in a voice stronger than he expected, "We have had a victory here." He paused and studied the faces of the people who turned to him. "Men and women have fought for the side of good." There was a ripple of agreement. "We have fought against the face of evil," his voice rose as he realized the truth of what he was saying, "and we have triumphed!"

The roar of approval was deafening.

It was a long walk back to the town gates. The ground that had been travelled so eagerly only a short time earlier now bore the weight of a litter fashioned from the canvas of a *Follower's* tent. Igon and Geir carried Cadmon's body while Fleta, Flint, Gode, Dell, Hulda and

Cwenhild paced by his side. Flint's mind was reeling with what had just occurred. What had happened to Martokallu? Was he dead or did he just retreat from the field of battle?

Flint was so wrapped up in his own thoughts that he paid little attention to anyone else in the victorious army. Vaguely aware of the spirit of elation that buoyed the soldiers around him, he gradually came to notice a disturbance in the crowd. Fleta and Hulda followed him as he left Cadmon's side and made his way over to the source of the confusion.

Surrounded by a circle of angry, yet cautious soldiers, stood the shirtless man Flint recognized from the battle. He hesitated a moment before forcing himself to step forward. "What is going on here?" he demanded.

One of the soldiers turned and indignantly informed Flint, "He is Kjell. One of *The Followers.* He was our commander back in Kallcunarth." Almost accusingly, he added, "We watched him die!"

Flint recoiled at that piece of information and looked back at the battlefield where they had left a team of soldiers to deal with the bodies of the dead *Followers.* He turned to a soldier he recognized and told him, "Take a group of men and run back to where they are burying the bodies. Tell them to be careful." On second thought, he added, "Tell them to burn the bodies." The man nodded and Flint watched him head off before turning back to the calmly smiling *Follower.*

The man regarded him with a quizzical look. In return, Flint studied the man as he recalled how the charred and battered-looking bow that he held had fired a flaming arrow. "Who are you?" Flint asked.

To the surprise of the watching men, *The Follower* smiled happily and said simply, "I am Kjell." There was a murmur of angry voices, but he continued blithely, "For many years, I have been a *Follower of Martokallu*. Now, thanks to an archer riding inside a metal bird, *The Follower* is gone and Kjell is back." He followed this strange statement with an open and happy smile before turning apologetically toward the man who had declared that he had seen Kjell die. "It was *The Follower* you saw die."

Hulda had a look of wonder on her face as she said, "I put fifteen arrows in you yesterday."

Kjell nodded serenely, "I thank you for that."

Fleta stepped forward. "This is the man who shot the flaming arrow and saved Hulda and me," she told the watching crowd. Flint nodded thoughtfully in agreement.

"Kjell," Flint asked, "what do you want?"

The smile that lit the man's face was almost beatific as he answered, "I want to live as a man lives. I want to see the beauty in the world. I want to know goodness."

This declaration startled Flint and the people around him. After a moment's thought, Flint turned to the bewildered soldiers surrounding Kjell. "Will you allow Kjell to join humanity again?" he asked. "Will you let him come with us?"

There were disgruntled mutters, but no one anything. Finally, one man declared, "I was standing too close when Martokallu appeared today. If he'd looked into my eyes for even a moment, I know he would've

332

taken my soul." He stepped toward Kjell with an outstretched hand. "If that's what happened to you, mate, and now you're free, I welcome you back."

Orma sat slumped in the rocking chair by the fire. Fleta was shocked to see that she had aged twenty years since they said goodbye that morning. Her eyes, when she opened them, were sunk deeply into black circles and the skin of her face stretched tightly across the bones of her face. Cwenhild crossed the room quickly and sank down beside her mother.

"There is no need to hold it any longer," she said gently. "Let it go."

"It is gone. He broke my shield," answered Orma wearily. "For hours he pounded against my energy and finally, it all just erupted, and the cloak was gone." She raised her eyes and let her gaze take in the faces surrounding her. "What has happened?"

Cwenhild answered quietly, "We have defeated Martokallu and his *Followers*, mother."

Orma's eyes snapped wide and she said, "He came himself?"

Cwenhild nodded, "Fleta and Flint fought him and he vanished with Flint's sword still piercing his stomach."

Orma's eyes found Flint and she immediately spotted the sword he wore sheathed at his waist. The blade was too long for the scabbard on his back so he had gently taken the one Cadmon had always worn.

Flint hitched himself a little taller, and forced himself

to tell her, "Cadmon is dead, Orma. Martokallu made sure of that." His voice trembled as he shared the news.

Gode's deep voice rumbled from the doorway, "Cadmon gave Flint the *Rising Star*."

Flint felt a rush of grief tinged with relief. He had not realized just how worried he had been about Gode's reaction. How could Cadmon have thought him worthy of such a powerful weapon?

Orma's eyes found his, and she said, "I think Cadmon chose wisely."

Chapter 47 - Death and Life

In the days leading up to Cadmon's funeral, events were a rush of confusion for Flint. Egbert enlisted Flint and Fleta's help and together they worked hard at the forge in Fasnul. They fashioned a casket to look like a smaller version of the armored vehicle, *The Hawk*. It even had the wings which could fold out of the way.

When it was completed, they loaded it onto a small, horse-drawn cart and drove through town toward the house where Orma had laid out Cadmon's body.

It was not a long trip, but by the time they passed through the narrow streets, a large crowd had joined the procession. At first, it was only a few curious children drawn in by the look of the elegant wings protruding from the cart. But, before they passed too many streets, townspeople began to leave their work to walk behind the cart.

It was a silent and respectful crowd that stood outside the house as Flint and Egbert unloaded the casket and carried it inside. They found Orma sitting vigil beside Cadmon's body. She rose slowly as they came into the cottage. Fleta went to her and took her hands. "Egbert has built a beautiful memorial for Cadmon," she said.

Orma moved aside to allow Flint and Egbert to set *The Hawk* coffin on the floor beside the table where Cadmon was laid out. Turning to look at Cadmon's body, Flint was swept with the feeling that Cadmon was merely resting. His wounds were not visible under the black clothing he wore, and his face, although pale, had an almost peaceful look. A wave of overwhelming grief shook Flint and he rocked back on his heels as if struck.

Coming to stand behind him and grasping his shoulders, Orma said, "It is never easy to lose someone. When he is a man who lived with passion and conviction, it is all the more difficult. We will mourn him, but we will not forget him." Flint felt a tear roll down his cheek and when he looked across the room, he saw that Fleta's face was wet as well.

For a long moment, everyone simply stood quietly looking down at Cadmon's peaceful face. Flint saw Gode unabashedly wipe tears from his face. When he turned to look at Orma, she dropped her hands from his shoulders and reached into a pocket to pull out a damp handkerchief which she used to wipe her face.

Stepping back and looking away from the body, she rubbed her hands together briskly and said, "We should be on our way. It is already getting late."

In contrast to her words, she abruptly halted as the casket caught her eye. Orma studied the intricate engravings on the metal casket. "Oh, Egbert, it is beautiful," she said running her finger over the feathery tracings on the back of the bird. Another tear made its own path down her wrinkled cheek. Watching her, Fleta felt her throat close up. "It will be a most fitting monument for a man who believed so fiercely in the fight for freedom in Abbarkon."

Just as she finished speaking, Flint looked up to see Gode, Igon, and Dell standing in the open door of the house. Wordlessly, they nodded at Orma and Egbert and then without waiting for an invitation, they stepped into the room. Positioning themselves along Cadmon's body, they gently lifted him while Egbert opened the lid to the casket. Settling the body carefully on the woolen blanket Fleta had placed inside, they stepped back and watched solemnly while Flint helped Egbert fasten the latches.

Orma moved aside while the other six each took a position beside the handles on the casket. As one, they lifted and started forward. The crowd outside the house had grown and when the people saw the casket, a murmur rippled through the crowd.

As if their appearance was a cue, someone near the back of the crowd began to sing. The sound spiraled clean and pure up into the clear blue sky, drawing tears from every listener. For a moment, the pallbearers stood frozen as they listened to the mournful melody. Finally, with Gode and Igon in the lead, they carefully made their way to the cart where the horse waited patiently.

Egbert climbed up onto the seat while Gode and Flint arranged the wings as if for flight. When Egbert nudged the horse into motion, and *The Hawk* began its final journey, the song ended and somewhere, a drummer took up a sombre beat. Moving at a slow, walking pace, the funeral procession wound through the streets toward the cemetery at the edge of town.

Flint straightened in his saddle and looked around at the other *Hawks*. They had left Fasnul earlier that day and were heading toward Kallcunarth for Sebastien's coronation ceremony. It was strange to remember that Cadmon would not be there.

Standing at the graveside the day before, Flint had felt empty and alone, even with Fleta standing at his side. She had reached over and taken his hand as they stood listening to Gode talk about his friend.

"He wouldn't want us to call him a hero," Gode had begun, which managed to draw several smiles. "But he was a man with a clear vision of what was wrong with this world and he worked hard every day, in an effort to make a change."

Flint hoped that all the fighting and killing that had been done in the name of justice would make a difference to the people of Abbarkon. As he rode along at the head of the column, he remembered his life as a servant for Duke Dedrick. The fear he lived with daily had almost been forgotten in the three years he had lived as a *Hawk*.

During the last year, he had felt his share of fear, of course, but it was not the helpless fear of a victim; it was the type of fear that makes you careful. That was how people should be able to live. That was the change that King Sebastien should be able to bring to his people.

They drew close to the open gates of Kallcunarth and Flint was lifted from his reverie by the sound of a low rumble. He searched for the source of the noise. Only when he passed through the gates and saw the people lining the streets did he realize he was hearing cheering. The people of Kallcunarth repeatedly shouted, "Thank you, Hawks," and "Long live King Sebastien."

The sound of the regular chanting made him realize that *The Hawks* were no longer a secret society of people fighting against evil. Riding beside Fleta, he watched wide-eyed as the crowd cried, "Hawks! Hawks! Hawks! Hawks!"

Flint thought of his previous entrance into the city and looked over at Fleta. He guessed by the look on her face that she remembered the same thing.

She grinned as she asked, shouting to be heard over the excited crowd, "Do you think they patched the hole we made?"

"It'll be the first thing I check," he responded with an answering smile.

When they arrived at the palace, a servant stepped forward to escort *The Hawks* to a barracks that had been set aside specifically for them. The coronation was to take place later that evening in the square just off the palace.

Flint was surprised to have a boy reach out and offer to take his horse to the stable. After a moment of consideration, he handed over the reins, as did most of the other *Hawks*. Apparently, they were to be treated as visitors today. That would probably change if they stayed any length of time, thought Flint as he made his way into the barracks. He peeked into several of the rooms, each of which had four beds.

Choosing randomly, he entered one and dumped his saddlebag beside a bed. Flopping down, he let his booted feet hang off the end of the sturdily constructed bunk. Dell, Gode and Igon followed him into the room. Before long, they were all reclining easily.

They would have to get cleaned up before the ceremony, but it seemed the first time in ages that there had been a moment to relax. They lay there in comfortable silence as each man followed his own thoughts.

A sudden clatter of footsteps in the hallway interrupted their musings. Flint heard a murmur of voices and the door to their room opened. Geir stuck his head in and said, "This man says he has a message for *The Hawks.*"

The four men sat up as a shaggy-looking young man was ushered into the room. He wore a common brown traveller's cloak but the elegant sword hanging from his belt and the polished black staff gave him away as someone more important than a mere messenger. "I have a message for *The Hawks,*" he declared imperiously.

Gode swung his feet to the floor and stood up. "A message from whom?" he asked warily.

In the same commanding voice, the visitor answered, "I come from *The Worshippers of Dreff.*

TURN THE PAGE FOR A PREVIEW OF

THE HAWKS

BOOK TWO:

The God Sword

Prologue

Egbert studied the thin, shaggy-haired man in front of him, trying to decide whether he should trust the message he carried. Leaning back in his chair and stretching out his feet, Egbert laced his calloused hands across his round belly. His leisurely motions belied the curiosity and excitement which seethed just beneath his placid exterior.

When Flint and Gode located him in the King's foundry after King Sebastien's coronation ceremony, they had presented a garbled account of the messenger's story. Obviously intrigued by the proposal that the small man carried, both Flint and Gode were eager to hear Egbert's opinion.

The inventor covered his amusement at their confusion about the man's insistence on speaking specifically with him. Egbert had understood the connection immediately, but he chose not to explain it to the younger *Hawks*.

When he was comfortable, Egbert said slowly, "Well met, Urravon." He nodded his head in an informal bow and then indicated the two younger men who hovered at his side and said, "Now, Flint and Gode here did pass on your message, but I think it would be good to hear it from yourself. Please explain to me, and take your time. I want to hear the whole story. Why have you come to *The Hawks* and what exactly do you think I can do for you?"

Chapter 1 - Dancing

The music was unlike anything Flint had ever heard. They never danced like this in Abbarkon. He supposed that he and his partner must look a little mismatched. The dwarf girl, who had pulled him to his feet, barely came up to his elbows. As he tried to follow her skipping feet, he thought back on the path that had led him to this fireside celebration.

Since the afternoon of King Sebastien's coronation, events had tumbled one on top of another. He was still not certain of all the details, but the messenger from Cheveral had definitely peaked Egbert's interest. A meeting of *The Talons* had been called that same evening.

Of course, the meeting could not take place in Hawk Hut, but it was not too difficult to attain access to a private meeting room in the palace. Asdis and Penn had been stationed outside the only door to prevent any eavesdropping: accidental or otherwise.

It was odd to sit down with all *The Talons*, knowing that Cadmon was not there to guide the discussion. Flint had seen Gode hesitate before stepping to the front of the room to welcome everyone and turn the meeting over to Egbert.

The man that Flint knew to be a very talented blacksmith and inventor stepped to the front of the room eagerly. "No doubt," he had begun, "you will be surprised at what I be saying today. But I know that you will be understanding why I believe this to be a rare opportunity." The corners of Egbert's eyes had crinkled as he beamed at his listeners. "We be invited to join the search for *The God Sword.*" No reaction had followed that announcement, so after a thoughtful nod to himself, Egbert had explained further.

"What I am meaning to say, is that there be a story about a sword that could be the ultimate weapon in our fight against Martokallu." At that, a rumble passed through the room. Egbert smiled and threw more fuel on the fire when he said, "A weapon that we must be searching for beyond the borders of Abbarkon." Flint remembered the increased tension that statement had caused. Immediately, questions had been fired from the floor.

No one was really certain what had happened to Martokallu after he left that battlefield with Flint's sword still embedded in his stomach. The idea of travelling past the evil sorcerer's fortress in the western part of the Chain of Thollcrawnow was a frightening one. As well, no one in *The Talons* was ready to leave the borders of Abbarkon so soon after King Sebastien had taken his crown. How could they leave the new King with a weakened support?

Flint had listened in fascination while Egbert gradually

brought all of *The Talons* over to his point of view. Not once had Egbert tried to force his opinion on the group. He merely took the time to explain what he knew about the request that the messenger carried. It had been a long story.

Egbert started by telling them about his father, Adler Martell. Flint was shocked to learn that Egbert was the son of a man who had held a very important hereditary post within the Temple of Dworgunul in Tsaralvia.

Adler had been barely seventeen when his father died and he had to assume the title of *Hammer of Dworgunul*. The primary responsibility of the role was the preservation of the stories of the past. Adler and his twin brother, Harbert, had been trained since childhood in the arts of storytelling.

From the beginning, Harbert had shown the true talent and passion for the role. Adler preferred to spend his time at the forge. However, Adler was the eldest, even if it was only by five minutes. For that reason, it had always been known that he would be the one to inherit the title. Often enough the brothers had talked about switching identities, but although they were physically identical, Adler's time at the forge had turned him into a powerfully built man while his brother always looked a little softer.

By the time they were seventeen when their father died, there was no doubt in anyone's mind about who was who. The day after the funeral, Adler was anointed *Hammer of Dworgunul* and Harbert took his pledge to support his brother forever.

For over a year, Adler sat in the chair of power whenever the leaders of Tsaralvia met. His task was to offer stories from the past that would confirm that the decisions being handed down were the right ones. For over a year, Harbert helped Adler review the stories and provide validation of the leaders' decisions. For over a year, Adler had neither the time nor the energy to visit the forge where he had worked every spare moment of his childhood.

Neither he nor Harbert were happy with the situation. Adler never felt that he did justice to the stories and Harbert knew that there were occasions when *The Hammer* should have provided more support.

One morning, Adler resolved to do something about the situation. He spoke with Harbert and let him know that he would be leaving.

The way Egbert told the story, it sounded as if Harbert had not offered any arguments. They talked about how to make it so that the elders would have to accept Adler's decision. Harbert even found something in the stories to support their decision. Adler left a letter saying that he was dead to the country and he would never again step up to be *The Hammer of Dworgunul.* He would leave the responsibility to his brother and head north to Abbarkon.

By dawn the next day, Adler was on the road. He carried nothing more with him than the clothes on his back, the stories in his head and a hammer he had made himself. His goal was to travel up to Abbarkon, find a village where he could become the blacksmith and spend the rest of his days at the forge he loved.

He made it to the furthest reaches of Abbarkon before setting up a forge in Brunow by the North Sea. There, Adler met and married Anya, and shortly after that, Egbert had been born. All his life, Egbert had heard the stories of Tsaralvia and Dworgunul.

As a child, he had accepted them as stories, but as he grew older, his father had shared more and more of *The Hammer* training. If Adler had stayed in Tsaralvia, Egbert would have been the next *Hammer of Dworgunul.*

After his father's death, Egbert had continued to study the history of Abbarkon, Tsaralvia and Cheveral. Flint recalled the shocked looks on the faces of Egbert's listeners when he revealed this background. Inside *The Hawks*, no one knew Egbert as anyone other than a brilliant blacksmith, weaponsmith and inventor. However, before joining the rebel group in Halklyen, Egbert had also been a well-known expert of the history in the three lands.

It was this reputation that brought the Cheveralian messenger to Kallcunarth looking for Egbert Martell. Apparently, the first months of the search had been quite fruitless. It was only after *The Hawks* were exposed as the group that assassinated the old King and led the battle against *The Followers* at Fasnul, that Egbert gained a large measure of fame.

The stories of the armoured cart and the repeating bow he had built were being told in every tavern around the country. This had evidently made the messenger's task much easier. Everyone knew *The Hawks* were going to be at King Sebastien's coronation.

By the end of the story, Flint was not surprised to see that every single *Talon* had voted to allow the mission to proceed. There was tremendous interest in the quest and Egbert soon enlisted a large group of volunteers who were willing to follow him through the mountains to Tsaralvia.

Now, Flint was shaken from his memories of the difficult trip that he and his eleven companions had just completed. Evidently, the dancing girl had been taking it easy on him. Just when he was beginning to feel comfortable with the steps she was leading him through, she suddenly increased the complexity. It took every bit of his warrior's training to follow her flashing feet. He could hear the music increasing in tempo and his entire attention was focused on matching her every move.

The blood pounding in his ears matched the beat of the drums and the fiddles were weaving a melody that led his feet in a never-ending pattern. A flourish of running notes brought the music to the end and Flint looked around to see that he and the girl were the only remaining dancers. A burst of cheering startled him and Flint found himself smiling sheepishly while he produced a self-conscious bow for the clapping crowd. The girl had no such reservations. She spread her smile over the happy audience and dropped into a deep curtsy.

Flint searched the watching faces for his friends. He spotted Kjell, the newest *Hawk* standing near the musicians. The man was definitely odd. His usual blissful smile was in place and he gazed back at Flint with a look

8

of complete happiness. Once, one of the most powerful *Followers of Martokallu*, Kjell had awakened from injuries that should have killed him, to find that his body had healed itself. At the same time, it had also rid itself of the enthrallment that had ruled his existence for almost three hundred years. Since that time, he had been enjoying all the aspects of human life.

The next face that Flint recognized was Hackett's. The one-armed warrior was chatting with Igon. The two huge men stood head and shoulders above anyone else in the crowd. Although they appeared to be enjoying themselves, Flint noted that their casual conversation masked their vigilant examination of everything that was going on around the fire.

A flick of Igon's eyebrow led Flint to glance over to the shadows where he spotted Dell slouching against a tree away from the firelight. The jester-smile painted on the mask he wore hid a terribly scarred face, as well as any expression that might have told Flint what he was thinking.

However, actually knowing Dell's thoughts was less important than finding out whether the plan had been successfully implemented. Flint watched for Dell's signal and smiled to himself when he saw him nod his head and slide off into the shadows.

Flint brought his attention back to his dance partner and reached out to take her hand. She gave it to him easily and laughed as he bowed in his best impression of the courtly manners he had seen at King Sebastien's coronation celebration. "You must excuse me, my lady," he said dramatically. "It has been a long day, and I fear tomorrow will prove to be even more exciting." Knowing that she would not understand a word he said, he continued his playacting. "I do thank you for the dance." With that, he brought her hand to his lips before letting it fall. As she giggled, he backed away from the fire.

Squeezing through the gathered crowd, he scooped up his baldric from where he had set it when the girl pulled him up to dance. Flint eased his arms through the webbing and shrugged to settle the weight of the double swords. He kept his face impassive, but as always, the act of wearing the swords reminded him that Cadmon was gone and a lump built in his throat. Almost desperately, he tried to swallow past it.

Egbert had redesigned the double scabbard to accommodate the longer blade of *The Rising Star* after Cadmon had declared that it would belong to Flint. Every evening, on the long trip south to Vaarndal, Flint had drawn his swords and run through the drills that he and Cadmon had developed. It had not taken long to accustom himself to the new, longer blade and he found it worked best in his right hand. The added reach it gave him was very effective when he practiced sparring with Igon or Gode.

No sooner had he left the circle of light than the drums started up again and the fiddles joined the chorus. Flint stood still for a moment to let his eyes adjust to the darkness and then headed carefully in the direction of the inn where he and the other *Hawks* were staying. The

Cheveralian, Urravon who had brought the message to Egbert was already back at the inn. He had not proved himself to be a particularly social man, preferring his own company whenever possible.

They had been in the town for three nights already and each evening as the music and dancing began, Urravon would disappear up to his room and no one would see him again until the next morning. Flint wondered how he was spending his time.

Smiling to himself as he strolled through the darkened streets, Flint thought about how much he had enjoyed the evenings of song and dance. From the moment of their arrival when Egbert introduced himself and entranced his listeners with stories, the townspeople of Vaarndal had welcomed *The Hawks*.

The days had been filled with training sessions that brought most of the town's children and many of the adults out to watch. There had also been meetings that Egbert arranged with the town leaders. Discussions had centered on the political climate of the area. Egbert wanted to know everything he could about the country they were visiting.

At sunset, fires were lit in the market square and the musicians brought out their drums, fiddles, viols and shawms. It seemed as if everyone in town joined in the nightly celebrations.

As he walked, Flint carefully scanned his surroundings. When he was certain that no one was watching him any longer, he changed direction and headed for the shrine where he expected to find an excavation underway.

THE HAWKS: BOOK TWO

THE GOD SWORD

WILL BE RELEASED IN 2013.

Paula Baker and Aidan Davies decided one day when they were jumping on the trampoline, that they would team up to write a book. Aidan's head is full of stories, and his mother, Paula loves to write. *Rebels of Halklyen* was written during the summer after Aidan finished grade nine.

They live in British Columbia, Canada with their family where she is a librarian and band teacher in a Middle School and he attends High School.